I0690504

DARKER PATHS

THE WITCHES OF CANYON ROAD:
BOOK TWO

CHRISTINE POPE

DARK VALENTINE PRESS

This is a work of fiction. Names, characters, places, and incidents are either the product of the author's imagination or are used fictitiously. Any resemblance to actual events, places, organizations, or persons, whether living or dead, is entirely coincidental.

DARKER PATHS

ISBN: 978-1-946435-13-2

Copyright © 2018 by Christine Pope

Published by Dark Valentine Press

Cover design by Lou Harper

Print formatting by Indie Author Services

All rights reserved. No part of this book may be reproduced in any form or by any electronic or mechanical means, including information storage and retrieval systems—except in the case of brief quotations embodied in critical articles or reviews—without permission in writing from its publisher, Dark Valentine Press.

HIDEAWAYS

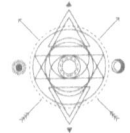

Miranda McAllister

Usually I felt better after I had made a decision, had gotten matters settled. Now, though, as I sat on Simon Gutierrez's couch and watched him smile down at me, I couldn't help but wonder whether I'd just made a terrible mistake. Yes, the man I was supposed to marry had just stomped on my heart and shattered it into about a million pieces—rejecting me as we stood on the altar at Loretto Chapel in front of the entire Castillo clan —but was disappearing with Simon so he could help me awaken my mostly dormant powers really the right response? The logical thing for me to do was to go back to the casita where I'd been staying at Genoveva Castillo's house, gather my belongings, and catch a shuttle down to Albuquerque so I could fly home to Arizona.

And yet….

The only person I had less desire to face than Rafael Castillo was his mother, the Castillo *prima*. There was no guarantee that I wouldn't run into both of them if I went back to get my things from the casita. I also couldn't see myself as being courageous enough to say the hell with it and take a flight home while still wearing my wedding dress.

Besides, if what Simon had just told me really was true, if he actually could help me get in touch with magical gifts I hadn't even known I possessed, then leaving now would prevent me from realizing my potential. Did I really want to be a *nunca*—someone born to parents of witch-kind but without any powers of their own—for the rest of my life?

That unspoken question seemed to settle things.

If Simon had taken any note of my apparent unease, he'd decided to ignore it. "I have a place where we can go. We'll be safe there. The Castillos won't be able to find us."

"You're sure?" I asked. "I mean, Genoveva is pretty powerful, and the clan is so big…."

"You'll have to trust me on this one," he replied. His night-black eyes were fixed on me, earnest, encouraging. "Just as I was able to hide my magical powers from them, I'll be able to hide us physically, too."

He'd hidden those powers from me as well. It was only a few moments earlier that he'd revealed he was also witch-kind, but from the de la Paz clan in southern Arizona. I supposed I would have to trust him to keep us well concealed, because he'd certainly done a good job at making me think he was a civilian, just an ordinary guy with no magical powers at all, someone who'd only been reaching out to a lonely girl in a new town.

And I'd have to believe him when it came to other matters as well. He hadn't hidden his interest in me, so for all I knew, this was just an elaborate ploy to get me alone so he could finally make his move. However, I refused to believe that. He could have tried to make a pass at me all the times I'd been alone in his apartment, but he hadn't. Right now, he seemed much more interested in helping me work with my buried powers than getting me in the sack.

Which was a relief. Yes, a very good way to get revenge on Rafe for leaving me at the altar might have been to sleep with Simon, but I didn't think I could go to bed coldly like that, driven by vengeance rather than love or desire. I'd been hanging on to my virginity my entire life, saving it for Rafe. Even though he'd rejected me in about the worst way possible, I wasn't willing to blithely throw that virginity away. I couldn't say what might happen as time went on, but for now I just wanted to have Simon as a friend and nothing more.

"Okay," I said. "I trust you. But how exactly are we going to manage this?" I remembered then that my meager belongings had been left at Rafe's house, all packed into two weekender bags in preparation for a honeymoon that had never happened. At least I could avoid going back to the casita, but it didn't seem as though there was any way to stay out of Rafe's orbit. "My bags are at Rafe's, and I can't exactly go roaming around Santa Fe in my wedding dress." I made a frustrated gesture at the heavy silk satin gown I wore, whose tight bodice now felt even more confining than when I'd put it on earlier that afternoon. More than anything, I wanted out of that damn dress. True, I'd taken off my tiara and veil a few moments earlier, but still, I was in no shape to go anywhere dressed like this.

"It's fine," Simon told me. "I can get your things for you."

I stared at him in disbelief. "How? Even if you can block Rafe from detecting your powers and realizing you're a warlock, he's not going to let you waltz into his house and get my bags."

"I don't have to go anywhere near Rafe's

house," Simon said calmly. "How much luggage did you have?"

"Um, just the two bags. Cat dropped them at Rafe's house because we thought it would be faster when it came time to leave town, but —"

"Miranda," he cut in, stopping the flow of words. "It's okay."

He came and sat down next to me on the couch, then took my hand in his. Part of me wanted to pull away, but I knew that would be horribly rude. Besides, something about his touch was reassuring—the warmth of his fingers, the gentle strength I sensed within him. I needed someone to calm me down, because my whole body positively thrummed with nervous energy, probably from that terrible scene at the chapel when Rafe had rejected me…and perhaps also from the realization that I'd just made a huge decision about my future.

"Think of everything you brought with you," he said, gaze meeting mine, open, friendly. "Don't tell me—just think."

This seemed like a pointless exercise, but I didn't want to argue with him. I remembered how he'd said a few minutes earlier that he possessed a number of different talents, not the one magical gift most witches and warlocks could call their own. Did those talents include magically transporting inanimate objects across miles?

A little shiver went through me at the thought. Just how many magical abilities did Simon actually command?

I supposed I'd find out soon enough.

So I sat there on his slightly saggy couch and felt how his fingers were entwined with mine, how his skin was smooth and warm. I thought of the few possessions I'd been allowed to bring with me here to Santa Fe, the mundanities of jeans and tops and jackets, a few precious items like the green tourmaline earrings my parents had given me for my eighteenth birthday and the thick bracelet of hammered silver that my grandfather gave me when I graduated from college. All the little bits and pieces that were supposed to help me create a new life here, far from where I'd grown up in northern Arizona.

And then there they were—a pair of dark wine-colored weekender bags, with my purse sitting on top of one of them. I let out a shocked sound and shifted on the couch so I could look at Simon. "You—you were able to bring them here, just like that?"

"Just like that," he said, voice and expression both slightly amused, as though he couldn't quite understand why I should be so impressed by such a simple feat. "Soon enough, you'll have learned to do these things as well. But for now, it's probably a good idea if you get changed."

I had my doubts as to whether I'd really be able to command those sorts of powers, but I didn't feel like arguing with him. All I wanted right then was to climb out of that heavy, ridiculous dress and get into something more comfortable. Even as I moved, I could feel one of the plastic bones from the bustier I was wearing dig into my underarm.

"Definitely a good idea," I agreed, then got up from where I'd been sitting. Simon's bathroom wasn't very big, but somehow I'd figure out a way to extricate myself from the wedding gown and get into some real clothes. After giving him a quick smile, I went and picked up both bags— since I couldn't remember which items were in which piece of luggage—and locked myself in the bathroom to change.

My face in the mirror was almost one of a stranger. No real surprise, considering I'd been made up earlier that day by an expert, and I wasn't used to the subtle contouring the makeup artist had used. But it was more than just the surface paint—those were the eyes of a woman who'd been hurt badly. Underneath the blush, my skin was far too pale.

Mouth compressed, I turned away from the mirror and began the arduous process of unbuttoning the row of tiny satin-covered buttons that fastened the back of the dress. I had a feeling this was the sort of procedure that usually required assistance, but there was no way in hell I was going to open the door and call down the hallway for Simon to come and help me get undressed.

About five minutes later, I finally had everything undone. With a sigh of relief, I let the gown slither to the floor, then stepped out of it and hung it from a hook on the back of the bathroom door. The rest of the process was easy enough—I traded my lace-topped thigh-high stockings for some boot socks, the bustier for a much more comfortable bra. A pair of jeans and a sweater, my favorite low-heeled brown boots, and I was done.

Well, except for the elaborate hair and makeup. I couldn't do much about the makeup without washing my face and starting all over, so I settled for digging out an elastic hair band from my cosmetics bag and grimly pulling my hair back into a ponytail. The long, loose curls the hairstylist had given me weren't damaged too badly by this process, but at least they didn't look quite so over the top when confined in such a way.

There wasn't much I could do with the wedding dress except roll it into as small a ball as possible and shove it in one of my weekender bags. Taking out the jeans and sweater had freed up a little space, although I knew the gown was going to end up hopelessly wrinkled. But then, what did it matter? It wasn't as though I was ever going to wear it again. Really, right then I could have cheerfully set it on fire.

I emerged from the bathroom to find Simon standing in front of the couch, zipping up the duffle bag that he'd set down on the cushions. Apparently, he'd been packing while I was changing and putting away my wedding dress. Somehow, looking at the bag he'd put together brought home to me the realization that we really were going to do this. We actually were going to disappear somewhere together.

That uneasy feeling returned to the pit of my stomach. Part of me understood how crazy all this was, that running off with Simon when I hardly knew him possibly wasn't the best response to Rafe's rejection. At the same time, I tried to remind myself that if I didn't take charge of my destiny now, the opportunity might be lost forever. Did I really want to go running back to Arizona with my tail between my legs, defeated and humiliated? I told myself that once Simon and I were settled and he'd begun helping me with my powers, I'd feel a lot better about the situation. Right now I was still jangly and upset from that horrible scene in Loretto Chapel. If nothing else, I needed a quiet place to go where I could calm down and better evaluate my long-range plans.

As soon as he saw me, Simon smiled. I couldn't detect anything in his expression except approval and relief that we were going ahead with our plans. He'd probably been worried that I was going to make some kind of last-minute protest. "Better?" he asked, taking in my jeans and boots with one quick glance.

"Much better," I replied. "But how are we going to get to this place you were talking about? I thought your car was in the shop."

For the briefest second, his smile wavered. Then he shrugged and said, "Oh, it was never in for repairs. I had to tell you that so I'd have a reasonable excuse for why I was riding the train."

Unease stirred in me again. "So you lied to me."

At once he stepped away from the couch and came over to where I stood. His gaze meeting mine squarely, he said, "Miranda, I hated to do that. But I couldn't tell you the truth about why I was here. Not at first, anyway. I had to sort of... ease into things, make certain that you really did possess some hidden powers."

I reflected that so much of what he'd told me over the past few days had to be lies—going to school at UNM down in Albuquerque, the car that needed repair...the family that had only come to settle in Santa Fe about a hundred years earlier. As he'd hinted, he needed some kind of cover story to give me until he could be sure that my powers really were something he could work with. I didn't like that he'd stacked falsehood on top of falsehood, but at least I could understand why he'd done it. And he was telling me the truth now, wasn't trying to hide the fact that he'd lied to me.

"What about this apartment?" I asked. "The job at the wine shop?"

"The apartment is an Airbnb," he said calmly, still meeting my gaze, expression open and frank. Maybe he'd told some lies to cover his tracks, but he obviously wanted me to know he wasn't withholding any information now. "And I was covering for someone at the wine shop, a guy who had to go back to Chicago for a few days for some family business. That's all."

That's all. Well, it was a pretty elaborate charade, as far as I could tell, but again, it hadn't been anything intended to hurt me. Exactly the opposite, really. He'd needed to look as though he had a job and an apartment here in Santa Fe, or the rest of his story wouldn't have made sense, and we wouldn't have gotten close enough for him to feel comfortable revealing the truth about himself.

"All right," I said wearily. Right then I just wanted to get the hell out of town. Although it seemed that Simon had his own ways of making sure we wouldn't be followed, I couldn't shake the feeling that the Castillos would track me down here if we lingered for too much longer. "Since your car is okay after all, let's get going. No point in hanging around here, right?"

"No point at all," he agreed. "Let me take one of your bags."

I wasn't about to protest. Right then I was just so damn tired that I thought I'd be lucky if I could make it down the stairs without stumbling. I nodded and handed one of the bags to him, then followed him as he walked through the short hallway to the front door. He paused to lock the door behind us, and afterward we headed down to the parking lot. Waiting there was a sleek newer-model compact BMW SUV. I looked at it with a raised eyebrow but didn't bother to comment. After all, it was pretty obvious that his starving student act had been only that—an act, with very little truth behind it. The de la Paz clan had a lot of money; it wasn't so strange that Simon would drive an expensive car.

He put the bags he was carrying in the back, then took my remaining weekender bag from me and stowed it alongside the others. In silence, I went up to the passenger door and let myself in. The vehicle was so new, I could still smell the leather upholstery. Had he bought it before he left Arizona? I'd noticed that it had New Mexico plates, but he could've acquired those sometime during the past couple of days.

"What about your family?" I asked as we

pulled out of the alley and headed west on San Francisco Street. "Your *real* family, I mean."

For a second, Simon didn't reply. Yes, he was in the middle of setting the self-driving controls, but I didn't think that was the real reason for the delay.

Then he said, "Back in Tucson, you mean?"

"Yeah. It's not like witches and warlocks generally leave their home territory for extended periods. Where did you tell them you were going?"

He shrugged. "I've been taking photography classes at the local community college. There was a workshop coming up within the right time frame, so I said I was going to take it. Since it's all about shooting in the desert, especially nighttime images, it meant I was going to be gone for ten days in places without a lot of cell service. It seemed the simplest excuse, and one they would have a hard time checking on. I already have a stockpile of images I can show them to prove that I took the workshop, so they won't be able to get suspicious about that, either."

That made some sense, I guessed. He couldn't have told his family the truth about where he was going, because there was no way they would have allowed him to come to another witch clan's territory and interfere with their business—especially when that business was something as important as the marriage of their *prima*'s only son to the daughter of the two northern Arizona clan leaders.

Not that what Simon had done could really be categorized as "interfering." It was more like he'd sat back and waited to see what would happen. For all I knew, he had some of the abilities of a seer, might have known that Rafe's and my cobbled-together romance would implode before it even got started. If that were really true, it might have been nice if he could have warned me…but then, would I have even believed him?

"What happens if this takes longer than ten days?"

He turned his head toward me and smiled slightly. "It won't."

"How do you know that?"

"Because I can already sense the power building in you. It wants to come out."

I wasn't sure I liked the sound of that; the picture that formed in my mind was one of a dam breaking, water flowing out and leaving destruction in its wake. I hadn't embarked on this escape with Simon because I wanted to hurt anyone or destroy anything. All I wanted was to have real powers like every other witch and warlock I knew. I was tired of feeling like a freak.

"Well, I guess we'll just have to see," I remarked.

The car turned right on a street whose name I

didn't catch. We passed restaurants and breweries and then came out into a more modern commercial area, with a big shopping center on one side. Across the street, though, was a cemetery, and I had to repress a shiver. I hoped its presence on our way out of town wasn't a sign of things to come.

Right next to the regular, old-fashioned graveyard was a national cemetery, the rows of identical white tombstones shimmering in my peripheral vision as we drove past. After that, we were on the highway, the houses of Santa Fe giving way to open country not so different from northern Arizona—juniper and piñon trees, scrubby dry grass spread over rolling hills. Only a few minutes passed before the car began to descend into a river valley, a line of cottonwood trees blazing like golden fire in the setting sun as they followed the water through the lowlands.

The car pulled off the highway at an exit for a place called Tesuque. I'd never heard of it, but that didn't mean much. Other than checking the climate and making sure I'd bring appropriate clothing, I hadn't done a lot of research on Santa Fe and its environs. I'd thought I would be able to discover these things in person, with my new husband at my side.

Well, there was a joke.

Although I'd resolved to put him out of my mind, I couldn't help but wonder what Rafe was up to right now. Was he worried at all about what had happened to me, or was he glad that I'd disappeared into thin air, that I wasn't his problem any longer? Even if that were the case, Genoveva had to be furious, just because at some point she'd have to provide some explanation to my parents as to why I'd disappeared.

My parents....

"I need to call home," I said.

"Of course you do," Simon replied, his tone unruffled. "You can use my phone when we get to the house. The signal isn't very good around here, so you'll need to use the wi-fi."

Just the fact that he hadn't argued or come up with excuses as to why I shouldn't call home made me relax a good deal. If—as I couldn't help worrying about, even though he'd given no indication that his intentions were nefarious—he really was up to no good, then the last thing he'd want was for me to let my parents know where I was. I knew they'd probably do their best to talk me into coming back to Arizona, but I would have to stand firm. I needed to give this a try. I had to see if Simon really could help me.

This area was nearly rural, the road now one lane in either direction, overhung by tall trees, their leaves a riot of autumn gold. We came to a crossroads with a funky-looking restaurant on one side, then turned past it and headed up toward the hills as the valley gradually sank into shadow.

"What was that place?" I asked.

Simon's gaze traveled toward the restaurant, then back to the vehicle's controls. As I watched, he disengaged the self-driving mechanism and took control of the car himself. "Oh, that's the Tesuque Village Market."

"It looked like a restaurant."

"It's a restaurant and a market. They sell local stuff. The food's good, though. We'll have to go there to eat soon."

I shot him a curious glance. "You're not worried about a Castillo seeing us? It doesn't seem like we're that far from Santa Fe."

"We're not, but they don't come here much. Besides, how many of them even know what you look like? And I can mask our witchy natures, so we'll just look like a couple of civilians to them."

This response sounded plausible enough. True, a large chunk of the clan had been present at the wedding, but I really doubted they'd be able to recognize me once I was back to my normal lip gloss and mascara and everyday clothes, rather than my elaborate wedding gown and hair and makeup. It was kind of a relief to think that Simon didn't intend to keep me locked up in a compound somewhere, that we'd be able to go out and eat at a restaurant like regular people.

He turned off onto a small dirt road, then paused after we'd gone about a hundred yards so he could roll down the window and enter the key code for the large iron gate that blocked our way. Maybe we really were going to a compound after all.

That seemed to be the case, because after we passed through the gates, we traveled along a small private road with carefully fenced-in grounds to either side. At this time of year, the grass appeared mostly yellow and dry, but it must have been lush and green in the late spring and summer. Tall trees, their leaves also golden yellow, were planted at regular intervals.

We came to a cluster of buildings, one of which was a detached three-car garage. Everything except the garage was built in what I'd learned was the New Mexico territorial style—steeply peaked roofs, wide porches. The place looked quiet, serene in the late afternoon light, and I felt myself relax at the sight.

Simon touched the controls on the steering column, and the door to the center bay began to open. As far as I could tell, the garage was empty except for a few trashcans lined up against one wall. We got out and retrieved our baggage from the rear of the BMW.

"This way," Simon said.

I followed him through a door on the same

wall where the trashcans were located, and then along a path that wound through a carefully tended garden, where a few hollyhocks and hydrangea bushes still bloomed, despite the time of year. Because we were approaching from the garage rather than the front walk, we came into the house via a pair of French doors that opened on the patio. I assumed Simon must have a key, but he didn't use one, only touched his fingers to the doorknob and used his inborn magic to let us in.

We stood in an enormously long hallway illuminated by recessed lighting overhead. An equally long, narrow bench ran along one wall, while against the other was a pair of antique tables topped by a matching set of vases filled with sprays of autumn leaves. Landscapes in serene hues lined the walls.

"What is this place?" I asked, my voice hushed. I'd only seen this one hallway—well, and the grounds as we drove in—and I could already tell it was the kind of property that no twenty-one-year-old kid could have rented by himself, even if said kid happened to be part of a prosperous witch clan. This was way, way beyond merely prosperous, and I felt a little like the beggar-maid heroine of a fairytale, sneaking into the king's palace.

He grinned as if he'd guessed precisely what I

was thinking. "It belongs to some rich Texas oil guy. The property was being rented by a Hollywood actor while he was doing a film shoot here in Santa Fe, but he left a couple of weeks ago. Now the oil guy is trying to decide whether to sell or not, so he needed someone to caretake the place in the meantime."

"That someone being you?" I inquired, not bothering to keep the skepticism out of my tone. That is, I could see why a place like this might need a caretaker, but I found it difficult to believe that anyone would entrust a multimillion-dollar property like this to someone barely old enough to drink.

"Yeah, me." His grin didn't fade. "I saw the ad and knew the property would be perfect. So what if I padded my resume a little?"

And, for all I knew, used a little magical persuasion to convince the property manager or whoever it was doing the hiring that he would be perfect for the job. I didn't ask, though; right then, I really didn't want to know if a talent like that was included in Simon's magic bag of tricks, because then I'd be forced to wonder whether he'd used it on me to get me to come here in the first place. My decision had been made, and I was too tired to start second-guessing every little thing, especially since I had absolutely no indication that

Simon's plans included anything beyond helping me discover my talents.

"Let me show you your room," he went on. "Since it's so late, I figured all we'd do tonight is get settled. I guessed you probably wouldn't want to get to work right away."

After the day I'd had, absolutely not. The trips that morning to the nail salon and the hairdresser and the makeup artist to get ready for the wedding now felt as though they had happened roughly a million years ago. "Sounds good."

I followed Simon down the hallway to a room that was almost the size of the entire ground floor of my parents' house in Jerome. Actually, it was really a suite, since it had a sitting room attached on one side, and then an enormous bathroom and closet on the other. That closet was bigger than the casita where I'd been staying at Genoveva Castillo's property, and I knew my few shirts and sweaters were going to look pretty forlorn hanging in that vast expanse. Although it seemed as though the entire house had been done in the same muted shades of beige and gray, with a few accents of pale green or soft terra-cotta, the effect wasn't dull at all, thanks to all the different textures the decorator had used.

No, the overall effect was just very, very expensive.

"I'm afraid to touch anything," I said, and Simon grinned.

"Don't worry about it. I mean, I had to sign a waiver that we wouldn't be throwing any big parties or anything while we were here, but a little normal wear and tear is okay. I already have a cleaning crew signed up to come in and go over everything, change the sheets and towels and stuff, after we're done with the place."

It was on the tip of my tongue to ask how long he'd been planning this whole getaway, but again, I wasn't sure I wanted to know.

He went on, "I'm going to stay in the caretaker's house. I figured it wouldn't feel as strange to you if we weren't sleeping under the same roof."

"You don't have to do that," I protested. Yes, it might have been weird to share the place with Simon, but on the other hand, the house was so big, I doubted we'd be tripping over each other.

"Really, I don't mind. The caretaker's house is bigger than the house where I grew up."

Absolutely wild. I'd noticed the other buildings as we passed by them on the way to the garage, but with the darkness of dusk creeping in on all sides, I hadn't been able to see a ton of detail beyond the basic design of those structures. It was a little mind-blowing to think that there was a secondary home here that was larger than most people's regular houses.

"Anyway, I'll let you unpack and get settled in," Simon said. "You can meet me in the kitchen when you're done. Then we can scrounge something for dinner, since I figured you probably wouldn't be up to going out tonight."

"No, I definitely am not." What I really wanted to do was crawl into bed and sleep for a hundred years, but since it wasn't even seven o'clock yet, I figured that wasn't a very good idea. "But maybe I should use your phone before it gets any later."

"Sure." He pulled the phone out of his pocket and handed it over to me. "It's unlocked."

"Thanks." Even though I'd asked for the phone, I hesitated for a moment before inputting my mother's cell phone number. What in the world was I supposed to say? As soon as my parents heard what had happened, they would know none of this was my fault, but…. I gulped in a breath, then quickly entered the digits on the keypad before I could lose my nerve.

The phone rang three times, then went to voicemail. What the hell? I would have thought my parents would be ready to pounce as soon as I called, considering I'd been in touch only an hour or so earlier, when Cat texted them a couple of pictures of me in my wedding gown. Then again, maybe they'd thought I would be so occupied with the ceremony and the reception afterward that I wouldn't have a chance to make any phone calls. It was sort of early, but maybe they'd gone out to dinner or something. While they might answer the phone if it rang during dinner at home, I knew they wouldn't do the same thing when out to eat, since they hated it when other people had loud phone conversations in restaurants.

Not sure whether to be disappointed or relieved, I took another breath and then said, "Mom, Dad, this is Miranda. Um…some weird stuff happened. The wedding's off, I guess. Not because of me," I added hastily. "Rafe got cold feet. Anyway, I'm all right, but I'm staying with a friend for a few days until I can figure out what I want to do next. I'll try to call again tomorrow. Love you."

I ended the message there, since I knew my mother could get Simon's number from the call log on her cell, and handed the phone to Simon. He took it from me and slipped it back into his pocket. "Maybe tomorrow we can go into Española and get you a phone of your own. It's probably safer than trying to go shopping in Santa Fe."

"There aren't any Castillos in Española?"

"Not that I know of. None here in Tesuque, either, which is a big part of why I thought this would be a good place to hole up."

"I wonder why," I said. "I mean, I know they have a branch of the family up in Taos, and that's a lot farther away."

Simon's shoulders lifted. "Haven't a clue. But it helps us out."

That was for sure. Of course Simon wouldn't have brought me someplace where the Castillos hung out, but still, I felt a little better knowing I wouldn't have to worry about stumbling over them in my immediate environs. "Okay," I said. "I'll get my stuff put away, then meet you in the kitchen…if I can find it in this place."

He chuckled. "It's not that hard. Just go back down the hallway and through the living room. It's at the other end of the house, but it's basically a straight shot."

"Got it."

A small wave, and then he exited the bedroom, leaving me to myself. I knew I should have gone to hang up my clothes, or put my toiletries away in the bathroom. However, I did neither of those things. Instead, I sat down on the edge of the bed and looked around at my unfamiliar surroundings, at the pale whitewashed beams overhead and the equally pale bleached-wood floor.

I'd vowed not to think about him, but I couldn't help wondering what Rafe was doing right at that moment.

TRACKS

Rafe Castillo

Cat left after about an hour, and Rafe sat on the couch in the living room and stared at the bottle of Avíon Silver tequila on the coffee table, wondering if he dared have another shot. He wanted to—more than anything, he wanted to blot out the pain and confusion he was feeling. Something had been taken from him, and he didn't even know how.

Or why.

After an interminable moment, he reached out and grasped the bottle and shot glass, then rose from the couch and went into the kitchen. He put the bottle of tequila back in the cupboard and set the glass on the counter next to the sink.

His stomach rumbled grumpily, and he knew he'd have to eat something soon to soak up the alcohol, even though the thought of consuming solid food made him feel sick.

Miranda was gone. They should have been at the reception by now, surrounded by family giving them champagne toasts. Everything had happened so quickly, Rafe didn't even know what had been on the menu, but since the event was being held at one of the family restaurants, he assumed that whatever that dinner was supposed to be, it would have been good. There would have been a first dance, cake, more dancing, more champagne. Not too much, though—he and Miranda were supposed to have hit the road for Taos as the reception was winding down. Anyway, another bottle of champagne would have been waiting for them in their suite at the resort.

Shit…had anyone called to cancel the reservation?

His head hurt. He didn't quite know what he was supposed to be doing with himself, but he guessed it wasn't standing here in his empty house and getting drunk.

There were things he could be doing. He could be calling Cat to have her notify the staff at El Monte Sagrado resort in Taos that no one would be using their fancy thousand-dollar-pernight honeymoon casita. He could be wandering the streets, looking for Miranda. Hell, he should be calling her parents to let them know she'd disappeared again, even though Genoveva had emphatically stated that she wanted Angela McAllister and Connor Wilcox left out of the loop, at least for now. Rafe knew his mother was hoping they'd locate Miranda soon, and all this nastiness could just get swept under the rug. Nothing to see here—we're all fine, thank you.

Only it wasn't fine at all. He had the overwhelming sensation that he was missing something vitally important about the whole mess, but he couldn't for the life of him think what that might be. His brain still felt fuzzy and not quite there, and he knew that sensation wasn't entirely due to the tequila. According to his sister Louisa, someone had gone in his head and messed around. Some kind of a spell, although no one in his family could say who would have a reason to cast such a spell.

Because now he had to circle back to the question he'd asked Cat only a short while earlier. Who would do such a thing...and why? Who would profit from wrecking an alliance between the Castillos and the northern Arizona witch clans?

No one, as far as he could tell. Miranda's

mother might have agreed to the bargain that sent her unborn daughter to the Castillos because she was up against the wall dealing with the dark warlock Joaquin Escobar and had no other choice, but circumstances now were very different. Everyone in the witch clans of the Southwest had been at peace for his entire life. Yes, the Castillos tended to keep to themselves, and yet that certainly wasn't any cause for enmity from the other witch families. As a rule, they tended to stay isolated, and one could say that the chumminess of the three clans in Arizona was the exception rather than the rule.

But someone had come along and stirred up trouble, for whatever reason. Rafe had wondered earlier whether the culprit was some previously unknown admirer of Miranda's, butting in because he didn't want to see the woman he loved marrying someone else. That sort of motivation was something Rafe could understand. She was beautiful and smart…and tougher than she appeared on the surface.

An image flashed in his head of the way she'd looked when he'd kissed her for the first time. Wary, and almost as if she'd wanted to bolt, but standing there in front of him with her cheeks flushed and her full mouth parted, her green eyes glowing. Absolutely beautiful, and so very desirable.

He wished he could remember how she had looked when she stood in front of him at the altar, but everything about that portion of his day was blurry, indistinct. Part of the spell? Maybe. He remembered driving to the church, and nothing after that until he'd come to himself in one of the meeting rooms at the cathedral, his immediate family clustered around him, demanding what the hell was wrong with him.

Well, now he knew. And he supposed he could say none of this was his fault, although he hated to face the reality that he was so weak, he couldn't even fend off a magical attack. Then again, he hadn't exactly been expecting one.

Maybe it hadn't been a good idea to send Cat away. At the time, he'd thought it better for his sister to head over to the restaurant where the reception was supposed to be held and check in with his parents, but now he wasn't so sure. She was good to have around, his little sister. The two of them had always presented a united front, since they were so much younger than their two older sisters, both of whom were married and settled and had families of their own. But he and Cat had always looked out for one another, and she'd always been a good sounding board. In fact, he'd joked on more than one occasion that if he ever were forced to kill someone, it was Cat he'd call to help him hide the body.

It couldn't be helped, though. She probably was performing a better service by going to the reception and doing what she could to smooth things over with the rest of the family than she would by staying with him and holding his hand.

However, Rafe knew if he remained here a moment longer, he would go crazy. He liked his house and had lived here alone for several years, but now it only seemed to mock him, to tell him he'd never bring Miranda here as his bride. Maybe that was only the truth, but he didn't want to face it now. He couldn't quite acknowledge that this all might be hopeless.

Damn it.

He went and got his jacket from the hall closet, then headed toward the garage. Thank God that Cat had driven him home from the cathedral in his own vehicle, rather than leaving it behind to be retrieved later. Yes, he could've called a Ryde and had one of the self-driving cars take him anywhere in town he wanted to go, but right now he wanted to drive himself. He needed to feel as though he was in control of something in his life.

Besides, he had this nagging sensation that he needed to go downtown, although he had absolutely no idea why. Not to drink—he knew he didn't dare have anything else if he wanted to stay safe behind the wheel. To get some food? Maybe, although he had a feeling it wouldn't be a very good idea to dine alone on this, of all nights. But he could always get some takeout from one of the restaurants there and bring it home.

Giving a mental shrug, he pulled out of the garage and pointed his Jeep west on Paseo de Peralta, then jogged over on Lincoln Avenue, which would bring him closer to the Plaza downtown. At least it was a Sunday night and therefore not as crowded as it would have been the evening before. Still, no one would have recommended Santa Fe's downtown as a place for pleasure driving, not with its narrow roads and one-way streets.

That strange feeling of being herded didn't lessen as he drove along, dusk now faded all the way into night. When he reached the parking structure on San Francisco Street, it was almost as if someone had poked him in the arm and said, *Here*.

So he pulled into the structure and parked on the second level, then sat there for a few moments, trying to figure out what the hell he was doing here. Yes, a little ways up the street was one of his favorite restaurants, Tia Maria, but it wouldn't be open now. Tia Maria was strictly a breakfast/lunch kind of place. And yet something had made him come here.

Frowning, he got out of the Jeep and headed over to the stairwell. However, he didn't descend to the street level, but instead walked up to the roof. Since nothing was going on at the Lensic Theater across the street, there wasn't much demand for parking; this level of the structure was almost empty. He raised his chin and breathed the chilly night air.

No, he really didn't breathe it in—he *sniffed* it, trying to detect something strange on the wind. This wasn't as effective as when he shifted into coyote or wolf form, but some of the traits he took on when he used his singular talent to become an animal of the wild seemed to stay with him, to be used when he needed them.

And he definitely sensed something off.

What it was, he couldn't even say. Something foul on the fresh currents of air, something that shouldn't be there. Eyes narrowing, he headed back to the stairs, walked down to ground level and then let himself out on the street. There was some traffic, not much, so he didn't have to wait long for an opening to cross San Francisco Street.

Once on the sidewalk opposite the parking structure, he paused again and inhaled deeply. Down here, there was a more muddled combination of scents—car exhaust, and cooking oil from a restaurant, a whiff of wood smoke. But there it was again, almost sickly sweet, like the smell of rotting flesh.

He walked slowly, hands in his pockets. Yes, it was definitely here—to be precise, somewhere near the wine tasting room just past the burger joint on the corner of Burro Alley.

At this hour on a Sunday, the shop was closed, its windows dark. Dark, too, were the windows of the apartment directly above it. Even so, Rafe found himself lingering here, watching the building for a long moment. Something about it tickled his memory, as though an important event had occurred here, but he couldn't remember what it might be. A little more than a year earlier, he'd come here with Tony and a few other Castillo cousins to sample the wares at the newly opened wine shop. He hadn't returned, though; the wine was good, but they hadn't offered any food at the time, and in general he didn't like to drink wine on its own.

The memory of the day he'd gone to the wine tasting room with Tony was very sharp and clear —it had been a mild day in early October, the trees just beginning to turn. They'd had two flights of wine, bought a few bottles, then headed down the street to the upscale pizza place there to get some real food. All this Rafe remembered without any trouble, and yet he seemed to sense something else far more important had gone on in this building in the recent past, even if he couldn't remember what the hell it might be.

Frowning, he moved a bit farther down the block, then cut down the alley so he might approach the building from the rear. How this would help, he wasn't sure, but he figured it couldn't hurt to try.

All was quiet back here. A pickup truck almost as old as his Wrangler was parked in one of the residents-only spaces, but the other ones remained empty. Well, the apartment over the tasting room had appeared empty; maybe it wasn't currently rented out.

Still….

Rafe walked over to the rear entrance of the building. The door was locked, but of course that didn't matter to a warlock. He touched his fingers to the handle, and it swung inward. After giving a quick look around and reassuring himself that he was alone, he went inside.

The odor was stronger here, as if it had concentrated itself in this dingy little stairwell. Breathing through his mouth, Rafe ascended the stairs and came to a small landing, the door to the apartment he'd noted now directly in front of him.

It had seemed empty, but he didn't know that for sure. As much as he wanted to simply let himself in and poke around, he figured it was smarter to cover his bases first.

He raised his hand and knocked on the door.

No answer, even though he waited a good twenty seconds or so for a response. Once again he knocked, and again only silence came back to him.

It should be safe enough.

He wrapped his fingers around the doorknob and stepped inside. The place was utterly dark, not even a nightlight to break up the gloom. Right by the door was a dual switch, so he flicked one upward. At once an overhead fixture flared to life, revealing a short hallway decorated with posters of local events—wine festivals, art exhibits —and not much else.

After moving farther in, he debated whether to turn on another light and decided against it. The light coming down the hall was enough to reveal that both the kitchen and living room were empty, as was the one small bedroom. Everything looked very clean and neat, nothing out of place, the bed made. In fact, when he peeked in the bathroom and into the closet, he saw no signs of occupancy at all, not one tube of toothpaste, not one lone sock lying on the closet floor.

It appeared the place truly was unoccupied. But what was with that sense of something dark and foul, something Rafe had never noticed before in his life?

He didn't know. All he did know was that something evil had once lurked here.

Unfortunately, that was all he knew. He certainly didn't have any idea why this place would be connected to Miranda or her disappearance.

Frowning, he turned and headed back toward the door, only to be confronted by a sturdy-looking woman somewhere in her fifties, who gave a little shriek of surprise and exclaimed, "Who are you?"

"I—" Rafe began, frantically thinking of some plausible excuse he could give for his breaking and entering.

Luckily, the woman didn't seem inclined to let him continue, saying briskly, "The apartment won't be ready until tomorrow. It should have said that on the Airbnb site."

Ah. So it wasn't really anyone's apartment, just a flat the owner—who he presumed must be the woman in front of him—rented out to people vacationing in Santa Fe. "Sorry," he said. "I came up, and the door was unlocked—"

"Hmph." The woman, who was probably around his mother's age but whose stoutness made her look a good bit older, gave an exasperated huff of breath. "People are so careless these days. I'm sure the man I rented it to forgot to lock the door as he left. The lock can be a little tricky, but—"

"Can you tell me where to find him?" Rafe asked eagerly, cutting her off. Could he be so lucky as to have stumbled onto an actual clue that might help him find Miranda?

The Airbnb owner huffed again and drew herself up to her entire five feet two inches. "No, of course I can't. It's very important to respect my guests' privacy—even if they don't seem to respect *my* privacy."

"Oh, well, normally I wouldn't ask," Rafe said. As he spoke, his mind churned, trying to come up with some story that might convince the woman to provide the information he needed. "But the guy who was just staying here really did a number on my little sister—told her he loved her and wanted to get married, then disappeared right when they were supposed to meet at the courthouse." That lie may have been a little too on the money, but if it worked....

Apparently it did, for the woman's expression softened, even as her dark eyes sparkled with righteous indignation on this mythical sister's behalf. "Oh, that's just wrong. I can see why your sister might have fallen for Robert, because he was a handsome young man, but—"

"His full name, then? My sister wouldn't tell me."

The woman's mouth tightened, but at least she didn't hesitate as she answered, "Robert Marquez. I think he came from San Antonio, but I'll have to check to be sure." She reached into the pocket of the heavy corduroy barn jacket she wore and pulled out her phone, then tapped away for a moment. "Yes, there's his confirmation email. Robert Marquez, San Antonio, Texas." A pause, and then she added, "That's really all I can tell you. It wouldn't be right to give you his address."

"It's all right," Rafe said. "It's something to go on at least. And I'm really sorry if I startled you."

"Oh, well." The woman shrugged. "It's not the first time I've surprised someone here when the flat was supposed to be empty. I hope you can get some satisfaction for your sister."

"So do I. Thanks a lot."

He nodded at her and let himself out, while she watched him go, her expression a mixture of curiosity and a little worry. Maybe she thought he was going to head to San Antonio himself to get some justice for his sister and her broken heart, and didn't want to be held responsible for the outcome.

Rafe didn't have anything like that planned. The Castillo family had several private detectives among its ranks, the closest of whom lived in Albuquerque. By now the whole clan must know about Miranda's disappearance, so it wasn't as though Rafe would be giving up any family secrets by contacting his cousin Daniel and asking him to follow up on this Robert Marquez person.

Then again, there was also the distinct possibility that "Robert Marquez" was really a mirage, a fake name that the person who'd stayed here had given to the owner of the Airbnb. That would be more difficult to pull off, just because the vacation rental site did some pretty strict vetting of the people who used its service.

Difficult, but not impossible. But Rafe figured he had to start somewhere, and this was the only lead he had at the moment.

Although he hadn't seen his cousin in more than a year, Rafe still had Daniel's contact information on his phone. Genoveva was very organized about keeping everyone in the loop, so to speak, and sent out an updated roster of Castillo relations every year. Some people probably would have preferred not to have their information disseminated to every single relative in the state, but they knew better than to question their *prima*. Luckily, the information didn't get abused too badly, except for now and then when someone decided to get a chain text message going and spammed everyone's inboxes.

His phone told him it was a little past seven. Right smack in the middle of dinnertime, but maybe private detectives didn't keep regular hours.

Rafe knew that Daniel wasn't married, had in fact gone through a nasty divorce a year or so earlier after less than a year of marriage, and so was less likely than most to be sitting down to a cozy dinner on a Sunday evening.

Walking quickly, Rafe crossed San Francisco Street and then took the elevator up to the second level, figuring that would save him some time climbing the stairs. Once he was safely inside his Jeep, he said, "Call Daniel Montoya."

"Calling," his phone told him, and Rafe settled against the seatback and waited for the call to connect.

Which it did after a few rings. "Rafe?" came Daniel's voice, clearly puzzled. "I just heard what happened. I'm sorry, man."

Sometimes family grapevines could come in handy, although Rafe still hated the thought of his personal life getting dissected by every aunt, uncle, and cousin twice removed. He cleared his throat and said, "It's—well, I can't really say that it's all right, but I'm trying to get through it. The thing is, I think Miranda's disappearance might be connected to a guy named Robert Marquez. I wanted to see if you could follow up for me."

"Sure," Daniel replied, interest sharpening his tone. "Do you have an address?"

"Not really. I think he's from San Antonio, though."

"Middle initial?"

"No."

A pause, during which Daniel was probably reflecting that his cousin hadn't given him very much to go on. Sounding resigned, as if he already knew the answer, "Date of birth?"

"Nope, don't have that either. But the woman who owns the place he was renting called him a 'young man,' so I have a feeling he's under thirty, maybe even under twenty-five."

"Well, that helps to narrow it down a bit. Give me a day, and I'll see what I can come up with."

A day. A lot could happen in a day. However, Rafe knew he couldn't quibble about the time-frame. For one thing, he was asking for a favor, a favor that might interfere with his cousin's paying work. Also, "Robert Marquez" wasn't that uncommon a name, and so it might take Daniel a while to sift through all the possible candidates.

"Okay," Rafe replied. He knew his cousin had to have noted his delay in making any kind of a response, but so be it. Patience was hard to come by when someone was missing.

"It's just—" Daniel began, then broke off. Curiosity clear in his tone, he went on, "If you basically dumped this girl while you were standing at the altar, then why are you looking for her now?"

Yes, the whole thing must appear pretty

strange when viewed from the outside. Clearly, although the story of the events at the church had already made the rounds, his family's speculation that he'd been influenced by some kind of terrible spell was not yet a subject of gossip. Rafe supposed he shouldn't be too surprised by that; his mother would do everything she could to keep quiet any stories about rogue witches or warlocks practicing dark magic in their territory.

"It's kind of a long story," Rafe said. "I made a stupid mistake. I'm trying to fix it now."

"Got it. Well, I'll do what I can. And I'll call you as soon as I have something."

"I appreciate it."

"No worries. Take care of yourself, Rafe."

Daniel hung up then, and Rafe let out a sigh and dropped the phone into one of the cupholders in the Jeep's center console. At least he had his cousin on the case, and that was something. It just felt as if he should be doing more.

Well, there was one thing he could try, although doing so in such a populated area carried its own risks. Still, he knew if he didn't make the attempt, he'd beat himself up for it afterward.

Jaw set, he backed the Wrangler out of its parking space, then went down to the ground level of the structure. A wave of his phone over the electronic meter at the exit to the garage, and the parking fee was automatically deducted from his account. Then he inched out onto San Francisco Street, turned left, then right and right again, squaring the block so he could come in at the apartment Robert Marquez had occupied from the side off the alley, where it was darker and there weren't any people around. In fact, Rafe didn't pull up to the building at all, but instead stopped the Jeep in an open area off the small parking lot, in a space clearly marked "No Parking."

That didn't matter. He didn't plan to be here for very long, and he knew the parking cops tended to be pretty lax on Sunday nights. But he was away from any streetlights, and the Jeep was sheltered by a large pine tree. No one would see what he was going to do next.

Transformations were always problematic. It wasn't so much that they were painful, but it wasn't like the movies, where a man would transform into a werewolf and shred the clothes he wore without any real concern for what would happen when he turned back into a man. No, Rafe needed a safe place to remove his clothing and stow it against his return. The back seat of the Jeep worked well enough, and he remembered to unlock the door and leave it slightly ajar so he could push it open with his nose.

Door handles were a bitch to work with when you'd already transformed into a coyote.

The coyote had always been his favorite animal to change into. Rafe couldn't really say why, except he thought coyotes tended to get a bad rap when they were really beautiful animals—and extremely successful as a species. Also, it wasn't that strange to see a coyote inside Santa Fe's city limits, since it seemed as though some of them looked on the city's streets as an easy means to cut from one wilderness area to another.

Anyway, while he'd been able to pick up on some of the dark magic that lingered in the area, he couldn't track it in human form. He needed a coyote's ultra-sharp nose for that sort of thing.

Clothes off, a deep breath, and the man who'd been sitting in the back seat of the ancient Jeep Wrangler was gone. The coyote who perched there now looked around quickly to make sure no one was lurking near the vehicle, then nosed open the car door and slipped out.

This area was alive with scents, from the pungent richness of the dumpster a few yards away to the sharp, aromatic smell of the pine tree he currently was using as shelter. Underneath all those ordinary aromas, however, was something dark and sickening, a smell that was unnatural, that was *other.*

Black magic.

The coyote trotted to the back door of the

building and sniffed around. Yes, the source of the wrongness came from here, but it also trailed along to one of the parking spaces at the rear of the structure. He sniffed here again, although the scent grew fainter, possibly because whoever the odor belonged to had gotten into a vehicle at this point.

And yes, he was able to follow the smell out of the parking lot and down the side street. As he approached San Francisco Street, however, it became so faint that he knew he wouldn't be able to follow it for more than a few more yards. No point in doing that, not when he had a much greater chance of being seen on that busy downtown route.

Tongue hanging out in disappointment, he retraced his steps and sniffed all around the parking lot. There were no other trails, though. Clearly, the person who'd been using the dark magic had gotten in his car and driven away. And if he'd headed out on San Francisco Street, he could have been going anywhere—turned right on Guadalupe to pick up the route to the highway that led to points north, or jogged over to Cerrillos Road and down to the southern, more commercial part of town.

A low growl escaped his mouth as he climbed up into the Jeep's back seat. He'd hoped this little excursion would have provided more helpful information, but the little he'd learned wasn't enough to work with.

As he turned back into his human self and began to grimly put his clothes back on, about all Rafe could do was pray that Daniel would come up with something. Otherwise, he feared he might never find the woman who had just vanished from his life.

SAFE SPACES

Miranda

Simon's instructions were clear enough that I didn't have any trouble finding the kitchen, vast as the house appeared to be. Even the kitchen was something to behold, with an eat-in area that was bigger than the dining room in our Flagstaff house, and an enormous six-burner stove and what appeared to be miles of pale granite countertops. Simon was in there already, standing in front of the massive built-in stainless refrigerator. The door was open as he appeared to survey the contents of the fridge.

However, he shut the door when he heard me approach, and offered me a smile. "Settled in?"

"Mostly," I replied. I had finally stirred myself to hang up my clothes—mostly because I didn't want them to get too wrinkled—but I'd only dumped my toiletries on the counter in the bathroom, too tired to figure out where I wanted to put everything away. That was something I could do when I got ready for bed. I lifted an eyebrow at the fridge. "Nothing to eat?"

"No, that's not it. I got some stuff at the grocery store and at Trader Joe's. I just wasn't sure what you liked."

"I'm not too picky." I went over and opened the freezer door, then peered inside. There were frozen pizzas and tamales, and also some fun snack-y type foods, like cheese-stuffed phyllo shells and an onion tart. I really wasn't that hungry, so I said, "Why don't we make up some of the snack food for now, and then see how we feel afterward?"

"Sure," he replied. "That sounds good."

We were both quiet for a moment. I got out all the items that looked particularly tasty, while he pulled out a cookie sheet and started the oven preheating. Then he went over to the wine fridge that dominated one wall.

"Something to drink?"

I hesitated. God knows I could've used a drink, but maybe it wasn't such a good idea to be drinking here with Simon. Then I told myself not to be silly. He hadn't made a single move on me, had been friendly and sympathetic, but nothing else. After all, just because Rafe had turned out to be such a jerk, it didn't mean the entire male half of the population would be the same way.

Still, I couldn't help making a token protest. "Won't the owner of the house mind if you drink his wine?"

Grinning, Simon opened the door to the wine refrigerator and extracted a bottle of what I thought might be pinot grigio. "This is TJ's wine —a whopping $7.99 a bottle. So you don't need to worry about drinking the owner's Beaujolais and Chateau Rothschild or whatever."

Maybe it was silly, but I did feel better now that I knew we wouldn't be dipping into the good stuff. "TJ's wine sounds great."

He nodded and got a couple of glasses out of the cupboard. Those glasses did look expensive— thin crystal, fragile as soap bubbles—but I decided I'd better not comment on them. I'd just have to be careful.

For a moment, he busied himself with hunting for a corkscrew, while I opened the packages of hors d'oeuvres and started placing them on cookie sheets. I was done with my task just as the oven beeped, apparently letting me know that it had reached the desired temperature.

"Should I go ahead and put these in?" I asked.

"Sure," Simon replied, even as he extracted the

cork from the wine. "I think there are some potholders in that top drawer by the stove."

The potholders were exactly where he'd said they would be. I wondered how much time he'd spent here, familiarizing himself with the house and its contents, because he seemed pretty comfortable. But then, he hadn't said much about the length of time he'd been in Santa Fe before I arrived. For all I knew, he'd lived here for a week or two, maybe more.

I slipped the cookie sheets with their assorted goodies in the oven, spent a few seconds fiddling with the control panel before I figured out the timer, then turned back around toward Simon. "You seem to know this house pretty well," I commented, hoping the words didn't sound too accusatory. I really wasn't accusing him of anything—I just wanted to know the story of how he'd ended up in this place.

He was in the middle of pouring some wine into the two glasses he'd gotten from the cupboard. When he was done, he came over toward me with both of them in hand, then extended one to me. "I picked up the keys about a week ago."

Well, that answered that question. "You knew I was going to be on that particular train to Albuquerque."

A lift of his shoulders as he raised the glass of wine to his mouth. "Yes."

Not sure how to respond, I took a sip of my own wine. Decent, but nothing to write home about. Which was fine. I still felt jagged from the way Rafe had rejected me at the chapel. I didn't really need any mind-blowing wine right then. "How did you know?"

To my surprise, Simon actually chuckled. "Miranda, it wasn't exactly a state secret that you were going to be leaving for Santa Fe on your twenty-first birthday."

I frowned. "No, but it wasn't like my parents hired a skywriter to advertise it to everyone, either."

His smile faded, a thoughtful expression on his face. For a second I worried he might step toward me, but he remained a respectful distance away. Thank the Goddess. I knew I couldn't deal with any forced intimacies right then. "True, your family didn't talk about it much. But still—your cousin Caitlin is married to my cousin Alex. There was some talk, although most people in the de la Paz clan probably don't know the whole story, except that you were going to marry someone from the Castillo clan. Still, it was easy enough for me to figure out exactly when you were leaving."

And there he was, waiting for me in Albu-querque like a spider sitting in its web. No, that wasn't fair. I did my best to brush the uncharitable thought aside. Maybe Simon had done a lot of plotting behind the scenes, but only because he believed he could help me. I couldn't exactly applaud his methods, and yet I hoped with all my heart that he was right and that he would be able to bring forth my hidden talents.

"I guess that makes sense," I said, my tone noncommittal, and took another sip of my wine.

"I know it all seems weird. I mean, it seems weird to me, too, but really, I had to be certain before I told you the truth about who I was. But as soon as I sat down next to you on that train, I knew I'd been right. I knew you had powers. They just needed a wake-up call."

Well, they'd certainly gotten that, although I wasn't sure who'd been doing the calling. I couldn't control them and had no idea when or where they'd manifest, but after talking to a ghost and teleporting a grand total of three times, I knew I could no longer claim to be a witch without any magic.

The timer *bing*ed, letting me know the food was ready. However, Simon was too fast for me, because he quickly set down his wine glass and went to pull the cookie sheets out of the oven before I was able to take more than a few steps in that direction.

"The plates are in there," he said, inclining his head toward the cupboard in question.

I got down the plates—heavy stoneware in a soft biscuit shade, with a raised pattern around the rim—and put them on the counter. Simon fetched a spatula and put a decent assortment of the hors d'oeuvres on both of the plates.

"Let's take this into the living room," he suggested. "It's not really the kind of food you have to eat at a table."

"All right," I responded, my tone a little dubious. I hadn't caught more than a glimpse of the living room on my way here to the kitchen, but it seemed like a fairly formal space, not the kind of place where I'd feel comfortable snacking. Then again, Simon had already told me he would have a cleaning crew come out once we were done with the house. And, thank the Goddess, the wine was white. A spill should have minimal repercussions.

Plate of goodies in one hand and wine glass in the other, I followed him out to the living room. Just like the rest of the house, the room was done in pale, neutral shades, the beiges and grays of the couched accented with soft coral and green tones. A pair of sofas faced one another across a large metal and travertine coffee table, which, I was happy to see, had been supplied with a stack of pale stone coasters. I took two and then set down my food and wine, while Simon did the same.

He glanced toward the large plaster-framed fireplace, and at once the logs within came to life. True, it looked as though it was a gas setup and not real wood, but still, I was impressed at yet another casual display of the powers he possessed.

For a moment, we were both silent as we ate and drank. It did feel good to get some food in my stomach, although I'd feared with the way it had been churning ever since I left the church, anything I ate might come right back up again. Now, though, both my stomach and my spirit seemed to be settling down. I couldn't say I was precisely calm, but at least my hands weren't shaking anymore. Maybe someday I'd discover the reason why Rafe had been so brutal to me. For the moment, it was enough to know that I'd wrested back some control. I needed to concentrate on myself, on healing the hurt he'd caused.

"Better?" Simon asked.

"Much," I replied. "Thank you."

His eyebrows lifted. "For what?"

"For this," I said, and gestured toward the living room with the hand that held my wine glass. "There's something very calming about this place. I do feel better, being away from Santa Fe."

"I'm sorry you had to go through that."

I shrugged. Probably he could tell how hurt I was, but I didn't see the point in wallowing in self-pity. Rafe didn't want me, and yet…it wasn't the end of the world. I'd show him.

I'd show everyone.

"It's for the best. I mean, I'd rather get dumped at the altar than get married to someone and have him walk out afterward. Now it'll be easier to move on." I swallowed some more wine and added, "Actually, I think I hated it there. So much pressure from everyone. Genoveva especially."

"I've heard she's kind of a dragon lady," Simon remarked as he picked up a cheese-stuffed phyllo pastry.

"Worse than a dragon. More like a Gorgon."

"Well, now you don't have to worry about her being your mother-in-law." He paused there and sent me a speculative look, dark head tilted to one side. "Were they all awful?"

"No, of course not," I said quickly, feeling compelled to defend the Castillos, although I didn't know precisely why I should care so much. "Rafe's sister Cat is awesome. And his cousin Tony is really funny and cute. Rafe's father was pretty nice, too. It was mostly Genoveva who was a pain in my ass."

"Guess we know who Rafe took after." Simon was frowning slightly now, straight black brows drawing together.

I wanted to tell him that wasn't really fair, but

then I realized I didn't need to stick up for my former fiancé. We'd had a few good moments—and a few scorching-hot kisses—but Simon was right. Rafe had treated me like utter shit. There was no other word for it, and no excuse, either. I hadn't deserved any of it, had done my very best to be honest with him, to be someone he'd want to spend his life with.

Still, I didn't feel like talking about Rafe. "Maybe," I said, then took another sip of wine. "Anyway, he's ancient history. He can drop dead, frankly. What's next for me?"

Simon's mouth curved in a smile. "Well, I hope you'll get a good night's sleep. Then tomorrow after breakfast, we'll go into Española to buy you a phone. When we get back, we'll…start."

He didn't elaborate, but I knew he meant we'd get started working on my magic. A little thrill went down my back at the thought. I really had no idea what that kind of magical training would even entail, because that wasn't how it generally worked with witches and warlocks—everyone had a specific talent they were born with, and they didn't need a lot of help learning how to use it. But Simon had told me earlier that he'd been studying old, old records from the de la Paz clan, stories about how they'd used magic long ago. He must have a plan. After all, he'd been able to detect my buried magic when no one else could.

"Sounds good," I said.

His eyes met mine, dark, penetrating. "Oh, I think you'll find it very…enlightening."

That night I had a hard time falling asleep. I knew part of it was simply being in strange surroundings, even if those strange surroundings involved a huge, comfortable king bed and impossibly high thread count sheets.

But even though I'd resolved to push him out of my mind, I couldn't keep myself from thinking of Rafe, of how this was supposed to have been our wedding night. My hand touched the empty space in the bed next to me, the space that he should have occupied in another bed, in the room reserved for us at the resort in Taos. Tears stung my eyes at the thought of that empty suite, of our canceled reservations.

Or maybe he hadn't canceled them at all. Maybe, once he knew he was blessedly free of me, he'd called one of his former girlfriends and taken her with him up to Taos. Maybe even now they were in that very bed, limbs entwined.

No. I quashed that thought with the same force I might use to crush a cockroach under my booted foot. Whatever Rafe had done to me, I couldn't believe he would be so callous as to go to another woman right after he'd dumped me at the altar. He might be an asshole, but he wasn't *that* big an asshole.

I hoped.

And I also hoped he was suffering agonies of conscience over what he'd done to me. Genoveva might have been a raving bitch, but she was also uniquely suited to give her son the maximum amount of grief about ruining her plans for a picture-perfect wedding between her only son and the daughter of northern Arizona's two clan leaders. It was definitely much more satisfying to imagine her chewing him out than it was to brood over him trying to rekindle past relationships.

As for me...as I'd told Simon, I needed to move on. Rafe was in my past. Now I needed to focus on my future, a future that, I hoped, would include me claiming my own powers.

Maybe Simon would be part of that future. I knew he wanted to be, but I could tell he was holding back, doing his best to be a friend right now and nothing more. His decision to sleep in the caretaker's house proved to me he was serious about giving me whatever space I might need. It still felt strange to be in this enormous house all by myself, but after we'd finished our impromptu dinner, he'd walked me over to the house where he'd be staying, just so I'd be familiar with the route—and also so I'd know he was really only a minute or so away, if anything went wrong.

Nothing would go wrong, though. We were safe and sheltered here. No one knew where I was, and I liked it that way. My parents only knew I was safe, but that would have to be enough for now. The next day, after we'd gotten a replacement phone for me, then I'd see about having a real conversation with them.

But I still wouldn't tell them where I was. I didn't want them to interfere. I needed this time alone with Simon. And when it was over, then I could start on the next stage of my life.

4

EMPTY SPACES

Rafe

HE'D SET HIS PHONE TO VIBRATE AND LEFT IT on the mantel downstairs, knowing that his mother would keep calling until he answered. When he'd gotten home the night before, he saw that he'd missed two messages from her while he was out prowling around in coyote form. That was when he turned off the damn ringer, knowing it would be hard enough to fall asleep without having to worry about Genoveva pinging his goddamn phone every ten minutes.

However, ignoring his phone couldn't prevent her from showing up on his doorstep at nine o'clock the next morning. Fearing exactly this sort of stratagem, he'd showered and shaved as soon as he rolled out of bed at a little past eight, but he'd barely had a few sips of coffee before the knock came at his front door. Rafe knew if he ignored it, she'd simply lay her hand on the doorknob and let herself in, so he went to answer her knock. At least that way he could pretend he had some control over the situation, even though he knew that was a lie.

"Morning, Mother," he said as she breezed in, perfectly coiffed and made up as usual, not a strand of dark hair out of place, expertly minimal cosmetics highlighting the elegant bones of her face. "Coffee?"

"No, thank you," she replied, giving his bare feet and untucked T-shirt a disapproving glance. "We need to talk."

"I assumed as much, or you wouldn't have shown up at such an ungodly hour of the morning."

"Don't be rude." Without waiting to see if he would follow, she marched past him and went into the living room, where she touched the controls to deactivate the room-darkening film on the windows. Rafe blinked in discomfort as bright morning sunlight flooded into the space. When he'd gotten home the night before, he'd had another two shots of tequila in an attempt to calm his jangled nerves.

Maybe that hadn't been such a great idea.

"I didn't know I was being rude." He sauntered past her and sat down on the couch, then propped his bare feet up on the coffee table. Genoveva winced, and he smiled.

However, it seemed clear enough that she had more important matters on her mind than his apparent bad manners. "We need to come up with a plan," she said. "Thank God that the members of our clan don't have any real contact with the Wilcoxes or the McAllisters, or the story would already be spreading like wildfire. However, we still need to do some damage control."

Scowling, Rafe swallowed some of his coffee, then sat up straight and put his feet on the floor so he could set the mug down on the table in front of him. "'Damage control'?" he echoed. "That's what you're worried about? Shouldn't we be focused on trying to find Miranda?"

"I assume we can all walk and chew gum at the same time," she snapped, her tone acid. "Of course we will do our best to locate your fiancée, but we also need to be able to work without any interference."

"Maybe we need that interference," Rafe replied. "I mean, anything could be happening to Miranda right now. The sooner we find her, the better…no matter who ends up helping us."

Arms crossed, Genoveva said, "If your fiancée is so talented a witch that she can tele-port away from all of us in the blink of an eye, then I have no doubt she can handle whatever situation she's found herself in. I am sure that she has simply gotten herself a hotel room somewhere so she can have a quiet place to think about what she wants to do next. In fact, your father is already making discreet inquiries to that effect. If she's in town, we will find her. In the meantime, we have to do whatever we can to keep Angela McAllister and Connor Wilcox out of our business."

Rafe wanted to tell his mother that her cavalier attitude wasn't helping, but she did have a point. The last time Miranda had pulled a disappearing act, she hadn't gone very far. And God only knew that hotels and motels and vacation rentals were thick on the ground in Santa Fe. It would take a while to search them all. "I didn't think Miranda's parents were an issue, considering you've practically banned them from Castillo territory."

Genoveva's mouth pressed into a flat line. "It isn't a ban. It's only that I had wanted you and Miranda to get a fresh start without any outside influence."

Of course, Rafe thought. *Inside influence, on the other hand, is an entirely different matter.* He scratched the back of his neck before responding, "Still, you made it pretty clear that they weren't welcome here, and it seems as though they got the message. I'm not sure why you think we need to worry about them butting in."

"Because they'll be expecting news about the wedding. Photographs. Luckily, Cat took some pictures of Miranda before the ceremony, so we'll just have to see what we can do with those."

"What do you mean by 'do'?"

"I mean, Rafe, that we need to make Angela McAllister and Connor Wilcox think that your wedding went off as planned. It's a good thing they knew you would be going to Taos for your honeymoon, and so they won't be expecting to hear from their daughter for the next week. Even so, we need to do our best to reassure them that everything's fine." Genoveva turned away from the window and gave him an appraising glance. "You've shaved. Good. I assume you have your tailcoat and the rest of your wedding outfit here?"

"Yes," he replied warily, beginning to see where this was going and not liking it very much.

"Good," she said again. "I'll need you to change into those clothes so I can get some photos. Your cousin Yvonne already got pictures of the chapel and the reception room, and Cat has given her the images she took yesterday of Miranda. Yvonne is fairly confident that she'll be able to composite them all together to create some images that should satisfy Miranda's parents...for now, anyway."

Rafe wanted to tell his mother that she was crazy. Unfortunately, he knew she wasn't. Ruthless, yes. She was determined to keep Connor Wilcox and Angela McAllister far away, satisfied that their daughter's marriage had gone smoothly and that she was now off enjoying wedded bliss in Taos. "They're going to find out eventually," he said. "Whether or not we track down Miranda. What then?"

"Then we will simply explain why we felt compelled to stall for time," Genoveva responded without hesitation. "And that is all we are doing. We need the opportunity to find your fiancée without outside interference."

"You don't think Connor and Angela would be able to help? They're powerful enough individually, but working together—"

"No," his mother cut in, her tone telling him that she had no intention of entertaining such a suggestion. "This is a Castillo problem, and we Castillos will solve it. And that means getting these pictures taken care of. Now go upstairs and change."

Rafe knew he could refuse. He could put his foot down and say there was no way he would ever go along with such a hare-brained scheme. However, he knew he wouldn't do that. For one thing, he didn't feel like getting into a shouting match with his mother. That would just waste energy better spent on other things—like finding Miranda.

For a moment, he wondered whether he should tell Genoveva about what he had found last night. But no, he didn't want her insinuating herself into his private search. She could do whatever she wanted with the resources of the rest of the clan, but he wanted to keep working with Daniel. Although he was close by, Genoveva probably wouldn't reach out to him for help. She could pull all the family togetherness and blood-is-thicker-than-water crap she wanted, but at the end of the day, Daniel's mother was a civilian, and so was his ex-wife. The Castillo *prima* might understand why it was important to bring outside blood into the family, but she sure as hell didn't have to like it.

As for the stench of black magic Rafe had detected, well, his older sister Louisa had already said as much when she informed him that she'd detected the dregs of a dark spell lingering around his person. Although he hated to think he'd been the target of a forbidden spell, better that than to think he'd intentionally turned on Miranda. At any rate, he'd only be confirming something Genoveva already knew, so he didn't bother to say anything.

Instead, he shrugged and said, "All right. I'll

put the damn monkey suit back on. Give me a minute."

She nodded and sat down on the couch, and Rafe went upstairs to his bedroom. At least he hadn't been so drunk last night that he'd tossed the tails on the floor, but instead had draped them across the bench at the foot of the bed. They were still a little wrinkled, but if his cousin Yvonne had the technical skills to combine separate photos of the chapel, Miranda in her wedding gown, and himself standing in his living room, and make them look realistic, then she could probably erase a few minor wrinkles.

He tried not to look himself in the eye as he struggled to get his bow tie in a proper knot. Even though he knew he'd been the victim of a spell, he still hated himself for what he'd said to Miranda. Now she would always hear those ugly words coming from his mouth, and he didn't know what the hell he was supposed to do to fix that.

But maybe telling her he loved her a few hundred times might start to erase the sting.

Did he love her, though? He'd shied away from that notion, even as he'd been forced to acknowledge the physical attraction they seemed to share. Instant love was something for *primas* and their consorts, although ordinary witches and warlocks tended to fall for each other pretty quickly, too. But Rafe didn't know for sure that he loved Miranda. Knowing she was gone was almost like a physical ache, and he thought of things about her that he didn't even remember noticing the first time—the way her deep green eyes lit up when she smiled, the lopsided dimple that showed in one corner of her mouth and not the other. The sweet music of her laugh, and the slightly throaty quality to her voice, something he'd always found sexy in other women and had never expected to be lucky enough to have in his fiancée.

The way she'd stood up to his mother, chin held high. And the way she'd kissed him, pure and passionate, as though every fiber of her being was invested in that embrace.

He scrubbed a hand through his hair, making it stand on end, then grimaced and smoothed it out as best he could.

Shit, maybe he really did love her.

And in that moment he knew he would do whatever it took to find her.

Still trying to pat down his unruly hair, he descended the stairs. Genoveva remained where he had left her sitting on the couch, which he supposed was a good thing. He knew she wasn't above snooping around while he was otherwise occupied, although she wouldn't have found too much incriminating evidence of his bender the night before. The bottle of Avíon Silver was safely back in the cupboard, the shot glasses he and Cat had used to drink the tequila stowed in the top shelf of the dishwasher.

He hadn't been expecting any praise for his appearance or his promptness, so he wasn't surprised when he received none. His mother rose from the sofa, phone in one hand.

"A neutral background would be best," she said. "Go stand over by the wall, in between the paintings."

No point in protesting. It was better to get this over with. He was itching to hear what Daniel had to say about "Robert Marquez." True, his cousin had said he'd get back to him by the end of the day, but there was always the chance he'd come up with something before then.

Expression as impassive as he could make it, Rafe went to the spot his mother had indicated and paused there.

"Smile, for God's sake," she admonished him. "You look like you're attending your own funeral."

He didn't want to think about funerals. That only led him to wonder what was happening to Miranda right now. Yes, her unruly magic had made her disappear in front of hundreds of witnesses, but that didn't mean she possessed the means to defend herself if she got into trouble. What if she hadn't actually gone to a hotel, but had reappeared in a rough part of town, wedding dress and all? She'd be easy prey. Santa Fe was a picturesque tourist city, a food and art destination, but that didn't mean it didn't have its darker side. Someone like Miranda, beautiful but sheltered, would attract predators like a gazelle with a broken leg.

"Now you're frowning even worse," Genoveva snapped.

Rafe did his best to shake those dark images out of his mind, plastering a false smile on his lips. It felt grotesque to him, but apparently his mother didn't find anything wrong about his appearance, because she lifted the phone and took a couple of quick pictures.

"Now turn slightly to your right."

Again he did as she commanded. He wondered where Cat was. Did she even know what their mother was up to, or had she slept in and so remained blissfully unaware? That wasn't like his sister, who tended to be an early riser. More likely, she'd put her foot down and said she didn't want any part of such a charade.

After an excruciating few minutes, Genoveva put her phone away. "This should be sufficient," she told him. "I'll get the images to Yvonne and see what she has to say. In case she needs more photos, make sure you hang that suit up."

"Yes, Mother," Rafe replied with a smirk. No need to return the tails to the rental place; the son of the Castillo *prima* would only get married in his own bespoke suit. It had been ordered and fitted months earlier.

Genoveva narrowed her eyes at him, but because she had gotten her way so far this morning, it seemed she didn't want to bother with any arguments. "Your father and I are going to meet with your cousin Marco," she informed him crisply. "We're hoping he can help us get to the bottom of this."

"He couldn't find her before," Rafe replied, then wanted to kick himself. He and Cat had worked very hard to hide that first disappearance of Miranda's from their mother, including Marco's failed attempt to locate the missing young woman.

From the way Genoveva's lips pressed together, she knew the story all too well. "Yes, so Marco informed me when I went to him to ask for his assistance. Regardless, I told him he needed to try again. Perhaps circumstances have changed. He was down for the wedding anyway, and I've told him we'll put him up at the La Fonda for as long as necessary, so he was agreeable to give things another try."

Of course Marco would agree to such an arrangement, especially if Genoveva threw room service and a bar tab into the bargain. And who knows? Maybe it would work this time. Magic didn't necessarily have to be consistent, even though when he'd failed in his first attempt at locating Miranda, Marco had been adamant that his talent for finding people and objects had never let him down before.

"All right," Rafe said. "I hope it works. In the meantime, I'm going to do my own digging."

"What kind of digging?" his mother asked, her tone telling him she didn't have much confidence in the outcome of said digging.

"A lead I'm following up on. Daniel's helping me out."

A sniff. "Well, I wouldn't put too much weight on his 'help.' A private detective who didn't know his own wife was cheating on him?"

Oh, for God's sake…. Rafe pulled in a breath and told himself that letting his mother know what a goddamn harpy she was wouldn't improve the situation at all. Anyway, making the affair sound as if it was Daniel's fault was a low blow. From what Rafe was able to tell, Daniel had a very successful agency, with two civilians working for him and a plush office in a high-rise in downtown Albuquerque. If he was guilty of anything, it was of being too busy to realize that his ex-wife's Pilates and yoga and Zumba classes were just a cover for her extracurricular activities.

"I don't know anything about that," Rafe said, his tone mild. Actually, anyone who knew him well would realize it was far *too* mild, but it seemed that Genoveva hadn't noticed...or just didn't care.

"Go ahead and work with him, if you want," she said. "In the meantime, I expect we'll get better results with Marco."

"That's for the best anyway," Rafe told her. "If we're both working this from opposite sides, there's a better chance we might come up with something useful."

"Possibly." She picked up her Chanel handbag and slipped her phone into it. "In the meantime, we should have enough to keep Miranda's parents at bay, and that's the most important thing."

"Does Dad know what you're doing? About Miranda's parents, I mean."

"I told him I would take care of it." Genoveva drew herself up to her full height and leveled a narrow-eyed look at her son. "He is very busy with his restaurants on top of contacting hotels about Miranda, and doesn't need to be drawn into our problem with her parents. It is the *prima*'s business."

"It's also his son's business," Rafe observed dryly, but his mother only waved a hand.

"And you're handling it, aren't you? No need to get your father involved."

Which was her way of saying that she knew Eduardo wouldn't approve, and so she wanted Rafe to keep his mouth shut. Fine. For now, he'd go along with her wishes, mainly because he didn't see what his father could really do to help.

"Got it."

She shot Rafe a suspicious look, but when he didn't say anything else, she seemed satisfied that he would keep quiet for now.

"I need to meet with Yvonne, and then Marco," she said. "Do try to stay out of trouble, Rafe."

Without waiting for a reply, she sailed down the hallway and out the front door.

Bitch, he thought, but the sentiment was a half-hearted one, something he'd thought about his mother far too many times before. His opinion of her wouldn't change anything; it never had.

He was just about to head upstairs and get out of those damned tails when his phone, which he'd left sitting on the mantel the night before, buzzed. For a second he thought about ignoring it in case that was Genoveva, calling about something she'd forgotten. But then Rafe realized the call could be from Daniel, and he hurried over to pick up the phone.

To his disappointment, the number displayed on the screen was his sister's. However, he'd been wondering what she was up to this morning.

No preamble, only, "Is she gone?"

"I see you knew Mother was coming over here this morning."

"Yes, and I tried to talk her out of it. Of course she didn't listen. Is the coast clear?"

"She left a minute ago."

"Good. I'm coming over."

Rafe didn't tell her not to. If nothing else, he could use the moral support right now. "Give me a couple of minutes—I need to get out of these tails."

A pause, and then Cat said, "I can't believe you went along with that stupid plan. It's cruel. Miranda's parents deserve to know the truth."

"If this drags on too long, I'll be the first to tell them what really happened. But for right now, it might not be a bad idea to keep them in the dark. Just until we can find Miranda."

Cat was silent. At last she let out a breath and said, "I don't like it."

"Neither do I, but desperate times and all that. Anyway, I'll see you in a few."

"Okay."

She hung up, and he took the phone with him as he went upstairs to get out of the tailcoat and tuxedo pants, and into an infinitely more comfortable pair of jeans and a long-sleeved T-shirt. Shoes, too, because although he preferred to go barefoot in the house no matter what the season, he didn't know what the day might hold, and it was better to be prepared.

When he was done, he headed back downstairs, phone in his jeans pocket in case Daniel should call. Not a moment too soon, because he'd just begun to take his coffee mug back into the kitchen when the doorbell rang.

Cat, of course. She must have washed her hair, because the long, night-black strands now hung straight as they usually did, all the intricate curls of her wedding coiffure from the day before long gone. "What a morning," she groaned as she stepped inside.

"That bad? I still have some coffee, if you need it."

"No, I'm good. I already had two cups. If I have any more, I'm going to be bouncing off the walls."

She moved past him and into the living room, and so he followed her. Ignoring the couch, she went to the window and looked out at the street.

"You expecting someone?" Rafe asked, half amused despite the situation.

"No, but I'm kind of surprised that half the clan isn't camped out on your doorstep this morning, wanting explanations."

He reflected that sometimes his mother could be useful, especially when it came to putting the fear of God in people. "I'm sure Genoveva told them to stay away and leave me alone."

"You're probably right." Cat went over to one of the couches and sat down. Like him, she'd dressed casually today, in faded jeans and a dark shirt under a suede jacket. "My phone started going crazy at around eight-thirty, so I turned it off. I don't know what the hell people expect me to do—I'm just an innocent bystander in all this."

"Yes, but you're my sister, so they figure you must have inside information." Although he didn't really feel like sitting, was way too full of nervous energy and caffeine, he forced himself to take a seat on the sofa opposite Cat's.

"Right. I don't know anything." She paused there for a moment, looking at him with an arched eyebrow. "Do you?"

"No." That was the worst of it—Miranda had been gone overnight now, and he had absolutely no idea what was going on with her or where she was. He was doing his best to remain calm because staying in a perpetual state of agitation wouldn't help the situation at all, but underneath his outward coolness, he could feel his stomach roiling, could feel the tension building up in his neck. "All I know is that something very strange is going on. Something dark."

"Like the spell that was apparently cast on you."

"Exactly." Rafe still hated the thought that he'd been so vulnerable, but damn it, the last thing he'd expected was someone to put the whammy on him. "Last night I had a weird experience."

"Another one?"

He ignored his sister's arched eyebrow and said, "Yeah, another one. I kept getting this feeling I should go downtown, so I did. And that was where I sensed more of that darkness, of something evil. I followed it to a flat above the wine-tasting room across from the parking structure."

Now Cat looked pale, the faint teasing expression she'd worn a moment earlier gone. "Why there?"

"I don't know." He flattened his hands against the knees of his jeans, once more overcome by the sensation that he was missing something big, although he couldn't begin to say what the hell it was. "The place is an Airbnb, I guess—I ran into the owner while I was snooping around. She gave me the name of the person who'd rented it out last, so I passed it on to Daniel."

"Smart," Cat observed. "I'm sure he'll be able to come up with something."

"Maybe. I don't know. I had to start somewhere. Of course, Genoveva doesn't approve."

His sister shrugged. "Why does that not surprise me? I think she hates the idea of anyone in the clan proving that life goes on after divorce, so it drives her nuts that Daniel is successful. But whatever. I'm just glad you found something that was worth following up on."

"I hope it's worth it," Rafe said grimly. "Right now, I honestly don't know. Genoveva thinks I'm wasting my time, so she's consulting with Marco again."

"Because that was so successful the first time."

"Well, we both know that, but I guess she needs to see for herself. Which is fine, since for now it keeps her out of my hair." He pushed himself up off the couch and went over to the window, more to work off some nervous energy than because he expected to see anyone outside. The street remained empty, except for one of his civilian neighbors, who was walking by with her big golden retriever Nellie. "Did you have to run the gauntlet to get out of the house?"

"Not really. I guess no one was quite bold enough to camp out on our doorstep, which was why my phone wouldn't shut up."

Rafe nodded. It made sense. If Genoveva had warned everyone not to bother him, then she definitely would have done the same for her own property. "Did you check the casita?"

Cat looked at him blankly. "No, I didn't. I mean, I looked in late last night after I got home, thinking I'd better feed that cat Miranda sort of adopted. But as soon as I opened the door, it bolted. I haven't seen it since."

Was that strange behavior for a cat? Since his mother had never allowed them to have pets growing up—and he hadn't bothered to adopt a cat or dog once he was living on his own—he really couldn't say. "Well, it sounded as if it might have been on the street before it wandered in, so I guess it should be able to manage on its own. Maybe it was just having a cat vacation and decided to go back home. We've got more important things to worry about right now."

"Should we check the casita again?" Cat inquired. "I mean, I can't imagine Miranda went back there—and even if she did, she would have let me know, wouldn't she?"

"You'd think, but this whole situation is so crazy, I don't even know what to say." Since almost anything sounded better than sitting around the house and stewing in his own juices, Rafe thought they might as well go take a quick look at the casita. Besides, if their parents were meeting with Marco, that meant they'd both be safely occupied for a while. Genoveva hadn't specified exactly where that meeting was supposed to take place, but Rafe guessed it was probably going to be at the La Fonda, since Marco was staying there. "Let's go. It's not as if I have anything else I can be doing right now. I have to wait for Daniel to get back to me, and I already cleared my schedule for the week because I thought I was going to be in Taos on my honeymoon."

"I'm sorry, Rafe," Cat said, and she did look truly sorry, her features taut with worry.

"It's all right." Well, actually, it wasn't, but the words were an automatic defense, a way to make her think he wasn't quite as upset as he knew he truly was. "Anyway, it's something to do. Maybe we can grab something to eat afterward."

"Sounds good. I had some coffee, but I just couldn't force anything else down my throat. But not eating isn't going to help, either."

No, it wasn't. He murmured his agreement, and they both headed for the front door, by unspoken arrangement going outside so they could take Cat's Mercedes SUV rather than his Jeep.

She climbed in behind the wheel, and he got in the passenger seat. A few minutes later, she was pulling into the driveway of the house where he'd grown up, although she didn't bother to park the vehicle in the garage. Instead, she parked where she'd stopped, and they both got out and headed for the side gate that would lead them onto the property.

All was quiet and still, although Rafe thought he could hear someone raking leaves in one of the yards that bordered the house. The sharp, metallic scraping noise made him want to wince, although he ignored it as best he could as he strode along the path that led to the casita. Once there, he paused at the front door, Cat a foot or so behind him, and knocked on the door.

"Miranda? Are you in there?"

Only silence met his query, and Rafe sent a glance over his shoulder at his sister. Maybe Miranda wasn't answering because she was still furious with him…and he couldn't really blame her for that.

Nodding in understanding, she stepped forward and knocked as well. "Miranda, it's Cat. We just wanted to make sure you're okay."

No response. The two of them stood on the step and looked at each other.

"Go in," Cat said in an undertone. "I really don't think she's here."

He had that same feeling as well. Holding back a sigh, he laid his hand on the doorknob and turned it, then opened the door.

Nothing appeared to be any different from the last time he'd been here. The vase of roses he'd sent as an apology after his and Miranda's first quarrel still sat on the little table by the window. The only thing that looked out of place was a bowl of water on the floor in the kitchen, presumably put there for the cat.

Which had taken a powder, so there was no

need to leave the bowl on the floor. Rafe bent and picked it up, then set it on the tiled counter.

"Miranda!" he called out, but softly. He could already tell from the waiting stillness that no one was here. Besides, the casita wasn't all that big. It would be hard to hide in a place this small.

Cat moved past him and went down the short hallway, headed for the bedroom. A brief silence, and then she said, "Rafe? I think you'd better come in here."

"What is it?" he asked, blood already going cold, horrible images of a murdered Miranda lying on her bed flitting through his mind.

"Just come here."

He hurried back to the bedroom, where he found his sister standing in front of the open closet and frowning. "What is it?"

"Look," she replied, pointing at the closet.

Staring at it didn't seem to help. All he saw was the door to the small walk-in closet standing open, the rod bare except for a few unused hangers.

"So?" he asked. "Miranda packed for our trip to Taos. You brought her stuff over to my house yesterday, remember?"

"Oh, right, I forgot," Cat said, looking crest-fallen. But then she lifted an eyebrow at him. "I left her bags right inside your front door because I was in a hurry, but I didn't see them today. Did you move them into your car?"

"No." He had the vaguest of vague recollections about noticing the two weekender bags sitting in his foyer when he came home yesterday, but he couldn't even say for sure whether that was a true memory, or whether he just thought he'd seen them.

"Let me check something." Cat left the bedroom and went into the bathroom, where Rafe heard her opening and shutting several drawers. Then she returned to where he was waiting, her expression one of undiluted worry. "Nope, nothing here, either."

"Which there wouldn't be, if she packed it for the trip." He pushed a hand through his hair, annoyed that he couldn't seem to remember whether Miranda's luggage actually had been at the house this morning. "I guess we need to go back to my place and look. I can't believe I didn't notice whether her stuff was still sitting in the entry."

"Well, you had a lot on your mind."

True, but he wasn't used to experiencing that kind of brain fade. Then again, he also wasn't used to having his mind taken over by some kind of dark spell that made him spew hateful words to the woman he was supposed to marry.

Rafe looked around the bedroom again. The

bed was made, and everything seemed to be in its proper place. It looked as if no one had stayed here in the recent past.

But there was *someone,* he thought fiercely. *She was here, even if we don't know where the hell she is now.*

He was just about to tell Cat that they might as well go when his phone buzzed in his pocket. After pulling it out, he saw it was his mother calling. So tempting to ignore the call...but what if Marco really had seen something, had been successful this time in locating Miranda even though his first attempt had been a bust?

"Hi, Genoveva," he said after running his thumb over the biometric reader.

Usually, she would have made a huff of annoyance at her son calling her by her first name. Now, though, she only said, her voice taut and brittle, "I need you to come to the hospital. Marco's collapsed."

5

PERMISSIONS

Miranda

"How far is Española from here?" I asked Simon as he walked with me out to the garage.

"About a half hour," he replied. It was warmer today, almost spring-like after the chill of the week before, despite the gold-leafed trees that surrounded us. The sleeves of his knit shirt were pushed up almost to his elbows, and I was sorely tempted to take off my jacket.

Still, I figured I'd better wait and see what the temperature was like in Española.

After a good bit of tossing and turning, I'd finally gotten a decent seven or so hours of sleep. It was enough to make me feel refreshed this morning—or maybe my mood had been improved by the luxurious shower I'd taken. I may not have been at the Monte Sagrado resort with Rafe, but it sure felt as though I had my own spa right here, thanks to the enormous marble bathroom that was attached to my bedroom.

I'd eaten breakfast alone, which felt a little weird, but again, I figured Simon was only doing his best to give me some space. The refrigerator and pantry had been well stocked with just about anything I might need, and so I'd indulged myself with an English muffin and delicious plum jam, and some great coffee. However, I wasn't sure I wanted all my mornings to be quite this solitary. Even though Simon was trying to be solicitous of my feelings, I would have rather had his company while I ate.

"You know, you could have come over for breakfast," I remarked, standing off to one side as he entered the security code for the garage door.

"I didn't want to seem like I was intruding." He went to the driver-side door of the BMW and got in.

After I'd climbed in on my own side of the vehicle, I responded, "I get it. But it seems sort of silly for us to have separate breakfasts when we're living on the same property. I know I wasted coffee because I couldn't figure out how to have that enormous coffeemaker brew just a single cup."

He smiled and shook his head, then backed

the SUV out of the garage. "Well, we don't want to be wasteful. So sure—I'll come to the big house for breakfast. Do you want to set a time, or should I text you?"

Since we were on our way to get me a new phone, texting would be simple enough. Then again, I thought it might be better to have a set schedule. That might make it easier to stick to a routine when it came to my magical training.

"Let's just set a time," I said. "Does eight o'clock work, or is that too early?"

"Eight is fine. I tend to get up early anyway."

I did, too. I wasn't sure if that made me a morning person, because I wasn't always overjoyed to be up at that hour of the day, but I generally got out of bed before seven. Even with having to make sure I was showered and more or less put together—I might not be thinking romantically of Simon yet, but that didn't mean I intended to let him see me with no makeup and in the oversized T-shirt I usually slept in—eight o'clock in the morning would work well enough. And that should give us plenty of time to practice magic.

"Good. Then let's plan for that."

"Sounds good."

We both were silent then, mostly because my attention was drawn to the changing landscape outside the car windows. In Tesuque, I felt sheltered, almost closed in, thanks to the hills on either side and the tall trees everywhere. Once we were back out to the highway, though, we were in almost a different world, with rugged mesas and dry, rocky land all around. As we headed into Española, though, the terrain changed again—it still rose and fell, but parts of it were quite flat, too.

"The Rio Grande cuts through here," Simon commented. "I guess that's why the town was founded in the first place."

I couldn't see the river, but I did notice more cottonwoods, and assumed they must be following the water. Otherwise, Española didn't appear to have much to recommend it—unlike the parts of Santa Fe I'd seen so far, this smaller town was full of strip malls and national chains, and really didn't look that much different from parts of Cottonwood or Flagstaff or even Phoenix.

There was one upside to the commercialization, though. We could shop here and get pretty much whatever we wanted.

Simon pulled into the parking lot of a large Walmart, and we both got out. The air here was even warmer than in Tesuque, mild and playful. Immediately I said, "Let me get out of this jacket."

"Sure," he replied, and waited while I tugged off my suede jacket and laid it on my seat.

Since we were only there to get one thing, it didn't take too long to pick out a no-frills phone for me and select a separate card with phone minutes so I wouldn't have to sign up for a plan. The whole time, though, I couldn't help shooting surreptitious glances at the other shoppers, trying my best to see if any of them were also witch-kind. But apparently Simon was right, and no Castillos lived in this part of New Mexico…or if they did, they weren't shopping at the local Walmart that morning.

"You're sure you don't want to get anything else?" Simon asked quietly as we headed for the checkout lines.

Since I had my luggage and toiletries, I had pretty much everything I might need. All right, my clothing choices might start to get a bit limited if this whole thing dragged on for more than a week, but I figured I'd make do. And besides….

A flush touched my cheeks. Apparently Simon noticed, because he asked, "What is it?"

"Oh, nothing," I replied. By that point we'd gotten to an "express" checkout line, although even that seemed to move about as quickly as a half-frozen stream in March. While the other people standing there didn't seem as though they could care less about my opinions, I still would rather I wasn't overheard. It would sound impossibly snobby to tell him I really didn't want to buy my clothes at Walmart, but that was what had passed through my mind. Most of my clothes came from cute boutiques in Jerome and Prescott and Flagstaff, or from department stores like Dillard's or Macy's. But if I tried to tell Simon that, I knew he'd think I was being a ridiculous snob.

He shot me a puzzled glance, but then shrugged and appeared to let it go. A pang went through me as I watched him pay for my phone and its accompanying minutes, but I knew better than to offer to purchase those items myself. I wouldn't put it past my parents to be tracking my bank accounts, even though I'd left them a message letting them know I was all right. For now, I had to let Simon handle this sort of thing. At least now I knew he was a de la Paz and not the starving college student he'd originally told me he was, and so I figured he could afford to manage the logistics. Even so, I vowed to pay him back as soon as I could.

We headed back to Tesuque. I knew as soon as we arrived at the house, I'd need to call my parents. And although I'd already called them the night before and told them I was okay, I still experienced a tremor of unease at the thought of talking to them. They were not going to be happy with my decision to stay here and learn how to use my magic with Simon. I knew they would pressure me to come back to Arizona, and I didn't want to do that. Twenty-one years of my life spent there, and I'd never shown a single sign of having any kind of magical ability. Three days here, and I was talking to ghosts and teleporting. My decision seemed obvious enough to me, although I doubted they'd see it that way.

All this ruminating made me realize that they'd never responded to my message from the night before. Or rather, Simon hadn't mentioned hearing from them, since I'd made the call from his phone. Once we were on the road again, I asked, "Did my parents ever call back?"

"They couldn't have," he replied as he pointed the SUV south and eastward. "The caller ID on this phone is blocked. They would have gotten the message, but they wouldn't have been able to respond."

"Oh." I supposed I should have thought of that, should have realized Simon wouldn't have allowed me to make the call if they could easily trace it back to him. The whole point was to fly low and avoid the radar. He hadn't come out and said it point blank, but I knew he didn't want me to give them any information about him. Of course I wouldn't; my clan was on good terms with the de la Pazes, and if I let too much slip, I knew it wouldn't take too long before someone in the other witch family figured out exactly who I was holed up with.

"It'll be fine," he said. "We'll be home soon enough, and you can use your new phone to call your parents."

"And then they'll have this number, and they'll be pestering me day and night to come home to Arizona."

He flashed me a quick sideways glance before looking back at the road before us. "You really think they'll do that?"

"Oh, probably. I mean, I understand why they would be concerned. And frankly, they're going to want me to get the hell out of Castillo territory." I let out a sigh and turned to gaze out the window for a moment. Now we were turning back onto the highway that would lead us into Tesuque, leaving Española behind. "Which means I'll just have to stand my ground."

"You're an adult," Simon said reasonably. "They can't force you to do anything you don't want to do."

On the surface, this was true enough. It wasn't as though I was my sister Emily, the *prima*-in-waiting, who was bound to Jerome and our clan, who couldn't just up and leave if she got a wild hair about suddenly wanting to see the world. Yes, I had clan loyalty to consider, but it wasn't quite the same thing. On the other hand, even if I wasn't the *prima*-in-waiting, I was still the *prima*'s daughter. I had certain responsibilities, even if I would never lead the clan.

Well, one of those primary responsibilities had been to get safely married to Rafael Castillo, and that hadn't turned out so well. Maybe the most important thing was for me to develop my powers so I could have something to offer the McAllister and Wilcox clans besides an advantageous marriage to a prominent member of a neighboring witch family.

"It's not that easy," I said, and let out a sigh.

Simon shifted in his seat and even began to lift one hand off the steering wheel, as if he intended to reach over and give me a reassuring touch. Apparently he decided that wasn't such a good idea, because after a brief hesitation, his fingers wrapped themselves around the steering wheel even more firmly. "I know you think you owe them something," he said. "But it seems as though you've done everything they asked of you. It's not your fault that this thing with Rafe Castillo fell apart. Don't you think you deserve to do something for yourself?"

"I am," I replied firmly. "Otherwise, I would never have come here with you. I would've hauled me and my wedding dress off to Albuquerque to catch the first flight back to Phoenix."

He chuckled. "And that would have been something to see. I get it. I can only imagine my parents' reaction if they knew I was here with you, in another clan's territory, rather than off taking pictures of stars in the desert."

"What're they like?" I asked curiously. Simon had said very little about his family, except to let me know he was part of the de la Paz clan.

A small lift of his shoulders. "What are anyone's parents like? I'm an only child, so they're protective. And it's hard to break away, to start making a life on your own. I knew I had to do that, though. And you need to do the same thing."

"I will," I said. Feeling more than a little daring, I reached over and touched the back of his hand, even though I knew he had stopped himself from doing much the same thing to me only a few minutes earlier. He didn't lift his hand from the steering wheel, but I saw the way a small shiver went through him as my fingers brushed against his skin. "Because you'll be helping me."

I sat at the table in the kitchen and stared at my newly unpacked phone. Simon was over at the refrigerator, pouring us both glasses of water. At last he spoke. "It's not going to make the call for you, you know."

Yes, I did know. Oh, some phones were

sophisticated enough that they did have the ability to carry on brief preprogrammed conversations, but this wasn't that kind of phone. I'd have to do the heavy lifting here.

Problem was, now that the time had come, I didn't have any idea what to say. Each dialogue I rehearsed in my head sounded progressively more ridiculous.

Simon came over to the table and set a glass of water next to me. When he spoke, his tone was gentle. "You need to get it over with. Just remember that they can't compel you to do anything. And if they're as awesome as you say they are—"

"They are," I cut in. "They're great."

"Then they'll understand. No one who loves you could possibly expect you to have stayed with Rafe Castillo, not after what he did."

My gaze flicked up toward Simon, but all I saw in his face was concern. His tone hadn't changed when he uttered the word "loves," which meant…what? I didn't really expect him to be in love with me, not when we still barely knew one another, but the attraction was there, whether or not he wanted to admit it right now.

Which was good. I needed to get my magic sorted out, and maybe then I could decide how I felt about Simon. I should be thanking him for showing so much forbearance.

And I needed to get this over with.

"You're right," I said. "I'm just being a coward."

"You're not a coward, Miranda." His voice was firm. "Don't ever think that about yourself. I'll be down the hall in the family room if you need me for anything."

"Thanks. But I think I'll be okay."

He offered me a reassuring smile. "I know you will."

After that he headed down the hallway. A moment later, I heard the TV come on, although not blaringly loud. Just enough to provide some cover so he wouldn't have to listen to my conversation come echoing through the corridor.

All right. I made myself pick up the phone, and then I went to the keypad and typed in the number for my mother's cell phone. In general, it was easier to call her than my father, just because he was often out in the garage or in the yard working, whereas my mother ended to have the phone right with her in case she was needed for clan business, or simply to be on call for babysitting duties.

Her phone rang. And rang. And rang. Just when I was sure it would roll over to voicemail as it had the night before, the call connected.

"Hello?"

Her tone was completely neutral, which I'd

been expecting. She didn't know the number I was calling from. I supposed I should be glad that she'd picked up at all, rather than letting the call go to voicemail.

"Mom, it's Miranda." There. I sounded much calmer and steadier than I'd thought I would. Maybe all the turmoil and stress of the past few days had actually been beneficial, had helped to toughen me up a bit.

"Miranda! Where are you? We got your message last night, but there was no caller I.D., so we had no idea how to get hold of you."

"I'm still in New Mexico." I paused, trying to think of the best way to phrase what I needed to say. "I'm with a friend."

"Yes, you said that. What friend? Where? And what happened with Rafe?"

I decided to respond to all those questions in reverse order. "He—I'm not sure exactly what happened, Mom, except he called the whole thing off while I was standing at the altar."

"He *what?*" Her voice practically vibrated with shock and anger.

"I told you—he dumped me." Gathering my breath, I said, "It's all right. I could tell things weren't going to work out between us. He didn't want to get married to me, and really, I didn't want to marry him, either. We didn't know each other."

A brief pause. Then, "What did Genoveva have to say about all this?"

"I honestly don't know," I replied. "I left, so I missed all the aftermath."

"You left," my mother said, her tone musing. "And now you're staying with a friend. What friend? Where?"

Obviously, she wasn't about to let any of that go. I couldn't even blame her, because I knew I would have been asking the same questions if I'd been in her position. However, I couldn't give her the answers she wanted, not and be able to work with Simon. I needed to keep him safely out of it.

"I'd rather not say," I told her. "Mostly because the Castillos don't have any idea where I am, and I want to keep it that way. There are some…things…I need to get worked out before I even think about coming home."

"What kind of things?" Her voice sharpened as she went on without waiting for me to reply, "Miranda, I know you must be hurt, and confused. But I really think it would be much better for you to come home."

"No," I said flatly. "I'm sorry, Mom. I know it's hard for you to understand, but I'm doing this for all of us, not just me. You have to trust me. Please…trust me on this."

A long, long pause. I held onto the cheap little phone, praying she wouldn't keep arguing with me. I could dig my heels in and be as stubborn as the next person, but I hated having to do that to my mother. I wanted her to understand and not ask any more questions.

At last I heard a gentle sigh come through the phone's tiny speaker. "But you're safe."

"Completely safe," I replied. "I'm fine."

"You do sound all right." Another silence, and then she added, "Okay. That is, I'm not sure how much we could do to force you to come home, since we don't even know where you are. But I suppose this is where I have to recognize that you're an adult and that you need to make your own choices. Just…be careful, and when you're ready to come home, you let us know."

"I will," I promised, relief rushing through me. "I honestly don't think it will be too long. Maybe a week, or just a little more."

"That still sounds like an awfully long time," my mother said. "Do you need anything from us? Money? More clothes?"

I thought of Simon buying the phone for me, of the way I'd refused to get any clothes from Walmart. What I had should last me a week, especially since I could do laundry here at the house. A small pang went through me as I recalled all the shops in Santa Fe that I'd never gotten the chance to explore. No doubt I would have been able to purchase plenty there to keep me happy, but that wasn't an option right now.

And clothes weren't important. What mattered was the work I would be doing with Simon, and nothing else.

"I'm fine," I said firmly. "I really don't need anything."

"If you're sure…."

"I am. Tell Dad I love him, and that everything is going to be okay. I just need some time."

"All right." A small hesitation, and then she asked, "What should we do about the Castillos?"

"Nothing," I replied. "I mean, if they reach out to you, then you can tell them I'm all right, but frankly, they don't deserve to know anything other than that. But you sure as hell don't need to call them."

"You're angry. I understand that. Somehow, though, we're going to have to figure out how to repair relations between our clans."

"Maybe," I said, thinking I was glad I wasn't *prima* and therefore didn't have to worry about the diplomatic side of the current situation. "But I think it's up to them to make the peace offerings, considering it was their *prima's* son who caused this whole mess."

My mother sighed again. "You're right. Well, your father and I will handle that, one way or another."

"Thanks, Mom." Should I say anything else? Probably not; the longer we spoke, the more chance she might be able to get information out of me that I really didn't want to share. "I need to go now."

"But I can reach you at this number?"

"Yes," I replied before adding quickly, "but only if it's an emergency, okay? I really need some time to myself."

"All right. Only in an emergency."

I heard the resignation in her tone and knew she wouldn't argue that point with me. She didn't like it, that much I could tell, but she'd respect my boundaries. My parents had always allowed us kids to make our own choices without butting in too much—unless those choices might bring us some kind of trouble. And also, they understood that I was an adult. Now that I was apparently on my own, they had to stand back a little and let me make my own way.

"Thanks. Love you, Mom," I said, then pushed the button to end the call.

Well, that was done, and with less damage than I'd feared. I had to hope my father wouldn't be too upset by the arrangement my mother and I had made, and try to call me himself, but I supposed that was a risk I would have to take.

I pushed the chair where I'd been sitting away from the table and stood, then went down the hall to the TV room, where Simon was watching soccer, of all things. Well, I'd caught him watching football just the day before, so I had to assume he liked sports, although otherwise he didn't give much indication of it.

As soon as I entered the room, though, he picked up the remote and shut off the TV. "You talked to them?"

"I talked to my mom."

"And?"

"I think we're good. She understands that I need this time for myself. I even got her to agree not to call unless it's an emergency, which feels like a minor miracle. So I guess that means I'm ready." For what, I wasn't completely sure, but I had to trust Simon, trust that he knew what he was doing. Otherwise, I shouldn't be here at all.

"Good." He got up from the couch and approached me. This time he did reach out to take my hand, to wrap his warm fingers around mine. "Let's get started."

6

INVESTIGATIONS

Rafe

HE STARED DOWN AT HIS COUSIN'S SLACK features, at the tubes attached to Marco's arm and chest. The beeping of the heart monitor seemed set at precisely the correct pitch to grind into Rafe's eardrums. "I don't get it."

"What don't you get?"

Genoveva's tone was even sharper than usual, but Rafe figured he could forgive her that much. This whole thing had to have been an enormous shock.

Doing his best to soften his voice, he said, "Why is Marco in the hospital? Why didn't Yesenia take care of him?"

Rafe's mother glanced toward her husband, who was standing off to one side, Cat next to him.

His sister's features were drawn with shock and sorrow, and Rafe knew exactly why. Marco was so full of energy, so lively…so goddamn *young*…that it didn't make any sense why he would now be lying in a bed here at St. Vincent's Hospital rather than off drinking somewhere with his Santa Fe cousins.

"I called Yesenia as soon as…this…happened," Genoveva said. She glanced over at Rafe's father Eduardo, who appeared almost shell-shocked, as if he still was having trouble processing the tragedy that had overtaken his young cousin. "Thank God we were speaking in Marco's room at the La Fonda, rather than out in one of the public spaces. His room had a little sitting area, and we were all seated at the table there. He was reaching out, trying to find Miranda, and then—"

"And then he went very pale, then stiff," Eduardo said. "And he slumped forward, his head on the table. We called Yesenia immediately, and—"

"And she came to the hotel room," Genoveva cut in, looking somewhat miffed that her husband had interrupted her narrative. "She said Marco had a stroke, but she should have been able to manage that. And yet when she tried to use her power to repair the damaged blood vessels, to restore the blood flow to his brain, it didn't seem to help at all. That was when she said we had better call an ambulance."

"Which we did, at once," Rafe's father said. He rubbed at his temple, as though he had a headache. Rafe couldn't really blame him; his father was used to having everything go his way, and so much had not gone his way—or anyone else's—over the past few days, it was enough to give anyone a migraine. "They brought him here. He's been stabilized, but I don't know how much that truly means."

Probably not a lot. "Stabilized" was hospital speak for "not in imminent danger of dying." Rafe glanced back at Marco, at his cousin's slack features. Strange, how much someone's personality altered their appearance. If he hadn't known that was Marco he was looking at, Rafe wasn't sure whether he would have even recognized him.

"But they're going to run tests, right?" Cat asked, speaking for the first time. Her arms were crossed tightly against her chest, as though she needed to hug herself to provide some reassurance that everything would eventually be okay.

"Yes," Genoveva said. "Cat scans and MRIs and something else I can't remember. I've called Sophia, and she's on her way down from Taos."

Sophia Delgado was Marco's mother. His father had died some years earlier, in a terrible wrong-way crash on the I-25. Rafe didn't want to think what his cousin Sophia must be going through now, to worry about losing her only son when she had also lost his father.

"He's in good hands," Eduardo said, although something about his expression told Rafe that his father wasn't quite as confident about modern medicine as he pretended to be.

Who could blame him? Most witch clans relied on their healers to handle these sorts of matters, although so much depended on the strength of a particular healer's talent. Some could heal everything short of death itself, while others could only manage broken bones and fevers, leaving civilian healthcare professionals to handle strokes and heart attacks and cancer.

Rafe had to hope the civilians would be on top of this one. "Was Marco having any luck?" he asked.

His father blinked at him. "'Luck'?" he repeated.

"With finding Miranda," Genoveva said, the usual sharpness returning to her tone. "But no, he hadn't. Then again, he'd only just begun to make his attempt when he collapsed. Really, Rafe, while I know it's imperative that we find Miranda, right now we have more important matters to concern ourselves with."

He gave an absent nod, not willing to argue the point. It was true that Marco's health should be uppermost in their thoughts…but at the same time, Rafe didn't see how he could do much good by being here. Marco certainly couldn't tell who was standing next to his hospital bed. His consciousness must be buried deep within, focused on healing the damaged nerves and blood vessels that had put him in this coma in the first place.

"Do you…?" Cat ventured, then paused as everyone focused on her. She cleared her throat, although she looked as though she regretted speaking up at all. "Do you think his collapse is connected to our search for Miranda?"

"I doubt it," Genoveva said crisply, although her reply had come almost too fast. Had she entertained that same unsettling thought before she pushed it aside? "Marco has been using his talent safely for almost fifteen years now. It is a horrible thing to acknowledge, but strokes happen, even in young, otherwise healthy people. Not that I would have called Marco the picture of health."

No, you wouldn't, you harpy, because he's not a perfect specimen, and you don't much like having to acknowledge that every single Castillo isn't perfect. Rafe scrubbed a hand against the side of his face, acutely aware of last night's tequila and this morning's coffee resting uneasily in his stomach, and how much he really needed something to eat. It seemed a horrible thing to be thinking about at a time like this, but he couldn't help himself. His stomach didn't care what was going on in the world; it just wanted to be fed.

"I suppose you're right," Cat murmured in answer to her mother's comment, although from the way she still frowned slightly, Rafe guessed that she was still far from convinced.

"What now?" he asked.

"There isn't much we can do except watch and wait," Eduardo said. "There are a few procedures they can try, but they'll have to hold off on most of those until the test results come back."

"But you don't need me or Cat here."

Annoyance flickered across Genoveva's face. "No, I suppose not, although one would think you might show a little more concern for your cousin."

"I *am* concerned," Rafe said evenly, doing his best to control his anger. Genoveva always did know the best way to provoke him. "But I also know that there isn't a damn thing I can do to make him better. So I might as well focus on trying to locate Miranda."

"With Daniel's help," his mother responded, disdain clear in her voice.

"Yes, with Daniel's help," Rafe told her. Part of him was annoyed that Eduardo would remain here as long as Genoveva told him to stay, which meant he wouldn't be contacting any local hotels in the near future. *Someone* might as well keep working on finding Miranda. His gaze moved to Cat. "Do you want to stay here, Cat, or would you like to come down to Albuquerque with me?"

Her relief at being asked this question was obvious, but she hesitated for a moment. "I—I don't know. Mom, would you rather I stayed here?"

"Oh, go," Genoveva said irritably. "Like your brother said, neither one of you can do anything to help, and you would have had to leave when Sophia got here anyway. We're already bending the rules by having this many visitors in the ICU."

Rafe hadn't even thought about that, but she was right. Only immediate family, and two at a time, should have been allowed in Marco's room. Then again, Genoveva always did manage to get her own way, whether dealing with her own family or the faceless bureaucracy of a hospital.

Well, she *almost* always managed to get her way. The last few days had been clear proof that the universe didn't always rule in her favor.

"Then we'll go," Rafe said, his voice calm. "Call us if anything changes."

"We will," Eduardo replied. From the way he had answered for his wife, it seemed clear enough that he didn't trust her to make a civil reply.

"Yes, call," Cat said, then slipped out of the

hospital room. Rafe joined her in the hallway, and together they walked over to the elevator. As she pushed the button, she said, "Thank God you got us out of there. I don't know if I could have stood another minute."

"Hospitals are rough," he agreed.

The elevator doors opened, and they both got in. Luckily, they had the elevator to themselves. "Oh, it's not just that," Cat said. "I mean, hospitals are worse for me, because they do tend to be haunted, even if the hospital staff would never admit to it. And there's hardly ever any romance or adventure about a death in a hospital. Just suffering." She paused there, her hands jammed in the pockets of her jeans. "No, it's that I was getting the most terrible feeling, almost like… pressure…bearing down from all sides. I've never felt anything like it before."

"You're sure?" Rafe asked. "I mean, I can see how Genoveva might have that effect on you."

Cat made a face. "That's not funny, Rafe. No, it was much more than Mom being her usual pain-in-the-ass self. It just felt…wrong."

"Do you still sense it?" Despite his attempt to keep his tone casual, he felt a flicker of cold move down his spine. His sister wasn't exactly a medium or even psychic, in the way that most people thought of the term, but having a talent that allowed you to talk to ghosts had to make you more sensitive than the average person, or even the average witch.

"Not as much."

The elevator doors opened, and they stepped out into the lobby. By unspoken agreement, they were silent as they crossed the space and went out through the glass doors that opened on the parking lot. After they got in Cat's SUV, she sat there for a moment, making no move to turn on the ignition.

"Are you all right?" Rafe asked, now feeling slightly alarmed. "Do you want me to drive?"

She gave him a wan smile. "No, I'm okay. And it does feel better out here." She pulled in a deep breath and pushed her long, sooty hair over one shoulder. "I don't know what the hell that was."

"I have no idea, but I'm glad you can't feel it out here." He hesitated for a moment; she'd said she was okay, but was she all right to make the trip down to Albuquerque? Even with the vehicle doing most of the work, you still had to stay alert in case something came up that the car's computer couldn't handle. Heading to Albuquerque wasn't quite the same as driving across town to go home, or even to get something to eat. People tended to speed on I-25, where it wasn't mandatory to engage a car's auto-drive function.

"Really, I'm fine," she said, clearly noting his concern, even though he hadn't said anything further. "Even to go to Albuquerque. Actually, Albuquerque sounds like a great idea. Right now I want to get far, far away from Santa Fe."

Rafe had to agree with that sentiment. Maybe it wouldn't look so great to the rest of the family that he and Cat had bailed to head south for the day, but on the other hand, there truly wasn't anything they could do here. Neither one of them was a healer, or possessed any sort of talent that might be remotely useful in this situation, such as brewing fortifying potions. It seemed like a better idea to go see Daniel in person, do their best to make some progress in tracking down Miranda.

Cat pushed the button to turn on the ignition, then backed them out of their parking space. It wasn't very far from St. Vincent's to the onramp for I-25, so within five minutes they were moving south, leaving Santa Fe behind them. As they were passing the National Guard Armory on the outskirts of town, she spoke.

"I still think they're connected."

"Marco's stroke and looking for Miranda?"

She nodded, hands clenched on the steering wheel, gaze fixed forward. "Maybe I'm being crazy. But it does seem like an awfully strange coincidence."

"Maybe," Rafe allowed. At the moment, he wasn't ready to pass judgment either way. "I mean, no one really knows exactly how we use our powers, how they affect us physically. It's not as if any of us are going to volunteer to go into a lab for some testing."

"That's for sure," Cat said with a small chuckle. She was starting to look a little more like herself now that they were away from the hospital, the tension leaving her jaw and shoulders.

"So what if Marco was straining to locate Miranda, really forcing it this time because the last time he tried this, it didn't work at all? What if that strain made him blow a gasket, so to speak?"

"I've never heard of anything like that happening before," Cat replied, her tone doubtful.

"Well, maybe not among our clan, but who's to say it hasn't happened somewhere else? You know the witch clans are terrible about trading information, which is kind of stupid, when you stop to think about it. There's a lot we could learn if we were just willing to share."

His sister didn't reply at once, but Rafe could tell from her thoughtful silence that she was mulling over his words.

"Possibly," she said at last. "Although in some cases, there were very good reasons why the clans kept themselves separate."

He thought of the rampage by Joaquin Escobar that had forced the bargain between his grandmother and Angela McAllister, and acknowledged that Cat might have a point. Still....

"All I'm saying is that you could be right in that there is a connection, but only because Marco was working too hard—over-clocking his processor, you know?"

"I suppose." She was quiet for a moment. "Although that doesn't explain the pressure I felt in his hospital room."

Which could have been anything. Nerves, or stress, or quite possibly the unseen force of many ghostly presences pushing on her all at once. Rafe decided it was better not to point out all these possibilities, just because he didn't want to sound condescending. His talent was utterly unlike his sister's, and so he had no real frame of reference. It could be frustrating when he tried to understand what she might be experiencing.

"No, it doesn't. And I'm the first to admit that a lot of weird shit has been going on lately. I wish you could've felt that dark presence I experienced downtown by the wine tasting room—then you could've told me whether this felt similar."

"Maybe when we get back to Santa Fe, you should take me by there, see if I can feel anything."

That wasn't a bad idea. She was more attuned to otherworldly vibrations than he, so possibly she'd be able to pick up nuances that he couldn't.

"And maybe ask the ghosts in the area if they've noticed anything out of the ordinary."

She nodded. "That's probably what I'd have to do anyway. Even though I did feel something strange at the hospital, it wasn't the usual strangeness of ghosts hanging around. This was something different."

Well, Cat wasn't a medium, or a sensitive. She had a very specific talent, which was talking to ghosts. And he didn't possess anything like her gift. Besides, it hadn't been what he felt downtown, exactly, but what he smelled. Too bad the scent trail had died away before he could follow it to its destination.

"We'll try that." His stomach growled, and he grimaced. In the seat next to him, Cat grinned.

"Sounds like we need to get some lunch down in Albuquerque before we do anything else."

"Probably. We might as well, because Daniel doesn't know that we're coming. When I talked to him earlier, I made it sound as though I'd wait for him to call me. But it suddenly seemed better to go down and see him in person."

"I get it. We can call from the restaurant before we eat—that way he'll have more time to get ready to see us."

And hopefully Daniel wouldn't have any appointments he'd have to cancel to fit them in. He did seem to be pretty busy. However, Rafe figured that he and Cat could come up with something to keep the two of them occupied until their cousin could see them.

"Sounds good."

They were quiet after that, each of them occupied with their own thoughts. Rafe was especially glad when they descended into the Rio Grande valley after passing the turn-off for Cochiti Lake; for some reason, he always thought of that as the demarcation point between Santa Fe and its environs and Albuquerque and its suburbs of Rio Rancho and Corrales, and he wanted to be well clear of Santa Fe for a while. In less than a half hour, they were inside Albuquerque's city limits and headed downtown.

Neither he nor his sister knew the city that well, but the car's nav system gave them several options for restaurants near the high-rise where Daniel's office was located. Since this would be breakfast for both of them, they decided on American diner food rather than New Mexican or something along those lines.

"Thank God," Cat said after the waitress had brought their food, a huge platter of eggs and bacon and hotcakes for her, an omelette loaded with meat and peppers and cheese for him. "I could really feel it those last few miles. All this stress on an empty stomach kind of sucks."

Yes, it did. Rafe knew he'd gone way past the

point where he didn't feel like eating because of said stress, and on to the other side where his over-tired body needed some fuel to keep it going. He'd called from the parking lot, and Daniel had said that his two o'clock had canceled and so Rafe and Cat were more than welcome to stop in. Despite the train wreck that the day had been so far, it did seem as though things were going about as well as could be expected.

They ate quickly but not too fast, letting the food fill their empty stomachs and the distance from Santa Fe provide some much-needed relief. Neither of them mentioned Marco, although Rafe noticed how Cat jumped visibly when her phone buzzed. She picked it up, looked at the caller I.D., then shook her head ruefully and put the phone back in her purse.

"That was just the dealership reminding me of my service appointment next week," she said, then picked up her glass of iced tea and took a long sip. "I'd completely forgotten about it."

"Well, life has been a little crazy lately."

There was an understatement.

"I know." Cat swirled her straw around in the iced tea, watching as the slice of lemon floating there was temporarily submerged beneath the ice before it popped back up again. "Do you think it will ever get un-crazy?"

He shrugged, about the only response he would allow himself right then. "I don't know."

And he didn't. Despite the friction between his mother and himself, Rafe knew his life had been fairly placid for the most part...until Miranda came on the scene. He didn't think she had caused any of this havoc directly, but it did seem as though it liked to swirl around her, as if she was some kind of magnet for chaotic energy.

"But," he went on, hoping he could help cheer Cat up a bit, "I have a feeling things will get better once we find Miranda. Coming down here is probably the best thing we can be doing right now, no matter what Genoveva might think."

His sister's expression did brighten slightly, which made Rafe feel better. "You're right." She glanced down at her phone where it lay on the tabletop. "It's almost two. We should pay up and get out of here."

A plan he wholeheartedly endorsed. He flagged down the waitress and gave her a couple of twenties without even bothering to look at the check. It was close enough, and it never hurt to give a big tip if the service had been even halfway decent. He knew he would never have the patience to put up with demanding customers all day.

Judging by the look of surprise and the bright smile their waitress flashed him, it had been a *very* good tip. Even better. His own day might have been shit, but that didn't mean everyone else's had to be.

He and Cat left the restaurant and drove over to Daniel's office. There was a parking garage next door, so at least they didn't have to waste time looking for someplace to park on the street.

When the two of them got in the elevator, they got a couple of sideways glances from the people who were riding up with them. Rafe glanced down at his faded jeans and hiking boots, and over at his sister's ensemble, which wasn't all that different, except that she wore black ankle boots and her jeans were in a little better shape. Still, they stood out in contrast to the two men in business suits and the woman in the silk blouse and expertly tailored knee-length skirt who also occupied the elevator, clearly professionals with offices here, or possibly some of their clients.

Whatever. Rafe knew he wasn't here to impress anyone. He supposed he should be grateful that his position in the de la Paz clan allowed him to pursue an offbeat vocation. Actually, he didn't have to work at all—his stipend from the clan would have kept him comfortable without any outside income—but he'd learned early on that an excess of sloth wasn't necessarily a desirable thing. At least with the pre-visualization work he did for virtual reality games, he was able to keep himself busy with something he enjoyed.

Daniel's office was on the fourth floor. Rafe and Cat got off there, leaving the silently judgmental stares of their fellow elevator passengers behind. Once the elevator doors closed, she let out a chuckle and shook her head. "Maybe we should have gone home first and changed."

"Why?" he asked. "I'm not worried about what a bunch of strangers think about me."

"No, I guess you aren't," she said easily. "Most of the time you don't seem to worry about what *anyone* thinks of you."

"I'll take that as a compliment," he replied, holding the door to Daniel's office suite open for her so she could enter the small reception area. Directly ahead of them was a gleaming stainless-steel desk, and sitting behind the desk was a pretty civilian woman probably around Cat's age, just as well-groomed as the people who'd ridden in the elevator with them. However, unlike that group, this woman offered them a friendly smile.

"Hello," she said. "Rafe and Cat, right?"

"Yes," Rafe responded.

"Daniel's waiting for you. This way." She got out from behind the desk and led them down a hallway that ended in a door. Opening it, she said, "Daniel, your two o'clocks are here."

"Thanks, Lisa."

Rafe and Cat went ahead and entered the office, which occupied a corner of the building and offered a panoramic view of downtown Albuquerque looking east, as well as a stunning vista of the Sandia Mountains. Daniel got up from behind his desk and came forward, offering a hand first to Cat, then to Rafe.

"Good to see you, Cat," he said. "And you, Rafe."

"I wish it were under better circumstances."

At that remark, Daniel's smile faded slightly. He was thirty years old, dark like most of the Castillos, but with hazel eyes he'd inherited from his civilian mother. Attractive, Rafe supposed, although he'd never been all that good at judging other men's looks, except possibly by the way women reacted to them. However, from the way Cat flushed a little at her cousin's greeting, it seemed clear what her opinion of Daniel's appearance must be.

Maybe that connection was something Cat should cultivate. They were cousins, but not close cousins, at least three or four degrees of separation. It was hard to keep track of all that stuff, and anyway, he'd never had to worry about hooking up with a Castillo cousin, since he'd been intended for Miranda McAllister for as long as he could remember.

Rafe shelved the idea of Cat and Daniel for

further consideration later. The last thing he needed right now was to get distracted by his sister's love life.

"Did you find anything?" he asked.

"Go ahead and sit down," Daniel said, indicating the pair of chairs that faced his large antique desk of burnished curly maple. That piece of furniture must have cost him a lot, but Rafe had to admit it looked impressive.

Cat and Rafe took a seat. She sent him a quick sideways glance, one he couldn't quite interpret. Was she worried that the news must be bad, since Daniel hadn't immediately given them any information?

After opening up the shining silver laptop that sat on his desk, Daniel went on, "Well, this is what I've found so far. Or rather, what I didn't find. Robert Marquez is a fairly common name, and I found 202 people with that name in the greater San Antonio area."

Great. Rafe had feared he might hear something like this from his cousin, but he hadn't known the number would be that high. "Needle in a haystack, huh?"

"Not quite that bad." He tapped away on the laptop's keyboard. "Since you said the Robert Marquez you were looking for was young but still an adult, I narrowed the search to those between the ages of twenty-one and thirty. That brought us down to ninety-seven people. Two of them actually had moved out of the area and not updated their information, so they're probably not the person you're looking for. For the rest, I sent a few spiders crawling across the internet to see if I could locate any evidence of them traveling to the Santa Fe area in the past month."

"Did you find something?" Cat asked.

Daniel nodded. "Two of the Robert Marquezes in question had vacationed in Santa Fe during the month of October. One of them stayed at the El Dorado Hotel, so he probably wouldn't be your guy, right, Rafe?"

"Probably not," Rafe replied. "I mean, I suppose he could've actually stayed at the hotel and used the Airbnb for his other activities, but that doesn't sound as likely."

One of Daniel's eyebrows lifted at the "other activities" remark, but he didn't comment on it. "I couldn't find any information about where the other Robert Marquez was staying. If he'd been using an Airbnb, you'd think it would have shown up somewhere, but I'll admit they lock their accounts down more tightly than most hotels do. It's still possible he was staying at the place you visited."

"Do you have a photo of this guy?" Rafe asked.

"Sure." Daniel turned his laptop around so

both Rafe and Cat could see the display on the screen. It was clearly a DMV photo of some sort, or maybe from a work I.D. The man in the picture stared straight forward, unsmiling, and appeared to be around Rafe's age, maybe a little older. That fit the parameters they'd set. As for the rest....

"He's kind of cute," Cat said. "I mean, that photo's not doing him any favors, but...."

"Which means he probably fits the Airbnb owner's description of him being good-looking," Rafe finished for her. His gaze swiveled back to the image on the screen. Too bad you couldn't tell from looking at a photo whether someone was a warlock or not. He didn't know much about the witch clan that ruled the part of Texas where San Antonio was located. The Montoyas, who'd been there almost as long as the Castillos had been in New Mexico. This Robert Marquez could be part of their clan, or not. It was impossible to know for sure.

Well, unless he went and paid him a visit in person.

"Do you have an address for this guy?" Rafe asked.

"Yes," Daniel replied, and then frowned slightly. "You're not thinking of going to see him, are you?"

"What else am I supposed to do? He's the only

lead I've got—and if it turns out he really was the person staying in that Airbnb, then the last thing I want to do is give him any warning that I'm coming."

"Mom will never give her permission for that," Cat said.

Rafe wanted to snap that he didn't give a rat's ass about their mother's permission, but he knew Cat had a point. It was considered common courtesy to ask a neighboring clan for leave to enter their territory. Then again, if Robert Marquez was part of the Montoya family and had come here to Santa Fe without asking whether it was all right, then he was just as guilty of violating clan etiquette. One would have thought that Genoveva should have detected the presence of a strange warlock in her territory, but she'd been distracted lately, what with getting ready to have Miranda come to Santa Fe, and laying all the groundwork for the wedding so plans could be put into motion without much forewarning. Rafe supposed she could have missed the subtle warning signs of such an incursion.

"I think she's otherwise occupied right now," he said evasively, and Cat raised an eyebrow.

"I doubt she's so occupied that she won't notice you disappearing for a few days to go racing off to San Antonio. That's a long drive, in case you didn't know."

He knew well enough, since he'd driven to Austin once, and the two cities weren't that far from one another. "Who says I'd drive?" he asked. "We're in Albuquerque—the smartest thing to do would be to head over to the airport and catch a flight. I could be in San Antonio in a couple of hours."

Cat turned a pleading gaze toward their cousin. "Daniel, please tell him he's being crazy."

"I'm not going to comment on the craziness of the plan, but Rafe's right. He could be there pretty fast." A glint entered Daniel's hazel eyes. "You want me to check flights for you?"

"Great, you're both crazy." Cat crossed her arms and settled back in her chair. "Or maybe I'm crazy, too, because if you're going to go tearing off to San Antonio, you sure as hell aren't going to do it alone."

"I don't think—" Rafe began, then stopped when he saw the mulish set of his sister's mouth. Clearly, if he was going, then she was going, too. He could waste his breath on trying to dissuade her, but he knew it probably wouldn't do much good. Turning toward Daniel he said, "Yeah, check on the flights."

At once his cousin began typing away. After a moment, he paused and said, "It looks like there's one leaving in an hour. Puddle jumper, but that's probably what you want anyway. Most of the bigger airlines go to the hub in Dallas."

A small plane on an obscure airline. That sounded perfect—and a hell of a lot better than spending ten hours on the road one way. Rafe got his wallet out of his pocket and fished out his credit card. Handing it over to Daniel, he said, "Go ahead and book it. Two seats."

As his cousin took the card from him, Cat shook her head. "I seriously can't believe that we're doing this."

"Oh, believe it," Rafe said. "I'm going to find Miranda, no matter what it takes."

Even if that meant going into a neighboring clan's territory without permission…and without his mother's knowledge. Right then, he wasn't sure which was worse. Not that he cared.

He had to do this, consequences be damned.

7

MEDITATIONS

Miranda

A SOFT BREEZE PLAYED WITH MY LOOSE HAIR. The day had continued sunny and mild, almost too mild for early November, although I could tell it was warmer here in this quiet corner of Tesuque than it had been in Santa Fe. We were in a river bottom in this part of the world, so I supposed the lack of altitude had something to do with the milder temperatures.

Simon and I stood in the garden, the sun shining down on both of us. He'd suggested that we work out of doors, since the weather was so nice, and I hadn't been about to argue with him. Soon enough real winter would descend, and the chance to stand outside for long periods would be gone until the following spring.

Where I'd be when winter and spring came, I had no idea. I supposed a lot of that would have to do with how these practice sessions went. A little thrill went through me as I thought of what it might be like to no longer be a *nunca,* someone other witches and warlocks looked at in pity.

"Think about your magic for a moment," Simon instructed me. He stood a few feet away, the breeze ruffling his short, thick hair. It was crisp and lively, with just the faintest wave.

I wondered what it would be like to run my fingers through that hair, then wanted to shake my head at myself. Thinking about Simon's hair had nothing to do with magic.

"What about it?" I asked. "I mean, I'm not trying to be a pain, but isn't our magic always just sort of…there? I thought the whole point was *not* having to think about it. Using magic is pretty much like breathing for our kind."

For a moment, he didn't reply, only stood there and watched me carefully. I couldn't detect any disapproval in his gaze, but he also wasn't smiling. At last he said, "Well, yeah, that's true… up to a point. But you could argue that there are lots of disciplines in this world that use focused breathing. Different kinds of meditation…yoga… even biofeedback. For most witches and wizards, you're right—they don't have to really think about it. But you're not most witches." He paused, head tilted slightly one side as he regarded me the way you might look at a lock that needed to be picked, eyes narrowed. "So tell me—when your magic kicked in and you had those experiences of teleporting, what did it feel like?"

"It felt…." I paused to consider his question. What the hell *had* it felt like? Mostly, I'd just been trying to figure out what the heck was going on. "I'm not actually sure. At first, I was just scared. I didn't know what was happening."

"But then…?"

"I don't know," I said, realizing that was not what Simon wanted to hear. Still, I needed to tell him the truth. "I mean, every time my magic kicked in, I was stressing out about something. It didn't feel good, I can tell you that much."

"Extremes of emotion—like when Rafe rejected you at the altar."

Did he really have to bring that up? I'd been starting to feel a little better about life, mostly because I'd gotten that phone call to my mother out of the way. Now, though, it was almost as if I was living that horrible scene in Loretto Chapel all over again, the strange glitter in Rafe's eyes, the cold indifference in his tone as he tossed me aside like a piece of garbage.

"I guess you could call it extreme," I muttered.

At once Simon came over to me and took my hand. Annoyed as I was with him in that moment, it did feel good to have his fingers wrapped around mine. His skin was warm and smooth, friendly. "I'm sorry, Miranda," he said. "I know you don't want to think about what happened. We need to get past that, though. You need to understand that strong *good* emotions can help you far more than negative ones."

"I know that intellectually," I replied. "It's just difficult to internalize, I guess."

"It's all right." He smiled, and the sunlight glinted on his even white teeth. "How about you just try breathing for a minute or two? Slowly, in through your nose and out through your mouth."

Since I was feeling jittery, I thought that following his advice was probably a good idea. Following his instructions, I pulled in air through my nose and gently released it from my mouth, and then did the same thing again. And again.

Slowly, the tense, angry sensation that had tightened the muscles in my neck and shoulders began to dissipate. I continued to breathe, savoring the bright, clean scent of dry, sun-warmed grass, the dark, rich aroma of fallen leaves against damp soil. I almost fancied I could smell the house itself, warm and snug under the clear, shimmering sky.

"Good," Simon said softly. "Now, while you're still breathing, reach inside yourself. Reach for the bright center of your magic. It's there…you know it's there. Without it, you couldn't have sent your-self from the chapel to my apartment…to me."

Almost against my will, my eyes closed. Somehow I knew I had to turn my focus away from the clear, shining beauty of that November morning and deep within myself. Simon was right. A *nunca* could never have done the things I'd done over the past few days. The magic was inside me. I just had to learn how to bring it out.

There. It was like staring into the heart of the sun, or into the depths of a volcano. Bright, so bright it almost hurt my eyes, even though I knew I was looking at the thing with my mind's eye and nothing else. Shimmering gold and copper, turning and twisting in on itself, practically vibrating with power.

Did everyone's magic look like that, or was there something special about mine, something about being born of a *prima* mother and a *primus* father?

Simon's voice was almost a whisper. "Do you see it?"

Afraid to open my eyes, I nodded.

"Good. We'll try something simple, some-thing you've already done before. Miranda, send yourself into the kitchen. You know you can do it —it's only a few yards away. It'll be easier than the teleportations you've already performed. Send yourself into the house."

Part of me wanted to argue, to tell him that I'd already tried this sort of thing and failed miserably. The magic did what it wanted; it didn't come on cue. And yet....

There it was, coiled and gleaming within me. I'd never seen it before. Maybe it had been waiting for this moment to reveal itself.

All right, magic. Send me into the kitchen.

At once the sensation of the sun beating down on my head was gone. Cautiously, I opened my eyes, saw that I stood next to the kitchen counter. The water glasses Simon and I had drunk out of earlier were still there.

"Goddess," I breathed.

I'd done it. I'd reached out to my magic and asked for it to do as I wished...and it had.

Footsteps at the back door, and then Simon was walking across the kitchen floor, coming toward me. He paused a foot or so away, then said, "You did it."

"I did, didn't I?"

"Hey." He reached toward my face and I almost flinched, not sure what he was doing. One finger touched my cheek and came away shimmering with moisture.

"Oh, jeez." At once I raised a hand to wipe away the tears, tears I hadn't even realized had been rolling down my cheeks.

"Are you okay?" Simon asked, dark eyes filled with concern.

"I'm fine," I said. "These are happy tears. I guess—I guess I just hadn't thought I'd really be able to do it."

He didn't say anything, only put his arms around me and held me close. It felt different from Rafe hugging me—the two of them were about the same height, but Simon was thinner, not as well muscled. As if that mattered. What mattered was the reassurance and compassion I could practically feel flowing from him into my own body.

Once or twice I'd thought about giving Simon a hug but had always stopped myself. Now I wondered why the hell I'd been holding back.

Still, I didn't want to give him the wrong idea. I knew I certainly wasn't ready to do anything more than exchange a hug. This embrace had been more to share the wonderful feeling I was experiencing, not an invitation to further intimacy.

I stepped back but made sure to smile at him so he'd know the small distance I'd put between us wasn't any sort of rejection.

Clearly, he wasn't offended, because he returned my smile as he said, "I'm proud of you. I knew you could do it, but it's not easy to overcome years of negative reinforcement."

"Now what?" I asked.

"Now," he said, "we practice some more."

It was strange to think of magic as something that needed to be practiced, but my magic apparently wasn't like anyone else's, and so I had to work with it in a way that was different from the way every other witch and warlock approached their powers.

Simon wanted me to do something simple at first. "Change your hair color," he said.

I lifted an eyebrow at him. We were back out in the garden, enjoying the sunshine. "I really don't think I'd look good as a blonde."

He grinned. "No, probably not. But that isn't the point. Your father can do illusions, right? So try casting an illusion over your hair."

That sounded easier than actually changing the color right down to the cellular level. I pulled in a breath and thought of my favorite color, a deep, deep green tinged with blue, almost teal.

Right before my eyes, I saw the long locks of brown hair that hung over my shoulders shift over to that same greenish teal. Wondering, I ran my fingers through it and saw that every single strand was that color. Or rather, there were variations in that teal green color, emerald and turquoise and dark aqua, just as my own hair varied, with glints of dark mahogany and near black buried within the brown. It amazed me that my magic could do something so complex and yet so real-looking.

"I like it," Simon said. "It's very anime…and it brings out the green in your eyes."

"Maybe I should keep it," I suggested, and he laughed and shook his head.

"Nah, I think I like the natural color better. But that does look cool. You could always change it up if you were going to a comic convention or something."

"Yeah, because I always hang out at those." I paused, and slanted him a sideways glance. "Do you?"

"I've gone a few times. It's fun. They have one here in Santa Fe, but you just missed it—it's held in the middle of October."

The words slipped out of my mouth before I stopped to consider their implications. "Well, maybe next year."

Simon's expression turned speculative, as if he was thinking over what I'd said and deciding whether or not he should comment on it. All he said, though, was, "Maybe." A lift of his shoulders, and he added, "Try turning it back now."

That was easier, since all I had to do was think of the way I looked every time I saw myself in a mirror. At once my hair shifted back to its regular brown.

"Good." Simon reached up to rub at the back of his neck. "It doesn't seem as though illusions are too much work for you, which is good. Sometimes they can come in really handy."

"Can you do them?" I asked, genuinely curious. He'd mentioned before that he had command of more than one power, but I still had no real idea as to the true extent of his magical talents.

"Sure," he replied. For just a moment, his appearance shifted to that of a popular actor, someone my cousin Jessica Rowe had a massive crush on, a man with warm brown hair and strikingly bright blue eyes. I blinked, startled, and once again Simon was standing there, the sun glinting down on his black hair.

"Wow, that's pretty good." Actually, it had been flawless, as far as I'd been able to tell. Since I'd never been around the real-life actor, I had no idea whether Simon had gotten the height right, but his face and general build had been perfect. "I guess if this warlock gig doesn't work out, you could always be a celebrity impersonator...or a stunt double."

"I'll take it under advisement." He was smiling now, clearly amused by my comment. "For now, though, I think the warlock thing is working okay for me." A pause, and then he said, "How are you with fire?"

"Well, I'm not a pyro or anything," I replied, my tone cautious.

"I meant, could you always call the fire, even though you didn't have any other magic?"

"Yes." That, and unlocking doors, had been about all I could do. But at least I'd been able to touch my finger to the wick of a candle and make it light, or get a fire going in a hearth without having to use a lighter or kindling.

"Good. Then that much magic has always been a part of you." He looked around at our surroundings, at the frost-yellowed grass beneath our feet. "Let's move over to the driveway. It's probably safer."

At first I wasn't sure what he was driving at, but then I realized that the spot where we stood was pretty combustible. "Right."

I followed him out of the garden and over to the driveway, which was very wide at that spot, spreading out from the narrow, nearly one-lane trail it was near the gate to the property, to an area wide enough to match the large three-bay garage. The gravel here was so immaculate, it looked as though it had been refreshed right before we moved in...or rather, right after the actor who'd occupied the place before us had vacated the property. It was so smooth and perfect that I really, really hoped I wouldn't scorch it too badly.

"Let's try a small wall of flames first," Simon

said, stopping about twenty feet from the garage door.

I gave a half-hearted chuckle. "Oh, is that all?"

He didn't smile. "You were able to perform an illusion without breaking a sweat, and also to teleport yourself into the house. This shouldn't be a problem."

Easy for him to say. Even though I had seen the evidence of my growing powers for myself, I still worried that I wouldn't be able to pull this one off. But I knew I had to try. I had to see just how strong my magic really was.

I drew in a breath and focused on the section of driveway where I wanted the flames to go. Nothing big, just something a few feet high and a few feet long. Enough to show that I could do it, but not so much that the fire I'd called would get out of hand.

And...nothing.

"It's not working," I said.

Simon came up to me, placed his hands on my shoulders. "You're tense. Why does this task frighten you so much?"

"Because...." I paused, trying to figure out why I couldn't bring the fire the way I'd been able to perform the other stunts he'd asked of me. According to Simon, it was only a matter of degree; I'd been doing something similar for half my life. "I guess because I'm worried about what will happen if I can't control it. There's no chance of anyone getting hurt if I cast an illusion on my hair, or even if I teleport into an empty kitchen. But fire…."

"You don't need to worry about that," he said, fingers digging into the taut muscles of my shoulders. He wasn't being gentle, but it still felt good…except that I still had to do my best not to tense up because of his closeness. Only a few inches more, and he would have been pressing against me from shoulder to groin. And yet his touch was almost impersonal, more like a massage therapist doing his job than someone who was looking for any kind of physical intimacy.

Since I didn't quite know how to react, I decided to do my best to ignore the fingers kneading the back of my neck. "I'm a worrier. It's what I do."

He chuckled, the sound warm and throaty at my ear. "Well, I suppose sometimes that's helpful, but right now, it's just getting in your way. I'm here. I'm watching. The second it looks as though you might lose control, I can take over. There's really no risk involved."

Those words did reassure me somewhat. I hadn't stopped to think that Simon could step in if the experiment went sideways…literally.

"All right," I said. "I'll try again."

Another breath, another glimpse of the core of

magic that burned deep within me. It knew it had the power; I just needed to get out of its way.

At once a wall of flame three feet high burst into existence a few feet from where we stood. No illusion here—I felt the heat of that fire coming toward me in waves.

"Awesome," Simon said. He let go of my shoulders and stepped back a pace. "Make it a little taller."

I nodded, and the fire rose another foot. However, it didn't advance, didn't move except for the natural flickers of the individual flames. "Good enough?" I asked.

"I'd say that was a more than adequate demonstration. Can you put it out?"

A blink, and the flames were gone. There weren't even any scorch marks on the gravel surface of the driveway, which made me let out a little sigh of relief. I supposed we could have fixed any damage one way or another—maybe by creating a helpful illusion—but better that we didn't have to go to those lengths in the first place.

"Perfect." He extended a hand, and I took it. "I'd say this calls for some lunch."

I was ravenously hungry. Was my hunger caused by all the magic I'd just been playing with, or simply because I'd eaten only an English muffin for breakfast, and that was now hours earlier? I couldn't say one way or another, but it definitely felt good to pull a bunch of sandwich makings out of the fridge and pantry and proceed to create quite a mess in the kitchen.

"I knew you could do it," Simon told me as he spread dijon mustard on some whole wheat bread. "You just needed to have more confidence in yourself."

Well, I would have been the first to admit that I was sorely lacking in confidence, at least when it came to magic. Then again, I'd had every reason to believe my powers…gifts…whatever you wanted to call them…were basically nonexistent.

"I think it's more than just confidence," I replied, carefully placing a slice of provolone on top of the mound of ham I'd slapped on a slice of bread. "It has to be something else."

"Like what?"

Since Simon appeared to be done with the dijon, I reached for it and spread a thin film of the mustard on a second piece of bread. Satisfied with the result, I finished assembling the sandwich and put it on one of the plates he'd set out. "I don't know for sure," I said. "Maybe it's this place."

One eyebrow went up. "Santa Fe?"

"I know that sounds crazy, but I just didn't

show any signs of magical ability until I came here."

He was quiet for a moment, appearing to consider my words as he finished up with his own sandwich. Once he'd put it on a plate, he said, "I never thought of Santa Fe as being particularly powerful that way."

It was my turn to raise an eyebrow. "Places are magical?"

"Of course they are. You've been to Sedona, right?"

"Lots of times."

"And you've never felt the energy there?"

Well, I always thought I could sense something special in Sedona, but I never knew for sure whether I was falling prey to all the hype about its supposed energy vortexes. Then again, the one thing the Wilcox and the McAllister clans had agreed on back when they were feuding was that neither clan could establish a branch there, supposedly because they didn't want either family to gain an advantage by gaining access to Sedona's mystical powers.

"I guess so," I said slowly. "But it isn't something I tried to actively work with, probably because I never thought I had enough magic for it to matter one way or another."

"Maybe it wouldn't have worked for you. I

don't know." Simon picked up his sandwich and took a bite. "Let's go sit down."

We took our sandwiches and some glasses of iced tea we'd poured for ourselves over to the kitchen table. After we'd both taken our seats, I said, "You think it wouldn't have worked because my powers weren't ready to wake up?"

"Possibly." He took another bite of sandwich, washed it down with some tea, and added, "Yours is a really rare case, so it's hard to say what would have worked and what wouldn't. Maybe Sedona's energies weren't the right kind to mesh with yours. I don't know about Santa Fe—I mean, it's a place that artists and musicians and writers have been coming to for more than a hundred years, so it has to have its own kind of energy, even if it isn't talked up as much. Maybe, for whatever reason, that energy did speak to you."

I wondered if that was what Rafe's grandmother had seen, the vision that had come to her while I was still in the womb. But then, if she'd seen that it would be this place that would finally bring me to my powers, you'd think she would have also seen that things between Rafe and me weren't going to work out so well.

Or so you'd think. Visions could be tricky things. My cousin Caitlin, who still functioned as the McAllister clan's seer even though she was married to a de la Paz and living in Tucson, had once said she really didn't have control over hers, that they'd come on her when she least expected them. And although her visions mostly did seem fairly literal, they weren't always helpful because they showed her things and places she didn't necessarily recognize. It must have been rough to have those strange images intrude whenever they felt like it, and although I'd bemoaned my lack of powers, I also was secretly relieved that I hadn't turned out to be the McAllisters' next seer.

As to what had awakened my own powers, I supposed in the end it didn't matter. What mattered was that they were definitely alive and kicking now, and I could control them. It was also gratifying to know that I could use several different talents, too, that, like my parents, an array of magic seemed to answer my commands. Even the two of them hadn't been able to manage anything more than the single innate power they'd been born with, until they'd figured out how to combine their energies. I wasn't like that, though; clearly, I didn't need anyone's help to teleport one minute and call the fire the next.

"Maybe it did," I said. "If that's the case, then I'm glad I came here, even with everything that happened with Rafe."

Simon ran a finger along the edge of his plate, not quite looking at me. "I thought you were going to let that go."

"I am," I said. "I will. But I also can't pretend that it didn't happen. For now, yes, I can ignore the Castillos. Eventually, though, we're going to have to come to some kind of reckoning, if for no other reason than our clans need to find a way to get past this."

He looked up, and his gaze met mine, dark and searching. It was hard not to look away, because I wasn't sure I wanted to see what I might find in those night-black eyes. However, I didn't detect much of anything, except possibly a bit of rueful surprise. "Spoken like the true daughter of a *prima*," he said. "And you're right, of course. But it will definitely help that when you talk to them again, you'll be coming from a position of strength. You won't be someone Genoveva Castillo can boss around."

Hopefully not, although I could still see how it might be hard to face down the Castillo *prima*, even if armed with a whole new set of magical talents. "Well, I doubt she'll want to have much to do with me," I told Simon. "I'm pretty sure most of the negotiations will take place between her and my parents. Since I'm not engaged to Rafe anymore, I should be mostly out of the picture."

"Good," Simon said, and I looked at him with some surprise. He went on, "That is, it will be good if they leave you out of their crap. Then you'll be free to do what you want with your life."

That would be a blessing. I'd spent so long thinking I had no control over anything, that I had to marry Rafe and try to make a life with him, that it was almost dizzying to contemplate what my future might be now. My life would no longer be shaped by plans made before I was even born. I could do anything, go anywhere.

Well, within limits. Witches and warlocks didn't just pull up stakes and settle in another clan's territory without express permission, and that permission was unlikely to be granted. We'd always stayed in our own little enclaves and hadn't ventured out much. But still, when I went back to Arizona, I could go where I wanted. I could stay in Jerome, or move up to Flagstaff.

Or even head south to Phoenix or Tucson, depending on what happened between Simon and me.

That thought sent a flush of embarrassment to my cheeks. It was way too early to be thinking about that sort of progress in our relationship. I still wasn't even sure how I felt about him. And I definitely didn't want to be one of those girls who immediately glommed on to another guy when their first relationship went south.

"That's kind of overwhelming," I said with a laugh that I hoped didn't sound too forced. "I think I'd rather concentrate on the next few days."

"We can do that. In fact, I was thinking we should go out tonight. You know, to celebrate."

The notion seemed somewhat daring, despite Simon's reassurances that he'd be able to mask our magical natures from other witches and warlocks. But then I thought, why not? Today I'd seen a real breakthrough. If that wasn't a cause for celebration, I didn't know what was.

"Yes," I said, "let's go out."

8

TRESPASSERS

Rafe

THE AIR HIT HIM AS HE EXITED THE PLANE,
warm, muggy, despite it being early November.
The plane they'd taken from Albuquerque to San
Antonio was so small that it hadn't even
connected up to one of the airports' two termi-
nals, had let its passengers disembark using one of
those rolling portable staircases.

Behind him, Cat dug her sunglasses out of her
purse and planted them on her nose. At least they
didn't have to worry about baggage claim, because
they hadn't brought anything with them. If the
situation went south and they ended up having to
stay here overnight, they'd have to shop for some
supplies, but Rafe hoped that wouldn't be
necessary.

"This way," he said, leading his sister across the tarmac and into the nearest terminal. He ignored the baggage claim and threaded his way through the crowds so they emerged on the walkway in front of the building. A long line of Ryde vehicles waited there, ready to take all the disembarking travelers to their various destinations.

He and Cat climbed into the nearest unoccupied vehicle, a low-slung van built for carrying lots of luggage. Too bad all that space was going to waste, but he couldn't worry about it now.

"Destination?" the Ryde's built-in AI inquired.

Rafe pulled his phone out of his pocket and pulled up the address Daniel had given him. "Um, 217 Sandstone Court."

"Thank you, sir. We will arrive in approximately twenty minutes if current traffic patterns hold."

"Great."

The van pulled away from the curb and waited for a few seconds for the pedestrian traffic in front of them to ebb. Then it navigated toward the access road, presumably so they could exit the airport altogether.

Which they did a minute or so later, heading toward downtown San Antonio's gleaming skyscrapers, although Rafe knew that downtown wasn't their destination, but rather one of the suburbs that seemed to surround the city. From this distance, the city didn't look all that different from Albuquerque, although the skyline was a bit more complicated, and of course there were no Sandia Mountains to lend a certain graphical outline to the landscape.

"What are you going to say to this guy?" Cat inquired, pulling her phone out of her backpack-cum-purse, presumably to check for any messages or missed calls. It didn't seem that she'd missed anything too important, because a second later she slid the phone back into her bag.

"Hopefully, nothing at all," Rafe replied. "I mean, if I get close enough and am able to tell that he isn't a warlock, then he definitely isn't our guy. That dark power I sensed down there off San Francisco Street couldn't have come from a civilian."

"And if you can tell he's a warlock?"

"Then we'll have a little chat."

Cat didn't look terribly impressed by his tough-guy reply. To be honest, Rafe wasn't exactly sure what he would do if this turned into a magical confrontation. Duels between warlocks—or between witches—might have occurred back in the bad old days, but they certainly weren't how differences of opinion were handled now. He supposed he was relying on the element of surprise; for one thing, he found it unlikely that this Robert Marquez would even know he was coming, and also, Rafe knew that his own power of transformation was a rare one. Probably Marquez wouldn't know how to react if the warlock confronting him suddenly turned into a wolf and leapt at his throat.

Of course, there were logistical problems to this plan, namely, that he wouldn't have the luxury of removing his clothes so they wouldn't get damaged during the transformation. And he hadn't brought any spares with him.

Hmm.

Cat's mouth quirked slightly, which meant she'd probably guessed that he wasn't quite as prepared as he should have been. To his relief, she didn't comment on his lack of a solid plan, but shrugged and said, "Well, I hope this guy's in the mood to chat. I'm here for moral support, but my talent isn't exactly the sort of thing you'd bring to a knife fight, so to speak."

No, it wasn't. Too bad that ghosts couldn't do much to affect the living. They could exert their will on inanimate objects—hence the furniture that got moved around at their cousin Tony's house whenever Victoria, the ghost in residence, got irritated with something Tony had done. However, she couldn't hurt Tony, couldn't do much except try to make his circumstances slightly uncomfortable. And since Tony was the kind of guy who pretty much took everything in stride, it all sort of rolled off his back.

Anyway, it wasn't as though Cat could call San Antonio's spirits to her defense if things got nasty. They wouldn't, though. It would turn out that Robert Marquez was just a civilian who'd come to Santa Fe at the exactly wrong time, and that would be the end of it.

Well, except for the part where they'd be back to square one in terms of locating Miranda.

By now they were well away from the airport, moving along a street that was your standard American suburban sprawl—fast food places, nail salons, tire stores, chain restaurants. It made him glad that he lived in Santa Fe, that his hometown was the sort of place where you could tell from a single glance precisely where you were, rather than this homogeneity of twenty-first-century commercialism. Well, to be fair, some of the sections of Santa Fe farther away from downtown didn't look that dissimilar from what he saw now, but he rarely ventured into those parts of the city.

The Ryde turned off the main drag and into a neighborhood of modest tract homes that had probably been built right around the year 2000. They were starting to look a little shabby now, but were still mostly well-maintained, the grass mowed, some late flowers still blooming in flowerbeds.

over at them, expression clearly puzzled. "Can I help you?"

He wasn't a warlock. Rafe wasn't sure whether to be disappointed that apparently they were no closer to finding Miranda, or relieved that at least he wouldn't have to get into a magical battle here in suburban San Antonio.

Cat stepped forward, and the man—who must be Robert Marquez, since his appearance more or less matched the photo Daniel had shown them back in Albuquerque—set down his wrench and stood up, expression shifting from one of puzzlement to obvious interest. Well, she was his sister, and so Rafe had never paid all that much attention to her looks, but it was clear enough from the male attention Cat tended to attract that she was pretty gorgeous.

"This is going to sound strange," Cat said. "But were you in Santa Fe a day or so ago?"

"Yeah," Marquez responded, still more interested than annoyed.

Smiling, she pulled out her phone and showed it to the man, who squinted down at the screen as she asked, "Have you ever seen this girl?"

At once he shook his head. "No."

The smile gone, a frown pulled at Cat's brows. "You're sure?"

"Yeah, I'm sure," Marquez said. "I think I'd remember if I saw a girl who looked like that. Or like you," he added with a smile, obviously doing his best to be charming.

Cat, however, was in no mood to be charmed. Frown still puckering her forehead, she asked, "But you were staying in an Airbnb downtown?"

"No. A cousin of mine lives in Santa Fe, so I couch-surfed at his place for a few nights." Marquez stopped there, a frown of his own altering his otherwise pleasant features. "What's this about? You cops or something?"

"No," Cat said quickly. "We're just—that is, the girl I showed you is our cousin. She's missing, and she was last seen in downtown Santa Fe. We had reports that she might have been hanging out with someone named Robert Marquez."

"Sorry to hear that." The man scrubbed a hand through his thick black hair. "I never saw her. You got the wrong Robert Marquez."

Well, shit. Rafe supposed he should have mentally prepared for this particular outcome, but he still couldn't quite tamp down the wave of disappointment that passed over him. It seemed obvious enough now that "Robert Marquez" had just been an alias used by the dark warlock—or whatever he was—who'd been occupying the Airbnb above the wine tasting room. The guy standing here in front of them now had nothing to do with any of it.

"It's all right," Rafe said, giving a subtle nod at

Cat so she'd know they were done here. In response, she began to move toward him.

"We're really sorry to have bothered you," Cat said. "Your name was the only lead we had."

"It's all right." It seemed he'd noticed the way she'd stepped back to be with her brother, because he added, "I wish I could have helped you more."

"No problem," Rafe said. "We'll let you get back to what you were doing."

"Sorry," Cat said again, and then the two of them were hurrying back to the waiting Ryde. They slid into the back seat, and Rafe shut the door behind them.

"Airport," he said, his tone curt, but the Ryde had been programmed to ignore those variations in tone.

"We will be there in approximately twenty-five minutes, given current traffic patterns."

"Great," Rafe growled, and they pulled away from the curb.

For a moment, neither of them said anything. At last Cat ventured, "Well, at least he wasn't a warlock. Because that could have turned into a real mess."

"I know." Rafe leaned back against the head-rest and expelled a disgusted breath. "What a waste of time."

"It wasn't a waste," she said, her tone a little too reassuring. Clearly, she wasn't happy about how things had turned out, either, but she wanted to sound supportive. "At least now we know that the 'Robert Marquez' at the Airbnb was a fabrication."

"And that's all we know. We don't know who took Miranda, we don't know where she is…we don't know if she's okay."

Cat reached over and patted his hand briefly, then returned to clutching the strap of her backpack/purse. "We don't even know if someone actually 'took' her, Rafe. I mean, she sure teleported out of that chapel under her own power, you know? True, we haven't been able to find her at any of the local hotels, but she could have gone farther than Santa Fe. For all we know, the dark magic you sensed downtown doesn't even have anything to do with this. It could be a total coincidence."

Yes, he supposed it could. He'd rather believe that, rather believe that Miranda had teleported herself off to someplace warm and tropical to recover from his rejection, than think she was being held captive by someone who meant her no good. Of course, that begged the question of what a user of dark magic would be doing lurking around downtown if he wasn't trying to kidnap Rafe's fiancée, but he wasn't sure he wanted to think about that right now. His head was beginning to hurt.

"Yeah, whatever," he said, but Cat didn't appear offended by his tone.

"It sucks, I get it," she said. "So we go home and regroup. I'll try talking to some more ghosts."

"Because that worked so well the first time."

"It's worth a try. Annalisa Jimenez usually hangs out down by Burro Alley. She might have seen something."

If he recalled correctly, Annalisa was a girl from around the turn of the last century who'd found herself in love with a priest, and hanged herself in her bedroom out of despair. No wonder she was still roaming around downtown, her spirit forever restless.

Rafe reflected that it must really suck to be a ghost.

"Sure," he said, not bothering to hide the weariness in his voice. "Why not?"

Cat shot him a sideways glance but apparently elected not to reply. She always had been pretty good at being able to tell when he was in a mood.

The Ryde van turned off at the exit to the airport. Rafe wondered how long they'd have to cool their heels while waiting for a return flight; he hadn't booked one because he hadn't known how long all this would take, although Daniel had reassured him that there were three flights to Albuquerque leaving between five and nine p.m., so at least it wasn't as if they'd be stuck here all night.

Well, no matter how long the wait, he knew he'd spend most of it in one of the airport's bars.

They pulled up to the curb in front of the terminal where they'd arrived an hour earlier. Rafe was just swiping his phone over the reader built into the back of one of the seats when Cat suddenly grabbed his arm.

"What?" he asked irritably. Good thing that little bobble hadn't screwed up the reader. He just wanted to pay and get the hell out of here.

"Witches and warlocks," she said in an under-tone. "Can't you feel them?"

Now that he was paying attention, he could. That tingle at the back of his neck wasn't his spider sense, but his witch blood telling him that there were more of his kind standing only a yard or so away. As his gaze traveled past the van's windows, he saw a small group of men and women, five in all, clustered near the curb. They appeared to be mostly in their forties, maybe a little older. Clan elders? It was hard to say, because not all clans even had elders, and when they did, the term "elder" didn't necessarily have anything to do with age. However, Rafe was pretty sure these must be some of the more powerful witches and warlocks in the Montoya clan, no matter whether they were elders or not.

"Guess we'd better see what they want," he said.

"You know what they want," Cat muttered, but she unbuckled her seatbelt with an air of grim resignation, as though she knew there wasn't much they could do other than try to get this over with as quickly as possible.

They both got out of the Ryde. At once the group of witches and warlocks moved toward him and Cat. The witch in the lead, a woman around his mother's age, stepped out a little in front of the others. She was dark, obviously of Hispanic ancestry just like Cat and himself, although her hair was dyed an improbable dark red. Arms planted on her hips, she said, "We need to talk, Mr. Castillo."

Rafe didn't bother to ask her how she knew who he was. Witches and warlocks had their way of ferreting out those sorts of things. "If it's some-place where we can get a drink, I'm all for talking."

A flash of irritation passed over her sharp features, but she said smoothly enough, "Certainly. This way, if you please."

She headed into the terminal, and Rafe and Cat followed while the rest of her group brought up the rear. He had no idea if their little procession looked as odd to civilian onlookers as it felt to him, but he guessed probably not. Like most witches and warlocks, they were all dressed normally enough, the men in jeans and cowboy-style shirts, the two other women also in jeans, although the witch who led the group was wearing a long tiered skirt and a knit top, along with embroidered cowboy boots. Well, this was Texas.

They all trooped into the airport bar, heading toward one of the booths in the back. "You two go ahead and sit down," said the lead witch.

Rafe could tell exactly what she was up to. If he and Cat sat down first, then the witches and warlocks would fill in around them, making it impossible for the two of them to attempt any kind of an escape. Not that he'd really planned to do any such thing, because doing something so foolish would only make the situation worse.

Still, he saw the flash of panic in his sister's eyes and wished he could do or say something to reassure her. Unfortunately, surrounded by all those hostile faces, he wasn't able to do much other than send her a quick smile as he slid into the booth. She followed suit, her body rigid with tension, and he hoped she would let him take the lead here. They needed to make sure they kept their stories straight.

The Montoya witches and warlocks took their seats next to them, although the lead witch grabbed a chair from a neighboring table and pulled it up so she could sit down on the opposite side of the table and face Rafe and Cat squarely. "I am Lupita Montoya," she said. "And I am the *prima* of this clan. What are you doing here, you Castillos? I had no warning about your arrival, no contact at all from Genoveva, the *prima* of your clan."

"I'm sorry about that," Rafe said, offering her a smile that generally worked fairly well on the female half of the population. The *prima's* expression remained stony, however, and so he decided that pouring on the charm probably wasn't the best approach to take here. "I'm Rafael Castillo, Genoveva's son, and this is my sister Catalina." He figured it was better to use his sister's formal name, since he got the impression that this Lupita Montoya was the sort of person who didn't have much patience with whimsy. "We had to come here on urgent business and didn't have time to ask for permission."

"Urgent and quick business," Lupita said. "Considering your plane landed only an hour ago and you're already on your way back to New Mexico. Or is it more that you were hoping such a lightning trip might escape our notice?"

Actually, he'd been hoping that very thing, but he wasn't about to admit that to the Montoya *prima*. "No, not at all," he replied quickly. "It's more that the business which brought us here didn't pan out."

"And what was that business?" asked one of the warlocks. His eyes were a startling blue, bright against his olive skin and black hair.

Rafe risked a quick glance at his sister. She nodded ever so slightly, indicating that she thought he should tell the truth—or at least as much truth as was safe to tell.

As he opened his mouth, though, he was interrupted by the arrival of the waitress, whose bleached hair was pulled up into a pouf of a French twist, and who wore dangling silver earrings in the shape of the state of Texas. "What can I get for y'all?"

Thank God. Lupita Montoya's mouth pulled tight in irritation, but the warlock who'd last spoken said, "I'll have a Heineken," which set off a round of drinks ordering. Rafe asked for a Dos Equis, since he doubted that he'd be able to get one of his beloved New Mexico craft brews here, while Cat requested a margarita on the rocks. Even Lupita unbent enough to order a daiquiri, and then the waitress went off to fill their orders at the bar.

"Now that we have that out of the way," Lupita said. "What were you going to tell us about your visit to San Antonio?"

"One of us is missing," Rafe said. He wasn't about to tell this hard-faced woman that the missing person in question was his fiancée, and the daughter of the leaders of the McAllister and Wilcox clans. Let the Montoya *prima* think they'd come here in search of a missing cousin. That should be good enough. "We had reason to believe that she might have been with a man from San Antonio. We went to talk to him, and it turned out he was a civilian who'd never even seen her. That's it."

Enough of this story was true that Lupita didn't appear to find much fault with it. Still, her head tilted slightly as she regarded Rafe for a long moment. "I can understand the urgency, but I still think there was enough time to contact me and ask for permission...or for help. We could have gone and spoken to this person and saved you a trip."

"We thought of that," Cat interposed just as Rafe began to open his mouth. "But the thing is, our cousin took off with this guy without our mother knowing anything about it. We were really hoping we could find her and bring her back sort of under the radar, so to speak."

"Ah," Lupita said, a knowing glint in her dark eyes. "I can see why you might have wanted to avoid notice. But your cousin wasn't here?"

"No," Rafe said, relieved that Cat had been able to dive in with a plausible explanation for why they would have come here without asking for permission. "Which puts us back at square one, I guess. We have another cousin who's good at locating people and objects, but only within a certain range. We were hoping the reason why he couldn't find her was that she'd gone out of state with this guy, but apparently that wasn't the reason."

The *prima* nodded but forbore from replying, since the waitress returned right then with their drinks. Once they'd all been handed out to their respective recipients and she'd headed back to the bar, Lupita said, "What will you do now?"

"Well, as you noticed, we're going home. There isn't much else we can do." Rafe picked up his beer and took a swallow. "We certainly had no plans to stay longer in Montoya territory than necessary."

"What does this girl look like?" the blue-eyed warlock inquired, adding, "Just in case she does happen to be somewhere around here, even if she isn't with the person you thought she might have come here with."

Cat's gaze flicked toward Rafe for a second. He knew what she was asking with that brief look —whether they should describe Miranda, or provide a description of someone else entirely. Since he felt as though he was up against a wall here, he figured it couldn't hurt to tell them this "cousin" was similar in appearance to his missing fiancée. If by some weird chance Miranda happened to wander into Montoya territory, at least they'd already be looking for her.

"She's a little younger than my sister," he said. "Long brown hair, green eyes. Slender, not too tall. When last seen, she was wearing a green leather jacket." That part wasn't quite true, of course, because when last seen, Miranda had been in a full-length silk wedding gown. But obviously he couldn't tell this group of Montoya witches and warlocks that, and he figured the green leather jacket was probably the most distinctive item of clothing she owned.

Lupita pursed her lips. "That will help. I am sorry you couldn't find her here. Is it possible she's still in New Mexico, although not close enough for your cousin with the gift of finding things to locate?"

More than anything, Rafe hoped that was the case. Marco had never said exactly how close things had to be for him to find them, but as far as Rafe could tell, his cousin's gift wasn't unlimited. It wasn't as though he could locate a missing cell phone on the other side of the planet. Maybe Miranda was just way, way north, up near the Colorado border in Chama, or all the way down south in the Carlsbad Caverns. He had no idea what she'd be doing in either of those places, but it was better than thinking she'd vanished into thin air, never to be seen again.

He couldn't face the possibility that the last time he'd ever see her was standing on the altar in Loretto Chapel, her green eyes widening in horror as he tossed her aside like a crumpled piece of paper.

"It's possible," Cat replied, once she realized Rafe wasn't going to answer right away. "And obviously, we'll head back to see what we can do there. But we really appreciate you keeping an eye out for Maria, just in case."

A nice, generic name…but also one that was close enough to "Miranda" that they could always claim a misunderstanding if any of the Montoyas happened to come across her in the future. Once again, Rafe felt a rush of gratitude for his sister's ability to think on her feet.

"It's no problem," Lupita said after taking a sip of her daiquiri. "Young people often do impetuous things—but I suppose you know that already."

Cat could only give a helpless lift of her shoulders. Had his sister ever done anything truly impetuous? Genoveva kept her on a pretty tight leash. Rafe wondered what would happen if Cat ever got tired enough of being controlled that she truly rebelled. He had a feeling that particular confrontation wouldn't be pretty.

And, now that he knew he couldn't do anything else here, he chafed to get back to New

Mexico. Thank God the Montoyas had allowed them to sit down and talk this out amicably, but he could only think of the minutes and seconds passing by. If he didn't get over to a ticketing kiosk soon, he and Cat would miss the next flight and would be stuck here for another two hours.

Although he didn't recall making any kind of a nervous movement, Lupita still gave him a knowing smile. "You wish to go. I understand. You have twenty minutes to make the next flight."

"Thank you," he responded. "Not that we don't appreciate your hospitality, but—"

"Hospitality? This?" She raised a penciled brow at him. "You and your sister should return some time for some real hospitality. The Montoya clan makes some of the best barbecue in Texas."

"That sounds awesome," Cat said.

"In the meantime, though—" Lupita made a waving motion with one hand, and several of the other witches and warlocks slid out of the booth so Rafe and Cat could extricate themselves. "Best of luck with finding your cousin…and if you should discover a need to return here, try to call first."

"We will," the two of them answered in unison. They both gave a half-hearted wave, and then hurried out of the bar in search of the nearest ticket booth.

"That was close," Cat murmured in an undertone once they were a safe distance away.

"Tell me about it." Rafe walked up to a kiosk and hurriedly slid his credit card into the slot. The machine read all his information, determined he was cleared for domestic flight, and sent the ticketing information to his phone. "Come on—they're boarding now."

As they hastened toward the designated terminal, Cat sent one last glance over her shoulder. "Do you really think they bought our story?"

"I hope so," Rafe said grimly. "Or else we're going to have a lot of explaining to do in the very near future."

9

BOUNDARIES

Miranda

ANY THOUGHTS THAT SIMON WAS TRYING TO woo me with a romantic dinner vanished as soon as I followed him into the Tesuque Village Market. Oh, it was cute, with its rustic interior and homemade murals on the walls, but it definitely wasn't the kind of place you'd take a girl if you were trying to score with her. Maybe in the summer, when it would be warm enough to sit out on the patio and watch the sunset, but definitely not now, when chilly nighttime temperatures banished any idea of dining *al fresco*.

Luckily, we were given a seat in a secluded corner, away from most of the chatter. Oh, the tables around us were all occupied, but it seemed that our fellow diners were much more interested in their own conversations than listening to anything Simon and I might say.

We both ordered wine, which made me feel a little reckless. Not that I had anything against drinking wine, but on top of coming out in public like this in the first place, it did seem as though I was rather throwing caution to the wind. I thought it might have something to do with my successes of that afternoon, of realizing that I had been able to tap into my powers, that I was no longer useless Miranda McAllister, helpless as any civilian. My birthright had asserted itself with a vengeance, and I finally felt as though I was my parents' true daughter.

If any Castillos did manage to confront me here, I thought I'd be able to hold my own against them.

However, it didn't seem as if such a confrontation was likely. Everyone else here in the restaurant was clearly a civilian, so it seemed as though Simon had been right when he said the local witches and warlocks didn't really hang out in Tesuque. Some of the tension that had never entirely left my body disappeared now as I realized we were safe enough here—and even more of that apprehension went away after my first two sips of wine.

Simon was studying the menu. "I've only had a few things here," he said. "But they were all good. I'm pretty sure you can order whatever you like." His eyes met mine over the top of the menu. "And I'm paying for dinner, Miranda. For one thing, it should be my treat, after all your successes this afternoon. Also, although I doubt the...people you left...have anyone with those kinds of skills in their ranks, it's better that you not use your credit card. They could be trying to trace you."

I forgotten about that possibility, but he was right. Probably my parents could have initiated a trace if they wanted to, but they knew I was safe and that everything was fine, and so they had no reason to do something like that. And I hadn't missed the way he was careful not to mention the Castillos by name. True, no one appeared to be listening to us, but even if you left the Castillo clan's magical powers out of the equation, they were still clearly a force to be reckoned with in Santa Fe society. It was probably better that Simon was being circumspect.

"Got it," I said. "I promise I won't argue with you about who's picking up the check."

"Good."

He went back to looking at the menu, while I did the same thing. Since I really hadn't had much of a chance to sample northern New Mexico cuisine yet, thanks to the topsy-turvy past few days I'd just survived, I decided on a combo plate with an enchilada, a tamale, and a taco. Despite the big sandwich I'd made for myself earlier that afternoon, I was hungry all over again. Using magic did seem to burn a lot of calories.

We placed our orders. Simon waited for the waiter to be out of earshot before he said, "I'm really proud of you."

Blood rushed to my cheeks. The lighting in the restaurant was fairly dim, so I didn't know how much of the blush he actually saw. Hopefully, not any. "Well, I think a lot of it was due to your help."

He lifted his glass of wine, seemed to study the dark ruby-colored liquid for a moment before he took a large swallow. "I don't know about that. I might have given you a little push in the right direction, but I don't want to take much more credit than that. If you didn't already have the innate power within you, nothing I said or did would have made any difference."

Maybe. Still, I knew it was that "little push," a way of helping me look at my power in a different way, that made my demonstrations earlier that afternoon at all possible. "I think you're being modest. You're a very good teacher."

That praise elicited a smile, although I could tell he was uncomfortable—his gaze shifted away from mine, and he seemed a little too interested in adjusting the napkin on his lap. Then he said,

"I'm glad you think so. This is the first time I've done anything like this."

"Same here."

We both chuckled a little, but that wasn't quite enough to relieve the tension. Was it only because we had to watch what we were saying, surrounded by civilians as we were, or because there was something else going on here?

Out of nowhere, I recalled the pressure of his fingers on my neck and shoulders. He was good at giving neck rubs, that was for sure. And even though that was all he'd done, I could still remember all too well how it felt to have him touching me.

I shouldn't be thinking about that. Not yet.

To cover my awkwardness, I reached for my wine glass, lifted it to my lips and took a sip. It was a malbec, rich and strong and a little fruity, something that should be able to stand up to the spicy food I'd ordered. And I knew I was doing my best to focus on my wine because it was suddenly hard to look across the table at the man who'd brought me to dinner.

"Have you thought about what you want to do tomorrow?" he asked, his voice casual...too casual.

Puzzled, I said, "I thought we were going to practice some more."

"Oh, we are. But what are we going to practice?"

Good question. I'd covered some basics today, but there were so many more types of magic I could explore. Suddenly, it didn't seem strange to think that I could try to make myself invisible, or call a storm cloud off a distant mountaintop. It was exhilarating, but also a little frightening.

"I'm not sure," I told him, then gave a wary glance at the occupants of the tables nearby. "Maybe I'll have to sleep on it."

Simon seemed to understand my reticence, because he nodded. "I understand. There is a lot to choose from."

Our waiter arrived with our food then, and once he was gone, we spent a few minutes eating in silence. Everything was excellent…and spicy hot. Good thing I had rice and beans to help cool off some of the burn from the restaurant's green chile sauce. Even that didn't get rid of all the heat in my mouth, and I reached for my wine glass again. Simon's mouth quirked.

"You grew up in Arizona and can't handle a little heat?"

"Northern Arizona," I said primly, then grinned at him. "Of course I've had spicy food, but there's spicy, and then there's *spicy*."

"If it gets to be too much, we can order some chips."

"I'm fine," I replied, determined to defend my honor as a native of the Southwest. No, I wasn't ever going to be one of those people who entered chile-eating contests on a regular basis, but I also didn't want Simon to think I was a complete wimp. Even though he was the teacher in our relationship, I still felt as though I needed to show I could hold my own, that I wasn't lesser in some way.

"All right," he said, still wearing that knowing smile.

I forged ahead, doing my best to ignore the rising heat in my mouth. When the waiter came by to see how we were doing, Simon ordered two more glasses of wine, since he only had a few sips left in his glass and mine was completely gone, thanks to swallowing way too much in a vain attempt to put out some of the fire. Maybe I should have protested, but two glasses of wine really wasn't that much, not compared to all the food I was eating. It wouldn't be like the afternoon when I'd fled from my disastrous lunch with Rafe at La Fonda and got completely wasted at the wine tasting room because I was drinking on an empty stomach.

"Stubborn, aren't you?" he remarked after the waiter had come back with our second round.

"Sort of," I admitted. "I guess I just don't want some green chile to get the better of me."

"I get it." He lifted his glass and I raised mine, since obviously he wanted to perform a little toast. "To Miranda, for digging in her heels and not giving up."

I clinked my glass against his. That was a sentiment I could get behind, mostly because I could tell he wasn't only referring to my dogged attempt to finish all the food on my plate. I could have given up. I could have gone home and washed my hands of New Mexico…and of magic. But I hadn't, and now I knew I could summon a wall of fire, could change my appearance, could teleport from place to place at a mere thought. If I'd given up, I would never have been able to do any of that.

"Thanks for this," I said, and he tilted his head toward me.

"For what?"

"Just…this." I gestured with my glass toward the restaurant. "Going out. Feeling normal. Doing something regular people do. I definitely did not feel normal in Santa Fe."

"I can't blame you for that. They're not exactly a normal group of people. I mean, I don't know all that much about the family, but it seems clear that the woman in charge is a little unhinged."

Once again I noted how he avoided mentioning any names. As for "unhinged"? I wasn't sure if I would go that far. Controlling, yes.

Domineering, definitely. But it was pretty obvious that Genoveva Castillo was fully in control of her faculties, even if you didn't much care for how she used them.

"Well, let's just say I'm *very* relieved she isn't going to be my mother-in-law after all."

Simon's eyes met mine. So dark, with that fringe of black lashes all around. "I'm relieved, too."

Uh-oh. I really hadn't meant it that way, but clearly he was just as pleased that I was now unattached.

Well, I'd worry about his remark later. Even with all the food I'd consumed, I could tell that the second glass of wine was starting to get to me. Not exactly in a bad way, but I knew I was a little tipsy. I'd have to watch it.

"So," I said quickly, knowing I needed to change the subject, "what do you do for hobbies, Simon?"

He stared at me blankly for a moment. "Hobbies?"

"You know, the stuff normal people do to occupy themselves when they aren't at work or school or watching TV or whatever."

"I know what hobbies are."

"Well, then."

"Photography, mostly. That was the reason I could convince my parents I was going on that night photography workshop/expedition. I've been pretty serious about it since my sophomore year of high school."

Photography. Yes, that was a nice, normal hobby to have.

"What about you?" he asked, his tone faintly challenging.

"Rocks."

"Rocks?"

"You know, those hard things that you walk on, or that make up mountains."

This time, he didn't bother to reply, only sat there across from me, fingers wrapped around the stem of his wine glass.

I relented, saying, "I guess it made sense, since I grew up someplace that was kind of geologically unique. But I always found rocks fascinating. I collected lots of them, had them all labeled on shelves." A pang went through me as I thought of those shelves of rocks left behind in Arizona. My parents would make sure they remained dusted and looked after, but the collection would now remain forever static, its final addition a gorgeous piece of rough tourmaline I'd found on the dirt road between Jerome and Williams.

"That's pretty cool," Simon said. His tone wasn't derisive or anything; he sounded genuinely interested. "Did you study geology at school?"

"I took some classes, but my major was European history."

"Why? I mean, why that and not geology?"

"Because…." I let the word trail off as I tried to think of a way to explain my decision. Both my parents had been surprised by my choice of major, considering all the hours I'd spent collecting specimens and looking them up and labeling them. "This is going to sound weird."

"Try me."

I took a fortifying sip of wine before I said, "Because I knew the history major would be interesting, but I wasn't exactly attached to it, you know? Whereas I really did love geology, and I knew I could get a degree and not be able to do a damn thing with it because I had to come here to marry Ra—well, to get married. So what would be the point? I could already tell that his mother wasn't the type who'd let her daughter-in-law go tromping around digging up specimens on the weekend. It was better to major in something I didn't care about so much."

For a long moment, Simon didn't say anything, only sat there and watched me, brows pulled together slightly, thin, mobile lips compressed. At last he leaned forward a bit, although he didn't try to reach out toward me. "I'm sorry."

I didn't ask him what he was sorry about. "It's

okay. It's not as though you had anything to do with any of it. But that's my hobby. I liked going on hikes, looking at the formations, gathering new stones for my collection. It was something I could do that didn't have any connection to mag—well, to the things I was expected to do and couldn't."

"I get it." He drank more wine, emptying his glass.

Taking that as a signal that he wanted the meal to end, I finished the last sip in my glass as well.

"Did you want anything else? Dessert?"

"Oh, no," I replied at once. "I'm so full, you're probably going to have to roll me to the car."

He smiled at my comment, and I could practically feel the tension dissipate. I'd told him some truths, and he didn't seem to mind, in fact appeared glad that he now knew a little more about me. This was how it was supposed to work, wasn't it? We'd each become more and more familiar with one another, and then....

And then...what?

I still didn't know for sure.

However, I didn't really need to worry about contemplating my immediate future, because the waiter came back, and Simon gave him a bunch of twenties and told him to keep the change. I was a little surprised by this, just because I knew so few people who carried any cash with them these days. It was so much easier to just wave your phone or your watch over a waiter's tablet.

But since he was trying to keep us off the Castillos' radar, I could see why Simon would use cash. No need to wonder where he got it; even witches and warlocks in their early twenties received a decent-sized stipend from their clans, enough money to live independently without ever having to get a job.

We went out to the car and drove back to the compound. The night before, I hadn't really paid all that much attention to how truly dark and isolated the place we were staying actually was, since I was safely inside and hadn't ventured out. True, solar lights guided us to the garage, and Simon clearly knew where he was going, but even so, I could almost feel the darkness of the woods that surrounded the property, feel the emptiness pressing in on me. The moon should have only been a day or so past full, and yet it wasn't visible. Probably it hadn't risen yet, or maybe we'd had a "day moon" and I just hadn't noticed it.

Either way, I was relieved when we pulled into the garage, and even more relieved once we were in the house. I suppose there wasn't any real need for Simon to accompany me there, since he was staying in the caretaker's place, and yet I was glad. I wasn't quite ready to call it an evening, although the house had satellite and I could've had my pick of shows to watch on TV.

I set my purse down on the kitchen table. "I need a glass of water. You want some, too?"

"Sure."

Good. Fetching water for the two of us would take up a little time. I got some glasses down from the cupboard and filled them up with water through the refrigerator door. "Here you go."

He took the glass from me, a small smile playing around the corners of his mouth. "The green chile still getting to you? Water doesn't really help, you know. You need chips or bread or something like that."

"Oh, I know." I took a sip, then said, "I'm mostly over it. There's just always that point you get to where you feel like your mouth is on fire, but I muscled past it."

"Good."

Another one of those silences fell, the kind I desperately wanted to fill with something but didn't quite know what I should say. Had he come in the house with me because he wanted a good night kiss? And if that was the case, what should I do about it? Part of me wasn't exactly put off by the thought of kissing Simon, although I knew it was far too soon to be doing anything like that. I couldn't stand on an altar with the man I'd thought I was going to marry on one day, then kiss someone else the next. It didn't work that way. Or at least, *I* didn't work that way.

"Thanks for dinner," I said. "It was really good."

"I'm glad you liked it. We don't have a ton of choices if we're trying to avoid Santa Fe, but there are some restaurants at the Buffalo Thunder resort in Pojoaque, and I've heard there are good places in Española, too…if you don't mind slumming."

I made a face at him. "Slumming? That's kind of harsh."

He chuckled, one eyebrow lifted at an ironic angle. "Oh, please. I saw the look on your face when I suggested you buy some things at Walmart. It's okay—you're the daughter of a *prima,* and your father is a Wilcox. I doubt you've ever had to look to see whether something was on sale before you bought it."

At first I wasn't sure how to reply, because really, if I put my indignation aside for a moment, what he'd said was only the truth. Money had never been an issue in my household. At the same time, I didn't want him to think I was a snob. And besides…. "Well, you're a de la Paz. Last time I checked, your clan wasn't exactly hurting for cash, either."

A strange expression crossed over Simon's face, one that came and went so quickly, I couldn't even tell exactly what it was. Annoyance? Impatience?

"Well, true, but it's still not the same as being part of the *prima*'s immediate family."

A half-hearted excuse at best, but I decided to let it slide. The matter certainly wasn't worth quarreling over…if that was even what we were doing. "Maybe, but I'm fine with going to Española to eat one night. Or up to Buffalo Thunder."

"Okay." He drained the rest of the water in his glass, then set it down. "Well, have a good night, Miranda. Don't stay up too late—we're going to have a busy day tomorrow."

"I won't," I said. Then I added, "But you're going to meet me here for breakfast, right?"

"Of course. That's what we agreed on." He smiled at me, but that smile didn't quite reach his eyes. "I'll see you tomorrow morning."

Then he let himself out through the kitchen door, and I stood there, wondering, glass of water still in my hands. Was he angry with me? Had he envisioned a different end to the evening?

Well, there wasn't much I could do about it now, even if I'd wanted to. And I wasn't sure whether I did. Things had moved fast with Rafe— partly because I didn't have much of a choice— and look what had happened there. Simon and I weren't under any kind of outside time pressure, so I sure as hell wasn't about to inflict some on myself for no reason. Things would happen, or they wouldn't, but it would be according to my own schedule, not Simon's expectations.

That sounded very sensible. About all I could do was hope I had the sense to follow my own advice.

10

WHISPERINGS

Rafe

THE WHOLE TIME THEY WERE IN THE AIR AND even after the plane set down on the tarmac in Albuquerque, Rafe had been tense, fully expecting that his phone would ring and Genoveva would be on the line, chewing him out for going to San Antonio on such a wild goose chase. But apparently Lupita Montoya wasn't the type to go telling tales out of school, because his phone remained blissfully silent.

After they got Cat's SUV out of the parking garage at Albuquerque's Sunport, Rafe called Daniel to let him know the San Antonio lead— and Robert Marquez—had been a bust.

"Sorry about that," Daniel said. "I knew it was probably a long shot."

"It's all right," Rafe told him. "But it means we'll need to keep digging."

"I'm not sure there's that much to dig, but I'll do my best. Bank records, probably."

Rafe didn't bother to ask his cousin how he could access that kind of privileged data. Even regular private detectives could ferret out information barred to the general public, and a private investigator who also happened to be a warlock could do far more than that. He realized he'd never learned what Daniel's particular talent was. It would be rude to ask, so he decided to set the matter aside for now.

"Thanks. I appreciate it. We'll be in Santa Fe unless something else comes up, so you know where to find me."

"Got it."

That was the end of the call. Rafe stuck his phone in his pocket and gazed moodily out the Mercedes' windows. By that point, the sun had already gone down, and whatever warmth it might have given the world had disappeared with it. He couldn't exactly shiver, not in the comfortable confines of his sister's SUV, but he still felt a chill.

"What now?" Cat asked.

"Not much," he replied. "More waiting, I guess. Heard anything from Genoveva?"

"She texted me during the flight, said that the results of Marco's MRI were inconclusive...whatever that means." Cat glanced over at Rafe, then just as quickly looked back at the road. "She wanted to know if I could sit with him for a few hours tomorrow afternoon. I said it wouldn't be a problem."

Which it wouldn't. Unlike him, Cat didn't have a "real" job—not that she needed one. She was, however, an accomplished textile artist, sold some of her hand-loomed pieces in the shops on Canyon Road and elsewhere around the city. Even so, she had plenty of spare time at the moment, since she didn't have any art shows coming up until closer to the holidays.

"Maybe I should come along," he suggested.

"You hate hospitals."

"Doesn't everyone?"

She tapped her fingers on the steering wheel. "Probably us witches and warlocks more than anyone, since we spend less time there. If one of our own is in the hospital, it usually means whatever is wrong is bad enough that a healer couldn't help." Another of those quick sideways glances— all she could really spare, since northbound traffic was still thick enough with people heading home from their jobs in Albuquerque that you really needed to pay attention. "But thanks. It would make it easier for me if you came along. And who knows—hearing the two of us talking might be better for Marco than me just sitting there playing with my phone."

"It probably would be. People in comas can still hear, or at least, that's what I've read." Rafe reflected that until Marco had been hit by this stroke—or whatever it was—he'd never known anyone who'd actually been in a coma. The condition had always been something he'd read about in a book, or seen in a movie or television show. "And it's not like I have anything else I could do with my time. I mean, I suppose I could contact my client and tell him I got back from my honeymoon early, but then I'm stuck with deadlines again, and if something happens with the search for Miranda—"

"Then you'd have to explain why you couldn't work. I get it."

Of course, if one of his clients dropped him, it wouldn't be the end of the world. It wasn't as though he needed the money. But his pride was involved. Rafe knew he was good at what he did, could pick and choose his projects. All it would take, though, was one failure to meet a deadline, and word would start to go out that Rafael Castillo was kind of a flake. When game launches involving millions of dollars of R&D were involved, flakiness was not tolerated.

Which meant he'd better hope this all got wrapped up in the next four or five days, because less than a week from now, he was expected to be back at work.

It's always a party, he thought.

"Well," Cat said, clearly picking up on his current mood, "we'll have to hope this doesn't take that long. True, San Antonio didn't work out, but…." She trailed off there, as if she'd just realized they didn't have any other leads to follow, and so whatever cheery pep talk she'd intended to give him would have fallen woefully flat.

However, he had to appreciate her attempt to keep him from wallowing in misery, even if there really wasn't much she could say to make him feel better. Miranda was gone, as gone as though she'd been sucked up into a passing UFO. Actually, that scenario would have given him some hope, since at least aliens tended to return their abductees.

If you believed in that sort of thing, of course.

"Maybe Daniel will find something else," Rafe said, since the silence that followed her aborted attempt to cheer him up was getting a little too drawn out.

"I'm sure he will," Cat said briskly. "He's really good at what he does."

Had he detected a particular note of admiration in his sister's tone? "He must be, or he wouldn't be able to afford that office and a couple of full-time employees." Rafe shifted in his seat so he could look at his sister a little more closely. "Are you interested in him?"

"Am I what?" They were right where the northbound I-25 intersected with Highway 550, and so she couldn't take her eyes off the road, thanks to all the people who decided to cut across the freeway at the last minute so they could exit in Rio Rancho. However, Rafe could still hear the incredulity in her voice.

"Interested in Daniel. I mean, he's a Castillo, but the connection is pretty distant. And he's successful."

Her mouth quirked, lit up by the glow from the Mercedes' instrument panel. "Rafe, are you trying to play matchmaker with me?"

"No, I—" He broke off there, since he realized that was pretty much exactly what he was doing. Had the impulse truly come from a desire to see his sister settled, or was it more that he was looking for something—anything—to take his mind off Miranda? "All right, maybe I am."

"It's okay." Cat paused for a moment, apparently trying to gather her thoughts on the subject of Daniel Castillo. "I mean, I see what you're driving at. He's a few years older than I am, but that's no big deal. On the surface, it seems like we might be good together. But he's not really my type."

"I didn't realize you had a type."

This time the sideways glance she shot in his direction was distinctly annoyed. "Everyone has a type, even if they don't want to admit it. Daniel's really good at fitting in with civilians. He's a successful business owner, Chamber of Commerce type. That's not really me. Besides, I don't think I could live in Albuquerque. Santa Fe's about as big city as I want to get. If I had my choice—" She stopped there, possibly worried she was going to say too much.

"If you had your choice?" Rafe prompted her. "If you weren't stuck living under Genoveva's roof, could do what you want?"

"I'd like to move a little ways out of town, have a place in the country. Someplace pretty and green, like Pecos or Glorieta. Or maybe even all the way up in Taos. I don't know. It's just that sometimes…."

"Sometimes you feel trapped." He could relate to the feeling all too well, even though he'd at least been able to escape to a home of his own, albeit a home less than a mile from the house where he'd grown up.

"Exactly. And I know I should be grateful for what I have, because so many people have so much less, but…it might be nice to be master of my own destiny. Anyway, I'm just babbling. And while I know Daniel's a nice guy and probably better than I deserve, I'm just not feeling it."

Rafe frowned, troubled by his sister's self-deprecating comment. She deserved everything the world had to offer, no matter what she might think. Unfortunately, he worried that if he tried to call her on her remark, they'd just get into a quarrel. They were both tired and discouraged, and so this probably wasn't the best time to really get into it. Instead, he only said, "I understand," and was quiet after that.

That silence followed them all the way to his house. When Cat pulled up in the driveway to let him out, she told him, "I'll come by and get you around one-thirty tomorrow afternoon, okay?"

"Okay," he said. That seemed like an awfully long ways off, but there wasn't much he could do about it. "See you then."

And as he went into the house, he wondered how he would be able to pass another night without knowing what was happening to Miranda.

Somehow, though, he survived. He didn't have much choice—he messed around on the computer, watched some television before going to bed early. As he wandered around the next morning, he realized there wasn't much he could do to tidy up the house, since it had already been cleaned in anticipation of Miranda's arrival. How the place could feel so empty without her, when she'd never even lived here, he didn't know. Maybe it was only that he'd anticipated her living with him in this house, and that was enough to make him note her absence. But whatever the reason, his footsteps seemed to echo more hollowly than they ever had before, and the hours until his sister was supposed to show up seemed to stretch out forever.

Eventually, though, one-thirty swung around. His phone pinged at him—a text from Cat, letting him know she was waiting in the driveway. He went out and squinted at the bright sunshine, faintly annoyed. How could the sky be so cheerful and blue, the air so unseasonably warm, when the woman who was supposed to be his wife had vanished without a trace?

He climbed into her SUV and shut the door. "Hey."

"Hey, yourself," Cat returned amiably as she began to back out of the driveway. "You look like shit."

"Gee, thanks." One hand went to his jaw; he'd forgotten to shave. Not that it really mattered one way or another. Sourly, he surveyed his sister. Unlike him, she'd obviously made some effort today, since she wore a long embroidered skirt, boots, and a wrap-style top with a bit of lace camisole peeking out from beneath. "You look nice."

"Thanks. I figured I'd better look as if I'd made an effort, just in case Mom decides to drop by and check up on us."

"You think she'd do that?"

Behind her dark glasses, Cat lifted an eyebrow. "What do you think?"

Of course she would. Genoveva loved sticking her nose in everybody's business, always firmly convinced that she knew better than anyone else. The odds that she'd swing by the hospital to check up on Cat were pretty high.

"Right."

A chuckle, and she turned left onto Old Santa Fe Trail, heading south toward St. Vincent's. "I'm glad you came along, though. I was kind of worried you'd change your mind."

"No, I said I'd come. I wouldn't leave you hanging."

"Well, I still appreciate it."

They were quiet for a moment as they drove along the old road, tall trees and adobe walls on either side. The street widened after a few minutes, taking them through a slightly newer part of town. Cat turned off toward St. Michael's so they'd be lined up for a proper approach to the hospital's visitor parking lot, then turned again.

It wasn't too busy that Tuesday afternoon,

which meant they were able to get a parking space fairly close to the front entrance. They both got out, went in, and headed toward the elevator. It was empty, giving them an unimpeded ride to the fourth floor where Marco's room was located. Just as they approached the door to his room, Sophia, Marco's mother came out, the lines of worry smoothing from her face the moment she caught sight of the two visitors.

"Perfect timing," she said with a smile. She was as slight as her son was round; he'd inherited his size from his late father. "Your mother said Cat was on her way, so I thought I'd slip out and get something to eat."

"How is Marco?" Cat asked.

Sophia's smile didn't exactly fade; it only grew tight, the strain more evident in the shadows around her dark eyes. "The same," she replied. "They're going to do a CAT scan later this afternoon. But at least his condition hasn't deteriorated, either. He's holding steady. But then, he always was a healthy boy."

Her voice caught on that last word—clearly he was still her little boy, no matter that he was a grown man in his mid-twenties. "Well, that's something," Rafe said, wishing he had something more encouraging to tell her. Problem was, he couldn't summon much enthusiasm for anything right now. As much as he told his brain to shut up and leave him alone, it kept summoning ever more gruesome possibilities as to what might be happening to Miranda at that very moment. Had she been caught by human traffickers? Had she lost her memory somehow, was shut up on a twenty-four-hour psych hold somewhere?

"You get your lunch," Cat said, her tone soothing. "Take as long a break as you need. We'll be here."

"Thanks, Cat." Sophia offered them another smile and then headed off toward the elevator.

Rafe expelled a breath. "Well, I guess we'd better go in."

His sister nodded and led the way inside. Just as Sophia had said, Marco seemed pretty much the same as he'd been the day before, tubes still running into his arm and his nose. At least it seemed he was able to breathe on his own, because his mouth was unobstructed. A ventilator lurked in the corner, though, waiting for the moment when it might be needed.

Two chairs had been placed up against one wall, and Cat and Rafe sat down in those. Thank God this was a private room, so they'd be able to talk without too much worry about being overheard.

"I'm glad Sophia seems to be holding up okay," Cat ventured.

"Well, she's a tough lady. Genoveva could

learn something from her. It is possible to suffer losses and not turn into a bitter harpy."

"Rafe." Cat's tone was reproving, but she didn't bother to admonish him beyond that. Whatever closeness had existed between her brother and her mother had been burned away years earlier, and she must have known there was no real way to repair the breach now.

"Whatever." He rubbed the palms of his hands against the knees of his jeans and wondered whether it had been a good idea to come here after all. What was he trying to prove, anyway? That he was a good son, a good Castillo who understood his place in the clan?

No, he thought suddenly, looking at Marco's slack features, at the bluish shadows under his eyes, he was here because Marco was his friend. Not just a member of the clan, not just a cousin. Rafe wished they could have been closer, because Marco was a decent guy and fun to hang out with, but the distance between Taos and Santa Fe was just great enough that they didn't get together as often as either of them would have liked. He knew then he would have come here anyway even if they hadn't been related at all, because it was the decent thing to do.

And because poor Sophia really looked like she needed a break.

"Anyway," he went on, knowing he needed to

say something to try to erase the wounded look in his sister's eyes, "I'm also hoping that Daniel might get back to me this afternoon. He texted this morning to let me know he was running a trace on a few things, but he had meetings with clients and didn't exactly know when he'd be able to be in touch. 'Running a trace' means he must have figured out a way to track Miranda's movements, right?"

"I guess?" Cat said, her shoulders lifting slightly. "I have to admit I don't know much about being a private detective. I assume Daniel isn't wandering the streets of Albuquerque with a magnifying glass or something."

The image her remark conjured was so ludicrous, Rafe couldn't help chuckling a bit. "No, I think he does a lot of his work online. Forensic data analysis, he said one time. Not that I know exactly what that's supposed to mean. But since he knows what he's doing, I have to hope he's got some kind of lead about Miranda, even if we can't figure out what that might be."

"I hope so," Cat said. "It's hard to understand how someone could just vanish without a trace like that."

"*Unghhh….*"

Rafe and Cat both paused and looked toward the bed. Marco didn't seem to have moved—until Rafe saw the way his cousin's fingers were clutching the thin hospital blanket. Was it possible…?

"Marco?" he ventured, hoping he didn't sound like a complete fool. "Did you say something?"

"*Unghh…Maahhhhh….*"

Cat's dark eyes were wide, the color in her cheeks gone. "Should I call a nurse?" she asked in an undertone.

"I don't know," Rafe replied. He got up from his seat and went over to the bed. "What're you trying to tell us, Marco?"

"*Teh—*" The syllable came out more as a huff of breath. "*Tess….*"

Now Cat was up and out of her chair, standing next to Rafe, her entire body tense. "Who's Tess, Marco?"

"*Tess…tess….*"

The beeping of his heart monitor began to accelerate. Rafe saw beads of sweat gather on Marco's brow and roll down his temples before soaking the hair next to his ears. "We don't understand," he said. "Who's Tess?"

"*Tess…uhhh….*"

The heart monitor was going crazy. The next thing Rafe knew, he was being pushed aside by a pair of nurses, one of whom looked at Marco's vitals and said, "Get the doctor," even as the other woman began to shove Rafe and Cat out of the room.

"You'll need to go," she said, the crispness of her tone allowing no room for argument.

"But he was trying to tell us something!" Rafe protested. "He was out of the coma!"

"No, he wasn't," the nurse said calmly. "Sometimes patients in his condition make vocalizations that sound as though they're trying to speak. His brain activity hadn't changed, though. And now his pulse is dangerously high, so we need to get that under control. You can go over there," she added, pointing toward the small waiting area that faced the elevator doors.

A pretty Asian woman wearing a white lab coat hurried into Marco's room, and the nurse who'd been speaking to them quickly turned away and went in as well.

Feeling helpless, Rafe said, "I guess we'd better go wait."

Face pale, Cat nodded. The two of them walked over and sat down on the hard chairs there, although they'd only been sitting for a minute or two before the elevator doors opened and Sophia stepped out, a Styrofoam coffee cup in one hand. Spying the two of them, she said, "What's the matter? Why aren't you in with Marco?"

"He, uh, had kind of an episode," Rafe began, but he didn't get any further than that, because

Sophia turned away and hurried toward Marco's room.

She wasn't even given the chance to get inside. The nurse who had shooed Rafe and Cat away a few moments earlier stood at the door, barring her from entry. Her words came clearly to the waiting area, even though she was some yards away. "I'm sorry, Mrs. Delgado, but the doctor's working on your son right now."

"I need to see him! What happened?"

"We're not entirely sure yet. He had a spike in cardio activity. We're trying to get him stabilized. If you could please go and sit with his friends, that would be great."

Even as she ended this sentence, the light next to the door turned red and began to flash.

"What's happening?" Sophia cried.

"He's coding. Please—we need to work."

Rafe got up from his seat then and went over to Sophia, taking her by the shoulders. "She's right," he said quietly but firmly. "Marco needs the doctors and nurses to do their thing, and we'd just be in the way. Come sit with Cat and me."

He could feel the tension in her thin frame, but she seemed willing to accept his advice, allowed him to guide her over to the waiting area. Cat took the cup of coffee Sophia had been holding the whole time, then helped lower her into one of the chairs.

A pair of nurses came out of the elevator, dragging a piece of complicated-looking equipment with them. Rafe had no idea what it was for, but he assumed it was something needed to resuscitate his cousin. Cat's eyes met his, full of wordless alarm. All he could do was stare back. Right then, he couldn't remember feeling any more useless. The only thing they could do was sit here and let the professionals do their work—and hope it was enough.

The minutes crawled by. Rafe could hear a murmur of voices coming from within Marco's room, but none of them spoke loudly enough for him to hear what they were saying. He didn't know which was worse—to not know at all what was happening, or to have some idea but still realize there wasn't a damn thing he could do about any of it.

At last the doctor emerged from Marco's room. Her shoulders were slumped, which told Rafe everything he needed to know. Still, his mind didn't want to recognize the truth. This couldn't be happening…could it?

Apparently Sophia guessed as well, for she slowly rose from her chair and went to face the young woman, who probably was only in her early thirties, barely out of her residency. "He's gone, isn't he?"

The doctor's gaze shifted toward Cat and Rafe

for a second. Possibly she was trying to determine whether they might be Marco's brother and sister, or if they were merely friends. "I'm sorry, Mrs. Delgado," the doctor said. "For lack of a more scientific term, his heart simply gave out. We're not sure why. Possibly damage related to the stroke, although none of the EKGs we ran seemed to indicate that was even a possibility. We did our best, but it wasn't enough, clearly." Once again her slender shoulders drooped. "I am so sorry."

Sophia nodded. Tears gathered in her eyes, bright and terrible, and ran down her cheeks, but she still remained almost preternaturally calm. "Thank you, doctor. I suppose you will want to do an autopsy?"

The doctor's finely arched brows lifted even further. "I'm not sure we need to discuss that right now—"

"I just want you to know you have my permission." Sophia pulled in a breath. "I want to know what it was that killed my son."

Rafe came to her, said quietly, "You can worry about that later, Sophia."

She nodded. "You're right. For now, I would like to be alone with my son."

The doctor said, "Of course. Come with me." Gently, she placed an arm around Sophia and led her into Marco's room. Rafe hung back, standing near the waiting area, not sure what to do.

Cat's fingers twined around his. "Rafe, what's going on?" she whispered.

"I don't know," he said. He didn't understand any of this. How could Marco be dead? Marco was a year younger than he was. The whole thing was crazy.

And what had Marco been trying to tell them? Who was Tess? Was she somehow connected to Miranda's disappearance?

It seemed that whatever Marco had known, whatever he'd been attempting to say, it had gone to the grave with him.

Now they would never know.

11

EXPLORATIONS

Miranda

Breakfast with Simon was surprisingly mellow—so mellow, in fact, that I wondered if I'd imagined the tension between us the night before, had allowed my semi-tipsy brain to manufacture undercurrents that simply weren't there. We'd goofed around in the kitchen, making bacon and pancakes, and started putting together a list of things we'd need from the grocery store the next time we ventured out.

As I said, almost relentlessly normal…and completely the opposite of what followed.

More practice, of course. This time, I indulged a childhood fantasy of mine and managed to turn myself invisible. That is, I could look down and see myself, but Simon claimed that I had completely disappeared, even though he could hear my voice and was able to feel my hand when I reached out toward him. So maybe it was some kind of weird magical stealth ability rather than being truly invisible, but the result was the same.

"Well, that was fun," I said, willing myself back to visibility. Even though I had been able to see myself the whole time, I still took a second glance down at my jeans and brown boots, relieved they were clear as day against the gravel driveway.

"It was," Simon replied with a grin. "And you've got one up on me. I've never been able to manage invisibility, no matter how many times I tried."

Interesting. Because he seemed able to master so many different magical abilities, I'd just sort of assumed he could do almost anything he put his mind to. "It's a fun trick, but unless you plan on a career in spying or bank robbery, I'm not sure how really useful it is."

"You're just trying to make me feel better."

"No, really," I said. "I mean it."

"What else do you want to try?"

Good question. There were so many possibilities out there, but I was interested in something a bit more subtle than being the new incarnation of the Invisible Man. "I want to know how you block your warlock nature. That seems like it would be handy to know. That way, I could change my appearance, block my witchiness, and go shopping in Santa Fe if I wanted to."

A flash of white teeth as he shot me one of his sly grins. "If you really want to go shopping, we can always head down to Albuquerque. There's probably less chance of running into a Castillo since they're spread a bit more thin there."

"It's not shopping, exactly, more...." I stopped to think about what I was that I really wanted to prove. "More that I think it would be awesome to slip in under their noses, and they'd never be able to tell."

"After what they put you through, I can see why you might want to thumb your nose at them."

We were standing out in the driveway again, since it was a good place to practice various sorts of pyrotechnics without having to worry about damaging anything in the multimillion-dollar property where we were staying. Simon came toward me and paused a foot or so away.

"Reach out," he said. "I know that we don't get that special 'tingle' or whatever you want to call it after we've been around each other for a bit, but if you focus, you can still sense it. Try it now."

I held myself still and let my newly developed powers drift out, touch his. Yes, there it was—that strange prickle at the back of my neck that told me I faced someone else with witch blood. But even as I felt that unique tingle, it vanished. For all that my witchy senses were telling me, I might as well have been standing next to a civilian.

"Wow," I said. "It's just…gone."

"Exactly. But it's really easy to do. You only need to think of the power at your core, your own witchy nature. Close your eyes and reach inside yourself. Feel it."

This was easy enough to do, because I'd felt that same power awaken in me just the day before, that center of brilliant, glowing light, warm and golden as the sun. I closed my eyes and almost immediately it was there, comforting, reassuring me that I possessed just as much magical talent as any other witch—actually, far more, since I wasn't confined to a single gift but apparently could encompass them all.

"I feel it," I whispered.

"Good. Now imagine blanking it out. It's not that it's disappeared—it's more like the sun during an eclipse when the moon passes in front of it. Do that now."

I nodded obediently, visualizing an eclipse, the darkening of the sun, the utter blackness that took its place. And the core of light within me dimmed and seemed to be gone, although I could still feel its strength, waiting for the time when I would call upon it again.

"You did it," Simon said. I opened my eyes to see him looking down at me with approval. "I can't feel your power at all. Now bring it back."

Eclipse over, the warm golden light of my magic flared out, thrilling in its strength.

Simon nodded. "And now I feel it again. It's really as simple as that."

"It's still amazing," I said. "To be able to hide my powers, just by thinking about it. My uncle supposedly was able to hide my father's powers from the McAllister clan, but I always heard that was a spell, not something my uncle could do on his own with his own innate abilities."

Simon shrugged. "I wouldn't know anything about that. I mean, I always heard that Damon Wilcox dabbled in some questionable stuff, so I suppose he could have found a spell to do basically the same thing. But obviously it's a lot easier when you're just doing it on your own."

That was for sure. I didn't really want to talk about my uncle, or the dark spells he'd explored before his death, long before I was even born. Certainly the topic never came up in my household; the few things I'd overheard about him were in whispered conversations, conversations that halted abruptly once the people talking realized I was around. I didn't even know what my uncle had looked like, because my parents didn't have any pictures of him out anywhere in either of our houses. I'd always gotten the impression that my father would have liked to erase Uncle Damon's existence altogether, that the topic was so painful he preferred to push it away and pretend he'd never had a brother to begin with.

"Much easier," I agreed, then went on, eager to change the subject, "So…what next? I've always thought it would be fun to control the weather."

"It's a useful talent, but one you need to be careful with. Nature has a balance of its own, and you don't want to mess with it too much."

"I won't," I promised. "I just want to see what I can do."

"All right." Simon looked up toward the sky— the day was still sunny and mild, but a few clouds wreathed the topmost peaks of the Sangre de Cristo mountains to the east. "It's easiest when you have something to work with. Making it rain when there aren't any clouds around is tough, because you basically have to make some clouds form out of water vapor before you can even think of doing anything with them. But there are a few." He pointed to the clouds I'd noticed, white and fluffy and looking as if they were stuffed with moisture, although it was too late for monsoon storms and really too early for snow. "Call them over here."

"'Call them'?" I repeated, looking at the

clouds in question with some skepticism. "How am I supposed to do that?"

"Think about the air currents, about the winds that drive them. It's not as if they move on their own. Find the wind and make it push them here."

That still seemed like a tall order, but I figured I should at least try. I drew in a breath and let my arms hang at my side as I focused on the power in my core. It was still there, waiting for me to tell it what I wanted it to do.

Show me the wind, I thought.

The sky remained as blue as ever, but now I thought I could see currents moving within it, odd translucent rivers snaking their way far above the landscape. And now that I could see those currents, I could try to get them to do my bidding.

Bring the clouds to me.

At first, it didn't seem as if anything was happening. But then I saw the clouds that crowned the mountaintops drift away, begin to move westward toward the spot where I stood. Not quickly, but anyone who was paying attention would have noticed that those clouds were no longer moving with the area's prevailing wind currents.

They drifted closer and closer, until at last they were directly overhead, blocking the sun. A chill went through me, even though a moment earlier I had been warm enough.

Simon spoke to me, the words soft, almost a whisper. "What do you want them to do?"

Good question. It seemed enough of an accomplishment merely to have brought them here. But then I thought of the fierce monsoon storms of July and August and September, the wild downpours of rain, the sharp crack of lightning, and how much I missed them as summer began to shift into autumn.

The clouds rumbled, seemed to turn darker. They pulsed with light from within.

And then a bolt cracked down from one of them, striking the lightning rod that graced the peaked roof of the caretaker's house. All at once, rain began to pour down, drumming so hard against the gravel of the driveway that it bounced back up a good several inches.

Simon and I shared one wild, wide-eyed glance, and then we both ran for the side door that would let us into the kitchen. It only took us a few seconds to get inside, but in those few seconds we were both soaked to the skin.

I hurried over to the drawer that I knew held the kitchen towels, and pulled out a couple and handed one to Simon before I began to blot my dripping hair. "Wow," I said. "I wasn't really expecting that to happen."

He wiped off his face, but from the way he was smiling, I could tell he wasn't upset with me for turning the two of us into a couple of drowned rats. "That's what I meant about weather being hard to control. The clouds can have a mind of their own. Did you actually want it to rain that hard?"

"Not really," I said, touching the now-damp towel to my cheeks. Good thing there wasn't a mirror around; I didn't want to know what that downpour had done to my mascara. "I was thinking of the monsoon storms, how much I missed them. And then the clouds just sort of let loose."

"That's the thing." He scrunched his hair with the towel, making it stick up all over his head. The effect was definitely punk rock, and I had to keep myself from smiling. Normally, that wasn't the sort of style Simon tended to sport. "With magic, intentions can have power. You need to think about what you want to have happen and be very clear about it to yourself. Luckily, all that happened to us was that we got soaked, but sometimes the side effects can be a lot more severe than some wet clothes."

I nodded. "I'll keep that in mind from now on." And I would. Over the past few days, magic had been something that just sort of happened to me, rather than vice versa, but I could tell I needed to work on paying attention to what I was doing.

"Good." His gaze moved upward, to where I could hear the rain still pounding down on the skylight. "Do you think you could get it to stop? I need to change, and I'd rather not get soaked all over again on my way to the caretaker's house."

"Sure," I said, realizing with some embarrassment that his dark T-shirt now clung tightly to his body, showing off muscles in his chest and shoulders that I really hadn't noticed before, since he tended to wear his clothing somewhat baggy. At the same time, I could see that my own shirt was doing much the same thing, only instead of revealing muscles, it was showing every outline of my bra. Blood flooded into my cheeks, but I told myself to focus on something more important, like getting those storm clouds to move away. I breathed in, imagining them now free of their burden of moisture and heading back to cluster around the topmost peaks of the Sangre de Cristos once again.

The drumming of the rain stopped abruptly, and a few seconds later, the gloom that had enveloped the house dissipated, sunlight returning now that the clouds were gone.

"I think it's safe now," I said.

"Sounds that way. How about we regroup here in the kitchen in twenty minutes?"

"Sure."

He let himself out, and I set the damp towel I'd been holding down on the countertop and hurried back to my room. The mirror in the bathroom revealed the utter wreck of my hair and makeup—and showed just how revealing my wet T-shirt really was. Muttering a curse, I stripped it off, but draped it over the shower door along with my jeans so I wouldn't be putting wet clothes in the hamper. It did feel good to get into dry things after having my soaked clothing stuck to my skin.

Twenty minutes. It wasn't enough time to blow-dry my hair, so I got out some of the serum I used when I wanted it to dry natural and wavy, and scrunched it in as best I could. Again, not enough time for full makeup, but once I'd repaired my raccoon eyes, I reapplied mascara and put on some lip gloss.

Did Simon even notice these things? Did he care? I was having a hard time deciding one way or another, although before we'd come here he hadn't done too much to hide his interest in me. Now, though….

Now he's giving you space. Isn't that what you wanted?

I thought so. I just didn't know for sure.

Shaking my head at myself, I went back to the kitchen. Simon was already there, studying the contents of the fridge.

"Is it lunchtime already?" I asked. My gazed moved to the digital readout on the stove. No, it was only eleven-fifteen. Maybe not an outrageous time for lunch, but I thought it was jumping the gun a little, considering we'd had breakfast at eight.

"No," he replied. "Not unless you're hungry, anyway."

I thought possibly I should have been, after all the magical energy I'd expended. But no, I could tell I wasn't quite ready for lunch yet. I shook my head. "I'd rather wait."

"Good, because I was thinking we should make a run to the grocery store."

"Into town?" I asked, a nervous thrill going through me. Technically, such a trip should be all right, since Simon had taught me how to block my powers. Even so, after all the morning's exertions, I was feeling a little tired. I would have rather given the magic a rest for a while.

"No," he said. "I wouldn't do that to you after all the work you did this morning. I was thinking we could go to Los Alamos."

"'Los Alamos'?" I repeated blankly, wondering whether I'd heard him correctly. It seemed like a long way to go just to do some grocery shopping.

"Yes," he said with a smile. "I know it sounds kind of funky, but I heard the Smith's there is like a temple of grocery stores...and I know you're not a fan of Española." I made a face at him, but he continued, still smiling, "So I thought we could go up there, do our shopping, have some lunch."

"Are there a lot of Castillos in Los Alamos?"

"There aren't any. Most of the people who live there work at the labs in one way or another, and when you're a witch or warlock trying to hide your identity, it's usually not recommended that you do something that requires a security clearance."

I hadn't even thought of that particular angle, but of course he was right. The witches and warlocks I knew in Arizona had all sorts of jobs, but none of them were FBI agents or worked for government labs or did anything that would require some kind of official organization to probe too closely into their personal lives. I eyed Simon, who still wore faint smile. "You seem to know a lot about the Castillos."

"I did my homework. I didn't know how long I was going to have to stay undercover until I met you, so to speak, and so I tried to learn everything I could about the Castillos, and about Santa Fe and the towns within driving distance. It never hurts."

No, I supposed it didn't. I thought of how I'd done my best to ignore most information about the city that would soon be my home, driven more by contrariness than anything else, sort of, well, *you can make me live there, but it doesn't mean I have to like it.* Which, in hindsight, had been pretty foolish. What was that old saying about forewarned was forearmed?

"Okay, Los Alamos it is." I paused, then looked down at my jeans and flats and patterned peasant blouse. "Is this okay?"

His gaze moved over me swiftly, almost carelessly. "You look fine. You might want to bring a jacket, though, just in case. It tends to be a little cooler there because of the elevation."

"All right. Let me go get my purse and a jacket."

He nodded, and I hurried back to my bedroom to fetch the items in question. Once there, I gave my appearance a quick once-over, but all seemed to be in order. If I'd known we'd be going out to lunch, I might have tried to put a little more work into my makeup, although I told myself that really didn't matter. Who was I trying to impress, anyway? A bunch of rocket scientists?

If that was even the sort of thing they did in Los Alamos. I knew the town had a national lab, and that it was where the atom bomb had been developed, and that was about the extent of my knowledge when it came to Los Alamos.

I went back to the kitchen, and the two of us got some reusable shopping bags from the pantry before heading out to the garage. Now it was all blue skies around us, the only sign of the downpour I'd summoned a few puddles on the walkway and on the gravel.

"How far do you think the rain extended?" I asked as we got into his SUV.

"I don't know for sure." He backed out of the garage, then touched the controls to shut the door. "That's something you'll need to focus on next time. Really good weather-workers can tell exactly how much area is being covered by the storms they call to themselves."

Frankly, I'd been so startled by the heavy rain that I hadn't even thought to reach out and see if I could determine my storm's area of effect. Next time, I'd know better—and I'd focus on exactly what I wanted the clouds to do.

If I was given the chance, of course. It was entirely possible that Simon would want to move on to a different skill, now that I'd proven I could call the clouds to me almost as easily as I could teleport or bring a wall of fire out of nothing. And really, at this time of year, it wasn't as though we needed a ton of rain. October had been fairly wet in northern Arizona, which was somewhat unusual. Since storms tended to keep heading east after they were done with us in Flagstaff and Jerome, I had to guess that Santa Fe and the surrounding areas must have gotten some of that same moisture.

We headed north on the same highway we'd taken to get to Española, only we cut off on another highway going west right after we passed the massive Buffalo Thunder casino and resort. This road was fairly wide, comparatively speaking, and seemed in better repair than some of the other highways I'd traveled in New Mexico. I mentioned this to Simon, and his shoulders lifted slightly.

"There's a lot of traffic to and from Los Alamos that uses this road. They keep it in good shape."

I nodded. It made sense. Did a lot of the scientists who worked there live in Santa Fe, rather than in Los Alamos itself? I could see how that kind of situation might be desirable, if the job was high-powered enough and paid well.

We crossed over the Rio Grande, where the cottonwoods were still blazing in all their golden glory. Seeing them sent a little pang through my heart. Back home, the trees would also still be bright with their autumn foliage. I remembered how I could see the line of the Verde River from my bedroom window in Jerome, how I'd watch every year to see when the leaves began to turn, a trail of gold with the majesty of Sedona's red rocks off in the distance. It had been so very beautiful.

Oh, it was beautiful here, too, if in a different way, but....

I knew I could go home. My time here in New Mexico had been chaotic enough that there hadn't been much time for me to feel homesick, but I knew the longing for Jerome and northern Arizona still lived deep within me, waiting to awaken. Really, there was nothing to hold me here, not now. A few more days of work with Simon, and then…well, I supposed I'd figure it out when the time came. Either way, there really wasn't any reason for the melancholy that had swept over me out of nowhere, especially considering my triumphs of that morning. I was making great progress. I had no reason to be downcast.

And yet….

Don't you dare make this about Rafe, I thought, resolutely staring out the window as the highway began to climb away from the river bottom, taking us up its steep path into Los Alamos. *I'd say he was pretty clear about what he thought of you. Obviously, every kiss you shared with him was a lie, or he would never have said those things.*

"You okay?" Simon's voice interrupted my thoughts, his tone gentle but also slightly worried.

"I'm fine." I shifted in my seat so I looked forward. "Just thinking, I guess."

I left it there, and although I could detect a faint furrowing of Simon's brow out of the corner of my eye, he seemed to understand that I didn't really want to talk. We drove in silence the rest of the way into Los Alamos, and I was glad of having new scenery to occupy me—the small airport on the very edge of town, the houses and apartment buildings that so obviously must have been built to house the people who worked here during World War II, or maybe right afterward. Then we came to the downtown section, which was clearly much newer, clean and bright and modern.

As was the Smith's, which seemed enormous to me, especially for a town whose population couldn't be all that large. Still, it was fun to shop with Simon, to choose items to make easy, homey meals—steaks and spaghetti and salad, and the fixings for chili and stroganoff and enchiladas. Good thing my Great-Aunt Rachel had taught me how to cook, because I knew I wouldn't have any problem putting any of these dinners together. Also, I had a feeling Simon would be fine being put on "chopping duty," which was always my least favorite part about meal prep.

Once we were done with our grocery shopping, we went across the street to a small restaurant/brew pub, had burgers and local beer. It was crowded in there, so we didn't have much of a chance to discuss my magical practice from earlier that morning…which was fine by me. Magic made me think about Rafe, about why I'd been sent here. It was much more comfortable to pretend that Simon and I were just friends going out to lunch, and he seemed to pick up the hint, talking about which meal we wanted to make first, and whether we'd have time to go on a hike up Tesuque Canyon, which he said was a popular spot and might still have some fall foliage to check out.

And even when we were alone in his car and driving back down the mountain, he didn't push me to talk about magic. Maybe he understood that everything I'd done so far had begun to overwhelm me, that I needed to get a little distance from it in order to give myself some breathing room.

Whatever the reason, I was feeling much more relaxed as we pulled onto the private lane that led to the house. I even smiled when I saw the tall roof of the main house come into view, the few fall flowers that still bloomed in the garden off the dining room. Even though I'd been here only a few days, it felt like I was coming home.

And if this borrowed house felt like home, what about the man who quietly guided the SUV into the garage, who took the lion's share of the grocery bags to carry into the kitchen? He was beginning to feel comfortable now, too, in a way that made me think wild, unbridled passion was highly overrated. The two of us got along extremely well. He seemed to understand me. What else did I really need?

I didn't know whether I could answer that question…didn't know whether I wanted to.

Maybe that realization should have frightened me. The fact that it didn't…I wasn't quite sure what I should do about that.

12

DISCOVERIES

Rafe

He and Cat sat in his living room, looking at each other, none of them sure what they should say. She'd wept on the way over here, but now she seemed to have more control over herself, although her eyes were still suspiciously bright.

"What did Mom say?" she asked.

Rafe had just put down his phone. The call to his mother was the first thing he'd done after he and Cat watched Sophia go in to sit with her dead son. They'd waited at the hospital until Genoveva arrived. It was her place as *prima* to take control of the situation, and after she'd gone to be with Marco's grieving mother, Rafe and his sister had left to come here. Neither of them really knew what else they should be doing. Of course the Castillo clan had seen its share of deaths, but no one as young as Marco, at least not as far as Rafe could remember.

Genoveva called only about fifteen minutes after he and Cat had arrived at his place. She was brisk, calm, letting Rafe know that Sophia would be staying at the house with Genoveva and Eduardo, since she couldn't very well be left alone right now. He told his sister what their mother had said, and she sighed.

"It makes sense—I know it would be terrible for Sophia to have to go home to Taos all by herself, but…." Cat stopped there and pulled in a breath. "I hate even thinking it, because it's so selfish, but it's going to be rough having Sophia at the house."

"No, I get it," Rafe said, and he thought he did. His sister was already on edge because of Miranda's disappearance. Now they had to deal with the tragedy of Marco's death, and Cat far more than he because of having Sophia basically in her lap until the funeral. All the Castillos were buried here in Santa Fe, even those who lived in Taos and Albuquerque and other parts of the state.

Buried. He ran a hand through his hair and then dropped it back to his knee. Marco, buried. What the hell was going on?

"Why don't you crash here with me for a few days?" he asked. "You can tell Genoveva that you thought it would be better for Sophia not to have so many people around."

Cat brightened for a moment at this suggestion but then shook her head. "No, that won't work. I know Mom will just say that I'm running away—and she'd be right—and then she'd give me a guilt trip for not wanting to stay and be there for Sophia. Which I should do. So…it'll be all right."

Rafe wasn't so sure about that, but he knew better than to argue. His sister's sense of family duty had always been a lot stronger than his own. "Okay, but if you need me to steal you away for a few hours here and there, just let me know. I'm sure we can manufacture some excuse."

The expression on Cat's face told him she wasn't so sure about their ability to fool their mother. She didn't protest, however, only reached for the glass of water she'd left sitting in front of her on the coffee table. No doubt she was wishing the glass held something a little stronger than water—a sentiment Rafe definitely shared—but both of them knew that drinking right now wasn't a good idea. There was a very strong chance that Genoveva might call again and need them to run an errand for her, do something to prepare for Sophia's stay at the house. Rafe couldn't really think what that might be, since the place was always immaculate and the freezer and refrigerator fully stocked, but he knew his mother well enough to believe she would think of something.

His phone buzzed again. *Here it comes,* he thought as he bent to pick it up, but then Rafe saw that the number displayed on the screen was Daniel's, not his mother's.

Had he found something? That would be the one bright spot in this otherwise miserable day.

"Hey, Daniel," Rafe said, watching as Cat sat up straighter on the couch, her gaze suddenly sharp. "You heard the news?"

"I did," Daniel replied in properly subdued tones. "My mother called me at the office. That's…rough."

"Yeah, it is. We're all kind of in shock right now."

"I can understand that." A pause, and then he went on, "I don't know if you want to back off on the Miranda thing for a while—"

"No," Rafe cut in. That was the last thing he wanted. He needed to make some progress in finding his missing fiancée, because even a few hopeful signs in that direction might help to restore his faith in the universe. Right now, he wasn't feeling too great about the state of the world, or at least his small corner of it. "We need to keep going, even—even though this has happened."

"Got it. Well, I don't have much news for you, unfortunately. All the traces I put on Miranda's bank accounts have turned up nothing. As far as I can tell, she hasn't touched her checking or her savings account since she left Arizona."

But what did that mean, precisely? That whoever had taken her wasn't interested in her money? Or, Rafe thought, his blood going cold, that she was as dead as Marco, and therefore had no reason to touch any of her accounts?

Something of the worry in his frozen silence must have communicated itself to his cousin, because Daniel said quickly, "Which doesn't necessarily mean anything. If she'd had sufficient cash on her, she could be using that to get by."

"She couldn't have had any money on her, Daniel," Rafe replied in biting tones. "She disappeared in her goddamn *wedding gown*."

Something about that comment appeared to pique Cat's interest for some reason, because she frowned slightly, then got up from the couch and disappeared down the hallway. What the hell was that about?

"Oh, right," Daniel said, sounding apologetic. "I forgot about that little detail. Well, in a way this is good news, because at least it shows she wasn't taken by someone who was after her money."

No, just her beauty, just her enticing body. Rafe had to shove that thought aside with an almost physical effort. He couldn't allow himself to think of someone using her, violating her, because then he thought he really would go crazy over his current impotence. Because he could pretend to be proactive, have his private detective cousin on the case, but, Rafe thought glumly, when you got right down to it, what he was doing right now was basically the intellectual equivalent of jerking off.

Cat came back into the living room, frowning. Clearly, whatever she'd gone to check on, she hadn't found what she was looking for. Well, that would have to wait until he was off the phone.

"Hey," Rafe went on, "I know you didn't know Marco that well, but stuff still gets around the family grapevine."

"That's for sure."

Daniel's tone was grim, and Rafe thought he knew why. His cousin's divorce had been unmercifully picked apart by a large portion of the Castillo clan, probably because divorce was so rare in their Catholic witch family. However, he knew better than to say anything on the topic, even in commiseration, since he understood that Daniel wanted to leave that whole mess behind him.

"Did you hear anything about Marco dating someone named Tess?"

"Tess? I don't think so, but I'll admit I don't pay much attention to that kind of thing."

"You're sure?" Rafe asked. It had been a long shot, but he couldn't help feeling a wave of disappointment at his cousin's reply.

"Pretty sure. Why? Is she someone who needs to be notified about his death?"

That consideration was something Rafe hadn't even thought of. "No. I mean, I don't know. Cat and I were at the hospital this afternoon, right before...well, right before. And even though Marco was in a coma and shouldn't have been able to speak, he had some kind of a fit or seizure, kept saying, 'Tess...Tess.' Cat and I couldn't figure out what he was trying to say, and then he was just...gone."

"Hmm." Daniel was silent for a moment, clearly pondering this new piece of information. "I don't know what that could mean. You should probably ask Sophia."

That was the most logical thing to do, and yet Rafe quailed at the thought of attempting to ask Marco's grieving mother if she knew anything about her late son's love life. "I guess I will," he said cautiously, "when the time feels right. It's just frustrating me, because it seems as though Marco was trying really hard to tell us something, and the message didn't quite get through. And now it never will."

"Don't say 'never,'" Daniel told him. "Sometimes you get an insight when you least expect it. Anyway, I have a client coming in at five, so I need to prep for that. I just wanted to let you know what I'd found—or hadn't found—about Miranda's accounts. And...I suppose I'll hear when the funeral will be happening."

"Yes, Genoveva's on that," Rafe said. "Probably on Friday, but we'll let you know."

"Thanks, Rafe. Hang in there."

He made a noncommittal sound and ended the call. Almost as soon as he swiped his finger over the screen, Cat said, "Her stuff is gone."

"What stuff?"

"Miranda's bags, remember? You were going to check to see if they were still sitting in the entry where I left them, but you never did, I guess because Mom called about Marco being in the hospital and we both sort of rushed out of here."

Oh, right. With everything that had been going on, he'd barely had a chance to remember to brush his teeth, let alone remind himself to go look for those mythical bags. Now, though, Cat's remark made him frown. "You're sure they're gone?"

She gave him what he always thought of the "Cat" look, head tilted slightly to one side, right eyebrow lifted at a quizzical angle. "Well, unless someone put a spell on them to make them invisible, yes, they're gone. Your entryway isn't so big that I would miss a couple of weekender bags sitting on the floor."

No, it wasn't. He reached up and rubbed the side of his head, pretty sure he had a headache coming on. Unfortunately, that was the least of his worries right now. "So, what are you saying—that someone broke in here and took Miranda's stuff?"

"Well, you don't have them, and I know I left those bags there for her so you guys could make a quick getaway after the reception." Rafe couldn't help but wince slightly at the thought of the wedding reception that had never happened, and Cat went on hurriedly, "Which means someone must have taken them. And there wouldn't have been any sign of a break-in if it was a witch or warlock who did it, right?"

"No, there wouldn't." Now his head was really hurting, but he ignored the ache as the import of his sister's words sank in. He'd already sensed some kind of dark magic in downtown Santa Fe, although he hadn't been able to pin it to a particular person. But what if that person—Robert Marquez, for lack of a better way to think of the man, although Rafe knew the name was only one the warlock had stolen to hide his identity—what if that person had come along while everyone was in an uproar and had taken Miranda's things?

Had taken them, in fact, because he was the one who'd kidnapped her. The answer was so obvious that Rafe wondered why he hadn't thought of it before this. Then again, there hadn't been any evidence to show that Miranda had been taken by force. She sure as hell had teleported out of the cathedral of her own free will.

Or...had she? Just because she'd pulled that disappearing act in front of Cat previously didn't mean that the same force was at work here. Maybe the warlock who'd stolen her had only made it look as though she was teleporting the way she had before. It would be a great way to deflect suspicion, because everyone—Rafe included—had just assumed that she'd teleported away under her own power.

Cat sat down on the couch next to him, face drawn with worry. "Rafe, what are you thinking?"

"I'm not sure yet. I get the feeling someone's taken her...but who? And why?"

"Well, she's the daughter of two wealthy and powerful people. And she was going to marry the son of the Castillo *prima*. That might be plenty of incentive for some unscrupulous warlock to swoop in, but if this was all about ransom or something like that, you'd think we would have heard from him. Or her," Cat added.

"I mean, I suppose a witch could be behind this as well."

"I don't think so," Rafe said. He wasn't quite sure why he felt so sure of that point, but some weird sixth sense was telling him that Miranda's captor had to be male. Once again he had the niggling feeling that he was overlooking something vitally important, but the more he tried to probe at it with his mind, the more it seemed to slip away. "I'm sure it's connected to Robert Marquez—I mean, the person who was using Robert Marquez's identity. Maybe we need to go back to that Airbnb."

"I thought that didn't go so well last time."

"No," Rafe admitted, "but that was because I was basically breaking and entering. Why don't I try to rent it? Then we'd have free rein to go through the place at our leisure."

Cat appeared to consider his suggestion for a moment, then nodded. "That sounds like a good idea, actually."

"All right, then." He rose from the couch. "Let me go get my laptop and see if the place is available."

As he headed upstairs to fetch his computer, Rafe wondered if once again they were following a dead end, a lead that really didn't mean anything. He didn't think so, though. Or at least, he really hoped not.

He unplugged the laptop from its charger and brought it back down to the living room, setting it down on the coffee table and opening it up so Cat could see what he was doing. It wasn't too difficult to find the Airbnb unit in question, since he already knew its location. And, thank God, it was currently unoccupied—it wasn't booked again until Thanksgiving week, which should give them plenty of time.

"How long should I book it for?" he asked, hurriedly setting up an account and getting his credit card information entered. Of course he'd never had any reason to use the service before this; witches and warlocks tended to stay put and not travel very much, and the times he'd gone up to Taos or headed south to visit Carlsbad Caverns, he'd stayed in regular hotels.

Cat pursed her lips. "Hmm…I don't know…three days?"

"All right." The unit wasn't all that expensive; reserving it for a day or two longer than he needed wouldn't be that big a deal. He requested a stay for three nights, starting tonight. Luckily, this particular Airbnb was set up for automatic booking, so he didn't have to wait for the owner to accept his request. The whole transaction went through in less than a minute, and almost at once he had several emails in his inbox, one confirming receipt of payment and the other a chatty little note from the owner with information about parking, the code for the door lock, that sort of thing.

"So we're set?" Cat asked as he closed the laptop.

"Looks that way. Let's head over and see what we can find."

"Are you going to pack?"

"'Pack'?" he repeated, not sure what his sister was driving at.

"Well, if you're really going to inspect the place, you might as well stay. Maybe you'll notice things you otherwise wouldn't. Besides, it sounds like the owner tends to come poking around. She's going to think it's weird if you don't have any luggage."

"She's going to think it's weird anyway, since she just found me there a day ago," he replied, then let out a breath. "But you're probably right. With any luck, she'll think I fell so in love with the place that I had to rent it right away."

Cat's skeptical expression told him exactly what she thought of that idea, but he would just have to take the risk. After all, he paid for the Airbnb fair and square. If the owner thought it was strange for him to be staying there, so be it. But with any luck, he wouldn't run into her at all.

"I'll go throw a few things in a duffle bag," he said. "Give me a couple of minutes."

"Okay."

Once again he went upstairs, this time to get the bag down from the top shelf of his closet. He didn't bother with any heavy-duty packing, only a spare pair of jeans and some T-shirts, underwear and socks, toiletries hastily stuffed into their own small leather bag. Fewer than five minutes had elapsed since he went upstairs. When he got back to the living room, it was to find Cat on the phone.

"Yes, Mom, I know," she was saying. "And I'll be home as soon as I can. I'm helping Rafe with something right now. Okay. Right. I know. See you soon." She ended the call and shoved the phone in her purse, a scowl of irritation creasing her brow.

"I see Genoveva is in her usual form," Rafe remarked as he set the duffle bag on the floor.

"Well, she's a little on edge. Dad is driving Sophia home to Taos so she can get some things together for a few days' stay, and Mom has been on the phone with the bishop, trying to get the funeral set up. He's doing his best to accommodate her, but I get the impression he's also been asking what the hell went on at your wedding."

"That's something we'd all like to know," he said, his tone sour. "But if Dad's off to Taos with Sophia, that means the two of them won't be back in Santa Fe for a while. That should give you enough time to come over and help me look at the flat. With any luck, it'll be haunted, and you'll be able to pick the resident ghost's brain."

"I don't know about the building itself," Cat responded, "but remember Annalisa, the ghost who hangs out by Burro Alley? That's close enough that she might have seen something."

Right. Cat had mentioned Annalisa when they were in San Antonio, but then they'd gotten broadsided by the Montoya witches and warlocks almost immediately afterward, and what with one thing or another, they hadn't had time to follow up. Just like Miranda's bags—loose ends that he shouldn't have lost track of. It almost felt as though some outside force was doing its very best to keep him off the scent.

Well, try all you want, he thought, *but I'm going down there now, and I* will *find something, damn it.*

"Yes, we'll talk to Annalisa after we check out the Airbnb," he said. "We'd better take two cars. That way I can stay, and if you need to head home unexpectedly, you'll have your own vehicle."

"Sounds like a plan."

They headed out, he to the garage so he could get in his Jeep Wrangler, Cat to the driveway to retrieve her Mercedes SUV. She didn't wait for him to back out, but headed west toward their destination, probably so she would have enough time to park in the structure across the street from the Airbnb and then wait for him. Since he was staying there, he'd have access to one of the parking spaces behind the building, which would make the logistics a bit simpler.

Sure enough, she was standing on the sidewalk in front of the wine tasting room, looking in the window a bit wistfully. As he approached, she said, "Maybe we'll get lucky and find a clue early on. Then we can come here and have a drink. I could use one about now."

"I wouldn't hold my breath," Rafe replied. "Luck doesn't seem to have been on my side lately."

Being Cat, she knew better than to try to tell him he shouldn't talk that way, or that he was being too negative. Instead, she said, "Then we might as well go inside and see what we can find."

"This way. The entrance is around back."

She followed him down the alley and to the small stoop where the back door to the building was located. Of course he didn't need a code to get in, but he dutifully entered it anyway, retrieving the numbers from the confirmation email he'd been sent. They went up the stairs and on into the flat, which looked just the same as the last time he'd been here. That made perfect sense; the owner had just had it cleaned, and no one had stayed here since.

"Any ghosts?" he asked after he'd shut the door behind him.

Cat moved into the living room and stood there for a moment, eyes shut. At last she shook her head. "No. This place feels unoccupied. But...."

"But what?"

"I don't know. It's hard to describe. Something about it doesn't feel *clean,* though. Like there's some kind of weird oily magical residue on everything."

To the naked eye, of course, the flat looked immaculate. But Cat was looking at the place with an entirely different kind of eye. Although she wasn't precisely a medium or a psychic, her gift for speaking with ghosts had given her a certain sensitivity to these sorts of things. And, considering the scent of dark magic he'd picked up when he'd prowled the area in coyote form, he thought she must also be sensing what he'd found, only experiencing it in a different way.

"I'm glad you can feel it, too," he said. "Because when I first came here, I wasn't totally sure, had to wonder whether I was manufacturing that residue because I needed to believe that something was very wrong about this place."

"No, there's something definitely here." Cat put her hands on her hips and surveyed the room, a faraway look in her dark eyes. "Actually, I think it's stronger in the bedroom." She crossed over to the short hallway, then went through the first door on the right. "Yes, I can feel it more in here."

Rafe followed her. He couldn't precisely smell the wrongness the way he had a few days earlier, but a weird crawling sensation began on the back of his neck. If he'd been in coyote form, he probably would have wrinkled his nose and snarled.

Again, the room looked ordinary and completely in order, the quilt in lively southwest colors lying smooth on the bed, the prints of past art and wine festivals all hanging perfectly straight on the walls. But there was something terribly wrong about it.

"Over here," Cat said, laying a hand on the dresser. "It feels even stronger here."

He went to her and began opening drawers, doing his best to ignore that creepy crawly sensation, which had now begun to move down his spine. "They're all empty," he said, after he was done with his inspection.

"Maybe not in it." His sister paused for a moment, surveying the simple oak piece of furniture with the sort of concentration usually reserved for observing a particularly nasty bacteria under a microscope. "Maybe *behind* it."

Because the dresser was empty, it was easy enough to move out of the way. At first the wall behind it appeared unmarked, untouched, but….

"Do you see that?" Cat asked.

Rafe squatted down so he could get a better look at the portion of wall in question. Yes, it looked as though someone had wiped it down, but not thoroughly enough. If you squinted and looked at it at just the right angle where the light from the window slanted against the plaster, you could see traces of strange diagrams etched with lettering he didn't recognize.

"What the hell is that?"

Her lips thinned. "I'm not totally sure, because this isn't the sort of thing I've ever really studied, but those look like sigils for some kind of spell casting—and not the good kind."

Well, her explanation seemed to reinforce Rafe's theory that they were dealing with some kind of dark warlock here. "Who would know for sure?"

"I honestly don't know," Cat replied, looking flummoxed. "Castillos don't practice this kind of magic. I mean, one time I found some old books in the library at home that had probably belonged to Grandmother—or maybe even Grandmother's grandmother. Anyway, I was just a kid and I was interested, so I started leafing through one. The book I found had diagrams like this in it. I didn't know what they meant, but man, when Mom caught me, she totally chewed me out, said I wasn't to look at those kinds of books ever again.

And the next time I checked, they were all gone. She must have locked them up somewhere." Cat let out a breath, then shook her head. "Maybe there's someone in the family who's studied these kinds of dark spells, but the only person who would know for sure is Mom, and you know she wouldn't tell us…and she'd demand to know why we were asking in the first place."

Rafe couldn't argue with that assertion, because it sounded exactly like something his mother would do. He raised himself up from his squatting position and said, "Well, at least we know there's some bad juju going on here." He paused, then asked, "Should I get a couple of pictures?" And he brought out his phone, ready to get some images of the patterns on the wall.

At once, Cat put her hand on his arm. "I wouldn't."

Puzzled, he stared down at her. "Why not?"

"Things like this…they have power. Even as digital images stored on a phone. I don't think you want that kind of energy traveling around with you."

A creepy little shiver wandered down Rafe's spine. He'd never thought about it like that, but she had a point. After returning his phone to his pocket, he said, "Okay. Then let's put the dresser back, and go down and see if we can find your ghost, pick her brain."

Cat appeared relieved by this suggestion, and that he hadn't argued with her about taking pictures. If the flat was giving him a crawling sensation all over, Rafe didn't want to know what it might be doing to his more sensitive sister. One thing was for sure, though—he didn't care how it might look to the owner if she came snooping around, but he sure as hell wasn't about to spend the night in this place. That duffle bag was going right back in his house with him.

They moved the dresser back to its original spot and headed downstairs to street level, then walked the half block to Burro Alley. It was a quaint spot popular with tourists, with a large bronze statue of its eponymous burro standing guard at the entrance, making sure only foot traffic got past. Luckily, since it was late after-noon on a weekday in early November, that foot traffic was at a minimum, making it easier for his sister to reach out to the ghost of the girl who'd killed herself over forbidden love for a priest.

"Annalisa!" Cat called out softly. "Are you there?"

A long pause.

"Annalisa?"

Another long, agonizing moment. A couple a few years older than Rafe walked past, carrying bags from the wine tasting room around the corner. They gave Rafe and Cat a single curious glance before continuing on their way.

"She's here," Cat murmured to Rafe. Then she said, "Annalisa, can I ask you if you saw someone here in the last day or two?" A few seconds of quiet, and she went on, "I'm not sure what she would have been wearing, but she's a few years younger than I am, with long wavy brown hair, almost to her waist. Very pretty, with green eyes. Slender, not too tall…you have?"

The relief that coursed through Rafe at hearing those two words was so strong, he almost didn't catch the next part of the exchange. But then he forced himself to focus, because clearly Annalisa wasn't done yet.

"Two days ago. She left with someone? Who?"

Rafe's pulse quickened, and he could feel his hands knot into fists at hearing Miranda hadn't been alone when Annalisa spied her.

"A young man with black hair and eyes, tall and slim," Cat said. From the way she spoke, Rafe guessed she was repeating Annalisa's words so he could hear them for himself. "They went around back to the alley and got in a white vehicle and drove away."

"Did she get the license plate number?"

Cat narrowed her eyes at him, obviously not pleased by this interruption. "Did it look like he was forcing her to go with him?" A long pause.

"Oh, so she got into the car herself and shut the door behind her. Anything else?" Cat appeared to wait, then told Rafe in an undertone, "That was all Annalisa saw. But she doesn't think Miranda was being coerced or anything."

Unless the guy had her under a mind-control spell. Once someone started playing around with black magic, it was really hard to know what was possible and what wasn't.

The description of the dark warlock kept echoing around in Rafe's head, though, teasing him, as if it should make more sense than it did. Young, and tall and slender. Black hair and black eyes.

Black eyes. Eyes so dark you couldn't see where the pupil ended and the iris began. Looking into those eyes was like looking into a black hole, a darkness without end.

The shudder that went through Rafe right then was so intense, Cat looked at him in alarm. "What's the matter?"

Memory came flooding back. The flat above the wine-tasting room. The voice telling him what he had to say to Miranda, hideous words designed to tear them apart, to send her running into the dark warlock's arms.

Voice tight, Rafe said, "I know who Miranda is with."

13

DINNERS

Miranda

I DIDN'T KNOW WHETHER THERE WAS A WITCH or warlock somewhere who possessed the kind of magic that would make meal prep a breeze, who could simply snap his or her fingers and conjure a casserole or a soufflé. Or maybe a spell existed in a grimoire someplace that could do the same sort of thing. I supposed it didn't really matter, because I knew my Great-Aunt Rachel would kill me if she ever caught me taking those sorts of shortcuts in the kitchen.

Because a few clouds had begun to gather toward sunset, and I could already feel the temperature dropping, I thought I'd make a big pot of spaghetti for dinner. Something about the aroma of homemade spaghetti sauce and garlic bread always made a house feel cozy. Besides, it would give Simon and me leftovers for the evenings when I didn't feel like making something from scratch and we also didn't feel like going out. And although he'd protested that he didn't want me to do all this work, I insisted. I liked to cook. It was relaxing and sort of zen when I got in the groove, and right then I wanted to focus on something that was completely nonmagical.

Despite my reassurances that I enjoyed the process, Simon couldn't help watching with some bemusement as I added tomato paste and wine and herbs in careful proportions to the large saucepan, with nary a cookbook in sight. "Where did you learn to cook like this?"

"My great-aunt," I replied, then picked up the bowl of onions and bell peppers he'd chopped for me earlier so I could sauté them lightly before adding them to the sauce. "I mean, my mother is a pretty decent cook, too, because Rachel taught her when she was younger than I am now. But I know Rachel liked me to come over and learn directly from her, and I always thought it was fun. My older sister wasn't really into it, and Rachel never had any children of her own, so I think she appreciated me learning what she had to teach me."

"That's cool," Simon said. "My mother was always a 'frozen meal from Costco' or pizza night kind of person. I didn't get home cooking much, except at the holidays when we'd get a bunch of homemade de la Paz tamales to bring home."

I'd had that opportunity once or twice growing up, when my mother's cousin Caitlin came up from Tucson with a platter of tamales from her husband Alex's aunt. Those de la Pazes definitely knew their way around a tamale, or at least, quite a few of them did. Rachel had taught me how to make tamales, and mine were pretty damn good, but they were still missing a certain something I detected in the de la Paz version of the traditional dish and could never seem to replicate.

"Those are good. I've had them once or twice."

"Right. From Caitlin?"

"Exactly."

He smiled, and a certain happy warmth passed through me. After all the magical exertions of the morning, it felt good to be doing something as ordinary as making spaghetti sauce. And it also felt good to be here in the kitchen with Simon, to chat about normal family things like cooking and holiday meals. When we'd gotten back from our little excursion to Los Alamos, I'd sent another text to my mother, just to let her know I was doing fine and would be making spaghetti for dinner. I thought she'd like to hear that, because it would let her know I was someplace with access to a kitchen and was able to do pretty much what I wanted.

I hadn't waited for her reply, but figured I'd check the phone once I had the sauce simmering away. Really, it should have been doing that for most of the afternoon, allowing the sauce to gain in richness as the hours passed. I had to hope it would still come out okay, even though I was sort of rushing things.

Watching me sauté the onions and peppers, Simon remarked, "You know, I really didn't bring you here so you could cook for me."

"I know," I replied, then shot him a grin. "But we both have to eat, and I like doing this. Really, it's good to give my brain a break. Magic is amazing and exhilarating, but…."

"It can be kind of exhausting. I know." He seemed to pause and think for a moment before adding, "I don't know much about them, but I wonder whether you should try making potions at some point. With your cooking background and your natural talents, you might be able to come up with some interesting stuff."

I'd never thought of that. Well, again, why would I, when before a few days ago, I had no idea that I had any magical gifts at all? Before, I'd had barely any alternatives to work with, and now I had almost too many. There weren't a lot of people in the McAllister clan who dabbled in potions, mostly because they did have an enormous potential to go wrong if you messed up something. However, I remembered that Zoe Sandoval, the *prima* of the de la Paz clan, was something of an expert.

"Does your *prima* do much of that anymore?"

"Much of what?" Simon asked, looking rather confused.

"Make potions. Wasn't that her talent, back before she even became *prima?*"

"Oh, right," he said quickly. "I'd forgotten about that. I guess it's because I always just thought of her as our *prima* and didn't think much about what her gift had been before she took over the de la Paz family."

I supposed that made some sense. Even with my own mother, I'd always thought of her as *prima* first and someone who could talk to ghosts second. And of course she had that grab bag of other abilities she could access as necessary, thanks to her bond with my father.

"Well, I'll think about it," I said, eyeing the onions and peppers in the pan. Since they looked cooked enough, I began to slide them into the rest of the sauce. "It's too bad it's late fall, because one talent I would have liked to try is coaxing growing things along. There were several witches in Jerome who had that green thumb, so to speak. It's a handy talent, but I don't much see the point in making plants grow now, when the next frost will just come along and kill them."

"Unless you kept it away." Simon had been standing on the other side of the island as I worked, presumably to stay out of my way, but now he came closer and leaned up against the counter a foot or so away from the stovetop. "You've already shown you can change the weather. You could create a warm zone where the frost never forms, or the snow never comes. If it was small enough, it wouldn't upset the overall balance of the weather in a certain area, but it would give you more time to grow things."

His suggestion was something else I'd never considered, but I didn't think I would want to do something like that. It felt far too much like open interference. Nature had its own patterns, and I knew better than to mess with them much more than causing a few random rainstorms.

"I could do that," I allowed. "But I think I'd better not. It's probably safer that way."

"Okay. I get it." Then his dark eyes sparkled with some inner mischief. "I guess we'll just have to think of something else to try."

"I suppose I can sleep on it." I turned burner way down, then glanced at the clock on the oven behind me. Five-twenty. The sauce needed to simmer for at least an hour. More would be better, though. "Dinner at seven? I want to go see if my mom responded to my text, but—"

"Go ahead," Simon said with a smile. "How about we meet back around six-thirty to get the pasta going?"

"And the garlic bread," I added. "Don't want to forget about that."

"That's for sure."

Still smiling, he let himself out the side door. A brief glimpse of him as he headed down the walkway that led to the caretaker's house, and then he was gone.

I felt a smile on my lips, too, and then shook my head. It was easy to be with Simon, partly because, while he of course was interested in exploring my talents, he knew when to back off and take it easy, seemed to know when I needed some time to myself.

A girl could get used to that sort of thing.

After double-checking that the sauce wouldn't simmer too high while I was gone, I went to my bedroom and picked up my phone from where I'd left it sitting on the dresser to charge. Sure enough, I had a new message from my mother.

I'm glad to hear that you sound so settled and happy. Your father and I still wish you would tell us where you are, but I won't press you on that. Take care, and keep in touch.

I texted back, *Thanks, Mom. Maybe soon. I'll let you know.*

Because really, it seemed clear to me that I could handle just about any kind of magic I put my mind to. At this point, it was all about practice and control, but I could work on that just as well back home in Arizona as I could here. Of course, there was something secure and sheltered and safe here, in our little getaway in Tesuque, but this idyll couldn't last forever anyway. This place was expensive...very expensive. Simon and I could pool our resources, and we still wouldn't be able to afford even a tenth of what it probably cost.

Anyway, it was probably a little early to be contemplating buying a house together. But we could go back to Arizona, and I could show my parents that my sleeping magic was now fully awakened, and then Simon and I could decide what to do next. He didn't sound all that attached to Tucson, so I didn't think it would be too hard to convince him to stay in Jerome with me. Of course, housing was always tight there, because the town was so tiny, but we could live in Cottonwood or Clarkdale for a while until something became available....

And you are getting so far ahead of yourself, it's not even funny, I thought, shaking off daydreams of Simon and me moving into one of the big Victorian houses on Paradise Lane, up where my parents lived part-time. *Just because things didn't work out with Rafe, there's no reason to jump into the picket fence and the cat and the kids with someone else.*

That inner voice sounded very sensible. I knew I'd better pay attention to it, because I knew that my need to belong could get me in trouble if I allowed it to. Much smarter to take it easy and wait to see how things progressed with Simon.

One way or another, though, I really didn't see myself staying here in New Mexico for much longer.

Simon had set the table and lit the tall, thin tapers in the holders of glazed bisque that stood like sentinels on the linen runner. He also found all the serving pieces we needed for our dinner, including a big pasta bowl and another bowl for salad, and helped me dish everything up.

"Is this guilt because I did all the cooking?" I asked with a laugh as he took the salad out to the dining room table.

"I wouldn't call it guilt," he said, his expression quite serious. "More like…wanting to help."

"Well, thanks for that. I think we're ready."

And we were. It was probably way too much

food for two people, but leftovers were always a good thing. Speaking of guilt, one of my guilty pleasures as a kid had been to sneak a piece of leftover garlic bread and heat it in the toaster oven for breakfast, even though I knew we were supposed to be saving whatever was left for another meal. I'd have to try that the next day and see if it still had as much savor as it did when I was ten years old.

We sat down at the table, which stretched away for what felt like miles from our two lonely place settings at the head. "Good thing you didn't make me sit at the other end," I said as I took my place to Simon's right, just below the head of the table. "We would have had to use semaphore flags."

"Or megaphones," he agreed, wrestling with the cork from a bottle of chianti we'd picked up at the grocery store. "I don't think I'd try to inflict that on you. I'm still trying to decide whether the Texas oil guy has a huge family, or whether he picked a table this big because he needed something that would fit in the space."

"Probably the latter," I said. "If he had a big family, you'd think they'd be here watching the house for him. I know I wouldn't let my father sell a place like this."

"I'm glad you like it." Simon finally got the cork out and set it on the table, then gestured toward my glass. I handed it to him so he could fill it up, then put it back down by my place setting. "How would you like to buy it?"

My eyes didn't exactly pop out of my head, but I could feel them widen. "Um, hate to break it to you, Simon, but I don't have four or five million extra bucks just lying around."

"You could, though." He finished pouring his own wine, then sent me a speculative look. "Or hadn't you gotten around to thinking about what you could do with those teleportation powers of yours?"

"To rob banks?" For a second, uneasiness swirled through me. He couldn't be serious, could he? Then I caught the dancing light in his black eyes and said, "Very funny. No, I hadn't thought about that kind of thing, because you know we're not supposed to use our powers for self-enrichment or to take advantage of others."

"Tell that to your Wilcox relatives."

I repressed the urge to stick my tongue out at him, because Simon had a definite point there. No one liked to talk about it, and as far as I knew, my father's clan was pretty much on the up and up these days, but I knew that the Wilcoxes in the past had indulged in a lot of shady practices to plump up their portfolios. They came out of the stock market crash in 1929 pretty much unscathed, and their investments and bank accounts had only grown by leaps and bounds since then. Still, even though some of their early methods probably wouldn't have held up to FCC scrutiny, that wasn't quite the same thing as teleporting into Fort Knox and walking out with bars of gold in my backpack or something.

"Anyway," I went on in quelling tones, "I don't think I'd want to settle down this close to the Castillos. The sooner I have them in my rearview mirror, the better."

"I can't blame you for that." Simon paused, then raised his glass in a toast. "To settling down wherever it makes you happy."

That was a toast I could happily make, so I clinked my wine glass against his and took a healthy swallow of chianti. It was fruity and full, and better than I'd expected it to be.

After that we were occupied with dishing out salad and spaghetti, and helping ourselves to some garlic bread as well. As I ate, I thought of how much fun this was, to be playing house like this, even though I knew our time here was limited. And there were other aspects to playing house....

I watched Simon from underneath my eyelashes as he ate. No, I thought objectively, he wasn't as handsome as Rafe, his face thinner, his features sharper. But I liked his thick, sooty hair, and those black, black eyes with their heavy lashes. It was an interesting face, one with good bones beneath it. And if I didn't have quite the same urge to hurl myself into Simon's arms, I told myself that was a good thing. There had been something about the way I reacted to Rafe that made me not quite myself. That lack of control could have gotten me in trouble, if it weren't that he'd been so clearly bent on sabotaging our relationship.

One way or another, I was well out of it.

And it was good for me to be friends with Simon first before anything romantic passed between us. I couldn't compare our relationship to the intense bond my parents shared, but I knew that in civilian couples, it was often far better for love to evolve from friendship. That way, you had something in common besides plain old lust.

"This is incredible," Simon said once he'd slowed down a bit, having made some serious inroads in his plate of spaghetti. "Better than I've ever had in a restaurant."

"Thanks." My cheeks heated a bit at his praise; I knew my spaghetti sauce was good, but only because Rachel had taught me to make it. "I'll have to let Rachel know. She's always happy when people like her recipes."

"Definitely." He set down his fork and sipped some chianti. "But I don't want to make you cook every night. Plus, I had an idea earlier this afternoon."

"Oh?" I asked, my tone guarded. I told myself that Simon wouldn't suggest anything that might get me in trouble, but....

He didn't seem put off by my obvious caution. "Well, I was thinking about how it seems fairly easy for you to handle a bunch of different types of magic. So I was wondering about you managing two different spells—for lack of a better word—at the same time. What would happen if you cast an illusion spell to alter your appearance…and also blocked your magical gifts so that no other witches or warlocks in the vicinity would know what you were?"

"That sounds hard," I said, feeling less enthusiastic than ever. It was one thing to expand my magical gifts, but quite another to push me past what I could comfortably manage.

"It could be, but it would also be an awesome test of your talents. I was thinking we could try it by going out to dinner tomorrow night in one of Santa Fe's best restaurants…which also happens to be just around the corner from Genoveva's house."

"Oh, no way," I told Simon, my voice flat. "Are you kidding? What if we get caught?"

"What if we do?" he responded. "It's not like she can put us in witch jail or something. She's no relation to you. Besides, you could teleport us out of there if anything went sideways."

"Teleport in front of a bunch of civilians."

"I doubt it would come to that." He stared at me, black eyes shining. "Come on, Miranda— don't you want to test your talents? And it would also totally give the finger to Genoveva Castillo."

His voice was hard as he said her name. I didn't know what Simon had against the Castillo *prima,* except that she'd done her best to coerce my family into making me marry her son. Since obviously Simon wasn't a fan of that idea, I could see why he might not be too thrilled with her. Still....

"Maybe," I said cautiously. "But I'd want to practice first."

"Of course," he responded. "We'll practice tomorrow. But I'll still make reservations at Geronimo."

I could have argued, I suppose. But part of me wanted the same thing Simon did—to show Genoveva Castillo that maybe she wasn't in quite as much control of the situation as she thought.

And who would turn down dinner in a five-star restaurant?

Not me.

I stared at myself in the mirror. All that day I'd practiced altering my appearance, right down to changing the plain dark T-shirt I wore over to a beaded wrap sweater, one I paired with slim jeans and high-heeled boots, since I hadn't actually brought anything that glamorous with me.

The face looking back at me from the mirror wasn't mine, though. I'd decided to go with someone who was around my same height and age—my cousin Jessica Rowe. Her hair was a little darker than mine, her eyes the same piercing blue as her father's rather than my smoky green, but otherwise we were fairly similar in appearance. I figured that was better, just because it was easier to hold the illusion and at the same time do that trick of hiding my true nature, that inner light which tended to announce itself to every other witch and warlock in the vicinity.

Simon hadn't let me off so easy when it came to him, though. I'd protested that there wasn't anyone in the Castillo clan who probably even knew what he looked like, and so I didn't know why I had to cast the illusion on him at all, but he still told me I needed to change his appearance as well.

"A really *extreme* change," he told me. "I know you can do it."

I had to hope his confidence wasn't misplaced.

When I met him in the living room, he looked at me in approval. "That's good—similar but not exact. How does it feel?"

"Fine," I said. "Once I set the illusion in place, it pretty much holds until I take it away."

"All right, then. My turn."

I pulled in a breath. Simon had said he wanted an extreme change, so that was what I would give him. My cousin Jason was as blond as his parents Levi and Hayley, tall and blue-eyed, with a definite Norwegian ski team captain vibe going on. I couldn't think of anyone who looked less like Simon, which made Jason's the perfect face to borrow.

Even though I knew what I was doing, I had to prevent myself from taking a step backward when the transformation was complete. The man standing in front of me was my cousin Jason's double, hair appearing nearly white under the bright illumination from the chandelier overhead.

"Go take a look," I instructed him, and Simon turned from me so he could go into the powder room down the hall and inspect himself in the mirror.

"Wow," he said. He didn't come back out right away, so I guessed he was leaning close to the mirror and looking at himself from all angles. I couldn't really blame him, since I'd done basically the same thing, just to reassure myself that the illusion was perfect. When he emerged, he was shaking his blond head. "This is incredible. Who is this guy, anyway? Some male model?"

"My cousin Jason."

"He looks like he should be the captain of a lacrosse team or something."

"I was thinking Norwegian downhill skier, but yeah."

A grin flashed across Simon's face. That was how I could tell he was still under there, despite the illusion—those might have been my cousin Jason's features, but the way he smiled was very much Simon. The difference was subtle, though, and I knew that no one we'd be seeing at the restaurant would be able to tell anything was off.

"We should get going," he said. "Our reservations are in twenty minutes."

"Okay."

I tried to ignore the way my heart pounded as I pulled on my jacket, then followed Simon out to the car. The closer we got to the heart of town, the more nervous I got. It didn't matter that the illusions were flawless, or that I knew I was safely blocking my magical nature, just as Simon was hiding his. I couldn't shake the feeling that somehow Genoveva Castillo would reach out from behind the walls of her compound and grab me as we passed, that she'd be able to see beneath the illusions and the spells we'd cast to hide our witch blood no matter what we did.

But then we were turning up Canyon Road, going much farther up on the street than I'd managed to explore in my brief time here in Santa Fe. We passed the restaurant, a place called Geronimo, then turned right so we could enter the parking lot from the proper side. It was extremely cramped and already full, but a valet appeared and said he'd take care of it for us.

Simon thanked the man and took a valet ticket from him before leading me slightly downhill to the restaurant's entrance. As soon as we were inside, I saw a large fireplace almost exactly opposite the door, and an elegant little bar off to my left. I didn't have time for any more of an inspection than that, however, because a girl around my age approached Simon and me, asked about our reservation, and then guided us to an intimate little room toward the back of the restaurant.

I noticed he hadn't given his own name for the reservation, but an alias—Robert Marquez. Probably just trying to be careful, although I wondered how he was going to reconcile the discrepancy between the name on the reservation and the name on his credit card. Well, Simon had been very careful so far, and so I had to believe that he already had all the logistics planned out.

As the hostess brought us to our table, though, a tingle at the back of my neck told me that the occupants of the table over by the window were also of witch-kind—a man and a woman I didn't recognize, probably around my parents' age. Of course my first instinct was to panic, but Simon only put a reassuring hand on my arm, presumably to help guide me into my seat. However, I knew what he was really doing was making sure I didn't react in a way that would draw their attention.

Heart pounding, I sat down on the banquette up against the wall, then murmured a thank-you to the hostess as she handed me a menu. Looking completely calm, Simon sat down as well, and accepted another menu from the hostess. She told us that our server would be with us shortly, then left the room.

I opened my menu and pretended to be perusing its contents, but really, I was only using it as cover so I could murmur to Simon, "What the hell are we supposed to do now?"

"Have dinner," he replied, looking magnificently unperturbed by the situation. "They haven't noticed anything, have they?"

Shooting the couple in question a quick glance from the corner of my eye, I shook my head. "Not that I can tell."

"And they won't. It's going to be fine."

Easy for him to say. Or rather, this was all easier for him because the worst that would happen if we were caught was that he'd be sent packing back to Arizona. I, on the other hand, would have a mountain of explaining to do.

The witch at the table did glance over at us, but after a panicky second in which I felt my heart begin to race again, I realized she wasn't looking at me at all, but instead had bestowed a single admiring look on my companion before returning her attention to the warlock opposite her, who was probably her husband. I supposed I couldn't blame her too much; my cousin Jason's looks attracted attention wherever he went, something I probably should have considered before I decided on him as Simon's avatar.

He smiled. "Better decide on what you'd like to eat, so we can choose a wine."

Fine. My panic began to subside, mostly because it seemed as though the pair of Castillo witches at the other table didn't have a clue that more of their kind were sitting only a couple of yards away. The spells seemed to be working. I couldn't ask for much more than that.

I looked over the menu quickly and decided on the filet mignon. Simon said he wanted the ribeye, and so that made the wine choice fairly easy. When the waiter appeared to take our order, Simon asked for one of the restaurant's Bordeaux wines, pronouncing the name of the winery with a lot more ease than I would have expected.

"You speak French?" I asked after the waiter had gone.

"Not really," Simon replied, reaching for his water so he could take a sip. "But it never hurts to teach yourself some of the pronunciation so you don't sound like an idiot when ordering at a fancy restaurant."

I supposed that made some sense, although it wasn't the sort of reply I normally would have expected from a guy my age. Then again, Simon wasn't exactly your run-of-the-mill twenty-one-year-old.

Because of the presence of the witch couple seated across the room from us, we couldn't really talk about my work with magic, or anything that might give away the fact that Simon and I were no more civilians than they were. Luckily, he went right into talking about the latest release in what he said was his favorite superhero movie franchise, coming out at Thanksgiving, and other commonplaces. He seemed to notice how tense I was, and so carried the bulk of the conversation himself—a relief to me, since all I had to do was smile and nod my way through most of it.

The wine was excellent, the food even more so…and I was finally able to relax just as I was having the last few bites of filet, because the pair of Castillo witches got up from their seats and left. It took all my effort not to hold my breath as they passed our table, but then they were gone, seemingly without noticing anything strange about the young couple sitting in the corner.

"Thank the Goddess," I breathed once they were gone. "When they ordered dessert, I thought I was going to lose it."

"But you didn't," Simon replied, still looking completely unperturbed. "And now they're gone…and I think they proved my point."

"What point?" I asked, still feeling a little off center, thanks to our near-miss.

"That you can maintain two enchantments at the same time without breaking a sweat. And while enjoying a very good Bordeaux. You truly are a marvel, Miranda."

I'd wanted to be annoyed with him for putting me in such a position in the first place, but it was hard to be too mad at someone who called you a "marvel." Still, I tried to sound nonchalant as I said, "Well, I don't know about that, but it wasn't quite as hard as I thought it might be."

He smiled. Right then I wished I could remove the enchantment, because it did feel strange to be having an intimate dinner like this with my cousin. However, I knew I didn't dare lift the illusion until we were safely home. "It's because you're so powerful. Most witches and warlocks couldn't have done anything close."

"Well, thanks." I toyed with my fork before setting it down against the rim of my plate. "All the same, I'll be glad to get out of here."

"You aren't enjoying your dinner?" he asked, eyes widening in mock astonishment.

"It's very good, but…."

"It's all right," he said, apparently relenting. "This has been a test, and tests are always kind of stressful."

"So we can go home once we've finished our wine?"

His lip curled. "No dessert?"

"No," I told him firmly. "We have ice cream at the house, if you want it."

"I'll be fine."

And after that Simon did take pity on me, because he finished his last few bites of steak and the last sips of wine in his glass, then asked the waiter to bring us the check. No dillydallying with a credit card, either—he dropped four hundred-dollar bills on the table, then extended a hand to help me up from where I sat.

"Ready?"

I nodded. Well, that was one way to get around the credit card conundrum, I supposed.

He had one "test" left, however. After we had the valet bring the car around and had climbed in, Simon turned so we were driving right past the Castillo compound, moving slowly.

"What the hell are you doing?" I demanded. "This is the last place we should be."

"No," he replied calmly, hands wrapped around the steering wheel even though the car was doing the driving. "You need to know that she doesn't have any power over you. Genoveva Castillo is a raging bitch, but she's also a very powerful witch. She should know you're here. And if she did know, what would she do?"

"Come out to confront us," I replied, my voice hardly more than a whisper. Adrenaline was sending spiky jolts of energy through my body, urging me to run. And yet I knew that if Genoveva really had been able to sense me, she would be here already.

Which meant she didn't know I was here. We were crawling past her house, her sanctum, and yet we might as well have been a couple of civilians for all she was able to sense our presence.

"Exactly. You see? You don't have anything to fear from her, or any of the other Castillos. You're more powerful than she is, Miranda."

A shiver went through me. I was just an ordinary witch. I wasn't supposed to be stronger than a *prima*. And if I was…?

I didn't know what to do about that.

"Take me home," I whispered.

14

IDENTITIES

Rafe

CAT WAS STARING AT HIM IN CONSTERNATION. "What do you mean, you know who Miranda is with?"

No wonder Rafe had kept having those strange spells where he knew he had to be missing something obvious, something right under his nose. It was because of the enchantment—or curse, or whatever you wanted to call it—that Simon had cast on him, making him forget. The spell had been broken at last, however.

"This guy called Simon," he said curtly. "Someone Miranda met on the Railrunner when she was coming up from Albuquerque."

"You didn't say anything about that to me."

No, he hadn't. Now Rafe wondered at the

omission, wondered why he hadn't asked for his sister's advice when it came to dealing with this unexpected interloper. He couldn't say for sure, except that maybe he was embarrassed at having a rival for Miranda's affections—Miranda, who should have been a sure bet, bound to him as she was. Just another aspect of the whole situation that he'd managed to screw up royally. If he'd said something to Cat about Simon, they could have come to the truth a lot sooner, since Simon's spell didn't seem to have affected anyone else in his family.

"We need to talk," Rafe said, then gave a quick glance around them. Burro Alley was quiet enough now, but it certainly wasn't the sort of place for an intimate conversation. "But not here."

"Upstairs?"

That would have made the most sense, since the Airbnb was only half a block away. However, Rafe immediately rejected that notion. The flat might have been empty, but it was still polluted by the residue of whatever foul magic Simon had used. For all Rafe knew, some kind of spell lingered there, sending every word spoken there back to its former occupant. Rafe had never heard of such a thing, but he didn't know much about dark magic. Better to play it safe. Besides, he'd already mentally vowed never to set foot in the place again.

"No, let's go back to my house."

Cat looked resigned at this suggestion, as though she wasn't terribly thrilled about heading back to his place when she'd barely gotten downtown but also wasn't going to protest. Like him, she must know that it was probably best to spend as little time in that Airbnb as possible. They'd already gotten the information they needed anyway.

"See you there," was all she said, and she hurried across the street to the parking structure, taking advantage of a small break in traffic.

Rafe went to retrieve his Jeep from the parking space behind the flat, then drove home. This was a time when he would have welcomed a self-driving mechanism in his car, just because he knew he was distracted, attempting to figure out how in the hell a powerful warlock like Simon could have slid in under his family's nose without anyone noticing. Miranda hadn't said anything about her acquaintance being a warlock, which meant she hadn't known. Which also meant that Simon must have had a way of hiding what he was from everyone, including her.

Son of a bitch.

Luckily, there wasn't too much traffic to worry about, and he was home in less than five minutes. Cat was knocking at the front door as he came down the hallway from the garage, and he hurried to let her in.

"Okay," she said without preamble, moving past him to go sit in the living room. "Now can you tell me what the hell is going on? Who is this Simon person?"

"Like I said, this guy Miranda met on the train. Only I have a feeling that meeting was planned. Simon had to be lying in wait for her."

"Why?"

Good question. It had to be more than Miranda simply being a beautiful unaccompanied witch. Yes, she had turned out to be stronger than anyone had thought—Rafe sure didn't know anyone who could teleport like she did—but was that the only reason?

"I don't know for sure," he said. "I'm doing my best to piece the whole thing together. But they met on the Railrunner, and they met again after that time she stormed out of our lunch at La Fonda. Miranda said that was just coincidence, that she'd gone into the wine tasting room for a drink and realized he worked there, but—"

"The wine tasting room under the Airbnb apartment?" Cat broke in. "Why didn't you say something while we were there? We could have gone in and asked about Simon, found out what they knew about him."

"Do you think someone who was able to hide

the fact that he was a warlock, who cast some sort of funky spell on me to say those horrible things to Miranda, would have told a bunch of civilians the truth about himself?"

"Well, I guess not," Cat said, looking deflated. "So where does that put us?"

"I don't know." Rafe scrubbed a hand over his bristly cheek. One of these days he should probably shave. "I mean, at least I know what the guy looks like, but I don't know how much that's going to help. I kind of doubt he's hanging around Santa Fe if he has Miranda with him. He'd want to make sure he was well out of our orbit."

"True." His sister seemed to think for a moment, idly playing with the straps of the backpack she used for a purse, her fingers running the heavy fabric between them as if they were the weft threads of her loom. "Still, if you know what he looks like, that's something. He's a warlock, so he had to have come from a clan somewhere. Tell me about him."

The last thing Rafe felt like doing was analyzing Simon's appearance, but he knew it was something that needed to be done. "He's around Miranda's age. Tall, but not quite as tall as I am, and thinner. Hispanic. Black hair and eyes—*really* black eyes, the darkest I've ever seen."

"He's Hispanic?" Cat asked, perking up a bit. "Well, that narrows it down. He's not one of ours, obviously, but what other clan could he have come from?"

"The de la Pazes, maybe?" Rafe rubbed his chin. That would make the most sense. He remembered thinking that Simon could have been someone who had a long-distance crush on Miranda and hadn't wanted to let her go. Maybe that's all this was—some kind of puppy love gone out of control. True, Miranda had claimed that she'd never met Simon before she saw him on the Railrunner, but maybe she was trying to cover up for him. Since Rafe knew he hadn't acted the most even-tempered around her, he could see why she might have been trying to protect her friend. "Or the Montoyas in Texas, but that doesn't make as much sense, since their paths wouldn't have crossed before now."

"Maybe you should contact Miranda's parents, ask if they know of anyone in the de la Paz clan who had a crush on her."

Rafe knew Genoveva would freak out if he got in touch with Angela and Connor, since they were supposed to be maintaining radio silence and pretending that everything was fine and he was off on his honeymoon with Miranda. Not that he cared too much about his mother's reaction. The lie was going to come out eventually, no matter what they did.

"Yeah," he said. "That's probably the best

thing to do." He dug his phone out of his pocket, went to his contacts lists, and then paused with his finger hovering over the number in question.

"What's the matter?" Cat inquired, clearly noticing his hesitation.

"I don't know. I'm just wondering whether we should go directly to the de la Paz *prima* and ask whether she knows if anyone from her clan has left their territory for an extended time recently."

"I think they're pretty tight with the McAllisters and Wilcoxes," Cat pointed out. "If you go around asking questions like that, I have a feeling it's going to get back to Connor and Angela pretty quickly anyway."

His sister was probably right. Rafe knew that part of his hesitation was probably simple cowardice. The second he talked to Miranda's parents, they'd know that something had gone terribly wrong, that the very people who were supposed to be their daughter's new family had been lying about her disappearance in order to avert an inter-clan war. Or maybe not war, but he had a feeling that relations between the northern Arizona witch families and the Castillos was going to be pretty frosty if he didn't get this straightened out soon.

With a sigh, he shoved his phone back in his pocket. Cat looked at him in alarm.

"What the hell are you doing?"

"We need to fix this ourselves," he said. "I mean, if it becomes inescapably obvious that we'll never be able to find Miranda without her parents' help, then yeah, we'll get in touch with them. Right now, though, we have a little grace period. They still think she and I are on our honeymoon. So let's use that time to our advantage, and think this thing through."

Cat still appeared dubious, but at least she stopped fiddling with the straps of her backpack and pursed her lips, obviously running through their options. "If you've seen Simon and know what he looks like, then maybe we should give Daniel that description along with any other information you have, see what he can come up with."

"Because he found out so much last time."

"He didn't have as much information to work with," Cat pointed out. "I'll bet he knows a police sketch artist or someone like that who could do a drawing for us. It'd be a lot easier when I talk to my ghosts, for instance. I could show them the sketch and see what they have to say."

Although Rafe wasn't completely on board with this proposition, it did make him think of something. He hated to even make the suggestion, but…. "What about Marco?"

At once her brows drew together. "What do you mean, 'what about Marco'?"

"Well…you talk to ghosts…." Rafe let the words trail off, hoping she would get the hint.

Which she seemed to do, although she looked even less thrilled with him than she had a moment earlier. "Just because someone dies unexpectedly, it doesn't mean they'll become a ghost. I didn't feel anything of Marco at the hospital after he died. I think he's moved on… and that's a good thing, Rafe. Do you really want to think of Marco's soul being in torment like that?"

Of course he didn't. Rafe wished he hadn't brought it up, but it was a question that needed to be asked. And of course he should be glad that Marco had been enough at peace with his life that he had moved serenely on to the next world. Being able to talk to his ghost might have made the search for Miranda a lot easier, though.

"No, of course not," he replied. Because he could tell she didn't want to pursue the topic any further, he decided he'd better let it go. Anyway, she'd looked so charged up about the prospect of working with a sketch artist that Rafe figured they might as well give it a try. Cat could be right. Visual aids often came in handy.

"Okay," he said, trying to sound more enthusiastic than he actually was. The last thing he wanted to do right then was go haring back down to Albuquerque, but he didn't think they had much of a choice. It wasn't as though they had any other leads to follow. "Let me call Daniel."

The sketch artist was a woman in her late thirties, pretty in a thin, intense way. She set up her supplies in Daniel's empty meeting room and then asked Rafe to describe Simon as carefully as he could.

"Um, he's tall and thin," he began.

"How thin?" she inquired. "Like, one-forty, one-fifty?"

"Probably more than that," Rafe allowed. "He had some muscle on him. He's just thinner than me. Maybe around one-sixty, one-sixty-five?"

"Okay," she said. "Start at the top. Hair?"

"Black."

"Eyes."

"Black."

"Complexion?"

"A little darker than mine."

"Face shape?"

Good question. The guy was thin—what else did the artist need? However, from the way she was looking at him expectantly, Rafe could tell she wanted a little more than that. "His face is thin, too. Um…his cheekbones aren't as prominent as mine. I think his jaw was a little wider than his cheekbones."

"Good," the artist said, working away on her large sketchpad. "Tell me about his eyes."

"Um, I already said they were black."

An annoyed little huff escaped her lips. Across the room where Daniel and Cat were seated, Cat also looked exasperated. Rafe got the feeling that if she'd been any closer, she probably would have smacked his arm and asked him whether he'd ever watched any police procedural shows.

To which he would have answered no, because those sorts of things didn't really interest him. But he knew he needed to be as accurate as possible now, or the sketch would be worthless. "His eyes are kind of deep set, but not too deep set," Rafe offered. "And his brows are fairly straight, but lift a little toward the ends."

"Do they meet in the middle?"

"No."

"Okay. Eyelashes?"

"Sorry—I don't pay much attention to men's eyelashes."

To Rafe's surprise, the artist smiled a little. "No, I don't suppose you do. All right, what about his nose?"

"Longish. Straight."

"Wide nostrils?"

"No."

A few seconds of silence while the artist worked on her pad. "Okay. Mouth?"

"Not wide. I remember it kind of curled, like he was smirking at me."

"Thin or full?"

"Um…sort of in the middle? I think his lower lip was fuller than his upper lip, but I can't remember for sure."

"That's good, Rafe," she said, her tone encouraging. What, did she think he was some kindergartner who had to be coaxed into doing a good job? He wanted to catch this guy. "How does he wear his hair?"

"It's a little shorter than mine, kind of wavy." Rafe closed his eyes for a moment, trying to remember. "I don't recall seeing a part. I think he might have combed it straight back, but I can't say for sure."

"That's all right. It's still enough for me to work with." She sketched in silence for a moment. "Any tattoos, earrings?"

"No earring. If he had any tattoos, they weren't any place that showed." Rafe scowled slightly. Again, that wasn't something he really wanted to think about…especially if the asshole did have tattoos somewhere under his clothes, tattoos that Miranda might have seen by now.

That thought needed to get right out of his head. He and Miranda might have parted on the worst of terms, but he didn't want to think that she would go immediately into Simon's arms, no matter how hurt she was.

At least, he hoped she wouldn't. But Miranda and Simon had been together for several days now. Who knew what was going on between them?

Anger flared in him, and Rafe tamped it down, practically visualizing himself stomping on it the way you might stomp on the last stubborn embers of a campfire to put them out. He didn't have the luxury of anger right now. If he didn't stay focused, he might never find Miranda.

"I think that's it," the artist said. She turned the pad around toward him so he could see the sketch she'd made. "What do you think? Close?"

Brooding dark eyes stared at Rafe from under level brows. The mouth of the man in the sketch was curled slightly, as if he were laughing at some private joke. Well, Rafe couldn't argue with that—the joke was definitely on him, considering Simon had managed to steal Miranda right out from under his nose.

"Yes, it's close," he said curtly. Too close. Just looking at the sketch awoke the anger in him again, and once more he had to push it aside. "It's very good. Thank you."

Daniel got up from where he was sitting and gave the sketch a quick once-over. "Excellent work again, Samantha. If you'll let me have it for a moment, I'll get it digitized."

"Of course." Samantha carefully tore the piece of paper from the sketchpad, then handed it to him. "It's always a pleasure to come to your office, Daniel."

Those words made Rafe shoot a quick glance at his cousin. Was there something going on between him and the sketch artist? True, she was probably at least six or seven years older than he, but....

It was impossible to tell from Daniel's reaction. He did smile at Samantha, but it was a polite, professional smile, with absolutely nothing of intimacy in it. Excusing himself, he left the room, presumably to take the drawing to a big commercial scanner so that it could be rendered into electronic form and then sent to Rafe's phone.

"Do you work with Daniel a lot?" Cat asked, her tone almost too perky. It seemed fairly obvious that she was thinking about the same thing Rafe was.

"When he calls me in. I also freelance for the courts. You know how it is." Samantha had turned brisk, as if she'd realized that Daniel's two cousins from Santa Fe had picked up on a few subtexts she would rather not have advertised.

"Yeah, I'm a freelancer, too," Rafe said,

figuring it was probably better to stay on neutral ground. The ploy worked, because Samantha asked him what he did, and for a few minutes they shared a lively exchange on graphics in the virtual reality industry, and how sketch artists like her could provide images that would be digitized and used as the basis for the game characters.

When Daniel returned, he looked pleased that everyone appeared to be getting on so well. However, all he said was, "The drawing has been scanned at a couple of different resolutions and sent to your phone, Rafe. Do you want the original sketch as well?"

For some reason, he really didn't. The thought of having his enemy's likeness lurking around the house in physical form seemed like bad juju. "You can keep it here at the office, if that's okay," Rafe replied, hoping his casual tone wouldn't belie his true feelings on the subject. "It'll be a lot easier to just show people the image on my phone."

"No problem. I have a file where I keep stuff like this." Daniel hesitated, then said, "Thank you again, Samantha."

She took the dismissal for what it was, offering everyone a quick smile before she gathered up her things and left the meeting room. Daniel turned toward Rafe.

"I kept a copy of the image, too," he said. "If it's all right, I'm going to run it through the criminal databases, see if I can find anything. If your guy's been busted for anything anywhere, I should be able to track him down. It might take a little while, though."

"That's all right," Rafe replied, although of course he would have preferred for Daniel to have told him that the process would only take a few hours. "In the meantime, we can start asking around in Santa Fe, see if we can find anything."

"Do you know what's going on with the funeral?" Daniel looked almost shamefaced as he made the inquiry, adding quickly, "It's just that if it's going to be on a weekday, I'll have to shuffle appointments around, and—"

"I haven't heard anything yet—" Rafe began, but Cat broke in.

"Actually, I got a text from Mom while you were working with Samantha. She had to go back and forth with the bishop, but the funeral is scheduled for tomorrow at 11 a.m." She glanced over at Daniel. "I know that's not a lot of notice, but—"

"It's all right," Daniel assured her. "I can make it work."

"And in the meantime, we need to get back to Santa Fe and see if anyone recognizes Simon." Rafe extended a hand to his cousin. "Thanks for everything, Daniel. I think this is going to help a lot."

"No problem. And, as I said, I'll run this guy through the databases. If he even has as much as a parking ticket, I should be able to track him down."

Cat beamed. "That's awesome, Daniel. Thank you."

"It's really no problem. Have a safe drive back to Santa Fe, and I guess I'll see you tomorrow morning at the funeral. If I learn anything before then, I'll call."

Thanking Daniel again seemed kind of over the top, so Rafe settled for telling his cousin he'd look forward to the call. He and Cat took the elevator down to the lobby, then crossed the atrium to get to the parking structure. She backed out of their space, then said, "It would be amazing if Daniel was able to get an image match from one of those databases he was talking about."

Yes, it would…unless that match showed that Simon was wanted for rape and murder somewhere, or had a penchant for burning down houses. Somehow, though, Rafe doubted that anyone as canny and calculating as Simon would allow himself to get caught if he really had committed such heinous crimes. No, it would probably be something stupid like a traffic ticket that laid him low…if they were lucky.

"I suppose so," he said.

Cat sent him a sharp sideways glance. "You

don't sound very thrilled about it. I'd think you'd want to catch up with this guy."

"I do…it's just that if I think of him as being a worse criminal than he already is, then I'm going to worry about Miranda that much more. You know what I mean."

Her lips pressed together, and she nodded. "Right. I guess I hadn't really thought about it that way. Well, maybe we won't need the database at all. Maybe someone in Santa Fe will recognize him, will say, 'Oh, that's the guy who rented my casita. And he seemed like such a decent person.'"

Having a local identify Simon would definitely be the easiest solution. However, Rafe knew that life seldom worked that way. It liked to play with you, torture you with false hope, draw things out a little longer to really make it hurt.

It didn't matter, though. One way or another, they'd track this bastard down…and then Miranda would learn the truth about what Simon had done.

15

SIGNS

Miranda

SIMON HADN'T TRIED TO KISS ME AFTER WE got back from our dinner at Geronimo. I didn't really know why, even though I'd halfway expected him to. But all he'd done was praise my performance again, then suggest we have some ice cream and watch a movie, which was exactly what we did. I had to admit that it was a good way to end the evening, a way to relax and exhale, and realize I'd managed to survive the ordeal. No, "ordeal" was probably the wrong way to think of that particular experience. Dinner itself had been wonderful, and although seeing the Castillo witch and warlock had been stressful, I'd passed the test. They'd had no idea who I was. If I wanted to, I could put on some appropriate illusion, hide my magical nature, and walk among them without them ever knowing.

Problem was, I really didn't want to do that. It was good to know that I could manage holding two different types of spells at the same time, but I sincerely hoped I wouldn't be put in too many situations where that kind of control would be required.

We ended the evening early, just a little after ten. Simon headed over to the caretaker's house, and I walked down the hall to my borrowed bedroom. As I turned down the expensive duvet and carefully set the decorative pillows on top of the dresser to keep them out of the way, I wondered again why Simon hadn't tried to kiss me. We'd just had dinner in a romantic restaurant, and I'd certainly fulfilled his expectations when it came to using my gift of illusion. One would think the time was right.

Then again, maybe I was looking at this the wrong way. Maybe I shouldn't be thinking about why Simon hadn't kissed me, but why I was disappointed that he'd never even tried.

Did I really want that kind of intimacy with him? Or was I only trying to use him as a substitute for Rafe?

I honestly didn't know. Once again I told myself that I had plenty of time to figure out my relationship with Simon. I shouldn't be worried about forcing anything.

Still brooding, I went into the bathroom and washed my face and brushed my teeth, then carefully applied moisturizer and some lip balm. When I slid into the king-size bed, one hand inadvertently moved to the empty spot next to me. Who did I really want to be there, anyway… Simon, or Rafe?

My mind recoiled at that thought. Of course I didn't want to sleep with Rafe. He was an absolute raging jerk, probably the biggest asshole I'd ever met, if I wanted to be perfectly honest. Still, I couldn't quite ignore the way his kisses had set my body on fire.

No, you will *ignore the way he got to you,* I told myself. *In fact, you need to forget him altogether. What-might-have-beens aren't going to help your current situation at all.*

That was for sure. I pulled the covers up to my chin and willed myself to put all that aside. A soft, comforting glow came from a nightlight in the bathroom, and the bed was supremely comfortable. I was safe here, safe from discovery by the Castillos. Now I needed to sleep, because I'd just had a crazy evening and was tired.

Darkness stole over me, soft and gentle. I didn't know how long I had been asleep before I heard soft footsteps in the hallway outside. That faint sound was enough to make me sit up in bed, eyes straining to see in the dim light.

"Simon?"

He came into the room. By that point, my eyes had adjusted enough to see that he was wearing only a pair of sweat pants, his smoothly muscled torso bare, painted with shadows. Without speaking, he approached the bed and then slid under the covers to lie next to me. Before I could open my mouth to protest, he was reaching for me, pulling me up against him. His mouth found mine, warm, insistent, tasting of mint from his toothpaste. At the same time, I could feel his arousal, feel his stiff cock pressing against my leg.

For some reason, I didn't try to pull away. Quite the opposite, actually—I clung to him, felt the wiry strength of the muscles beneath my fingertips. His hands moved under the tank top I wore to sleep in, fingers closing on my breasts. I gasped in delight, feeling how aroused I was, how a deep throbbing had begun between my legs, signaling my need for him.

He pulled off my tank top, grasped the elastic waistband of my panties and pulled them down. Now I was naked, but I didn't care. I gasped again when his fingers slipped inside me, stroking even as his mouth closed on my breast. Oh, yes, this was what I'd wanted, even if I'd been too much of a coward to admit it to myself.

I reached for his sweatpants, loosening the drawstring, pulling them down. He didn't have any underwear on beneath the sweats. Good, because then I had him in my hand, thick and heavy, so ready. Just as I was ready.

In the next moment, I was beneath him, feeling his weight on top of me. I could sense how he was at my entrance, just beginning to push his way in, about to take the virginity I'd stubbornly hung onto but now couldn't wait to get rid of.

And then the wrongness of it hit me, and I pushed away at him—and realized I was pushing at air, that I was now sitting up in bed, gasping, as if I'd somehow known I would have to make some kind of physical effort to break myself free of the dream.

My hand reached out and once again touched the empty space next to me. The sheets were cool beneath my touch. No one had been lying there. The dream had felt real, but that was all it had been—a dream. I'd been thinking about kissing Simon, and my brain had manufactured a sex scene with him. That was all.

Still, it had felt real. *Too* real. I pulled in a deep breath and another, willing my heart to slow down. The horrible thing was, I could tell I was still aroused, an ache between my legs letting me know that my body had responded all too well to the phantoms my mind had created. It might have only been a dream, but it had been a damn realistic one.

So what did it mean? That I really did want to sleep with Simon?

The thing was, when I tried to imagine being with him, I somehow couldn't. I could get about as far as kissing him, and not any further than that. For all I knew, even though he'd rejected me, I couldn't quite shake off the belief that I was supposed to be married to Rafe. After all, I'd spent my whole life moving toward that eventuality. Maybe my subconscious mind viewed any kind of intimacy with Simon as a sort of cheating. Stupid, I knew, but emotions weren't always logical.

I lay back down and drew in a breath. The dream had been unnerving, but it was subsiding now. Sooner or later I would forget it.

And I hoped it would be sooner…much sooner. Otherwise, I didn't know how I would be able to look at Simon the next morning and manage to avoid blushing like a damn rose.

A long shower didn't help much. Neither did a lengthy spell of blow-drying my hair and then using a big curling iron to set it in long, loose waves. It seemed that no matter what I did, I couldn't erase that goddamn dream from my mind.

Because I'd spent so much time on prep, I was running late for our usual eight o'clock breakfast time. Simon was already in the kitchen, just lifting the carafe of coffee off its warming plate when I entered the room.

"Oh, there you are," he said, with the faintest of sideways glances at the clock display on the stove. Eight-twenty. I really had been running late. "I was starting to wonder if we'd called off breakfast because of our big dinner last night and I'd just forgotten."

"No, it was my fault," I said hastily. "Sorry about that."

"It's no problem. It's not as if we had any concrete plans for the day. Besides," he added, giving me an admiring glance, "you look really nice today."

Even though the look hadn't been lascivious at all, I couldn't prevent the blood from rising to my cheeks as I recalled the way he'd touched my breasts in my dream, how our bodies had been just about to lock together before I woke myself up. "Oh, thanks," I said. "I suppose I figured I might as well make an extra effort, just in case there was something particular you wanted to do today."

"I hadn't planned on anything, but we can figure something out." He poured coffee into a pair of mugs and then extended one to me. "Here you go."

"Thanks." The aroma of the coffee rose to my nostrils, and I breathed it in, then blew on the surface of the liquid. I desperately needed to get that coffee cooled down enough to drink. "So what, then? More magical practice?"

"Probably." He took a cautious sip of his own coffee. "It never hurts to get as much practice as you can, although your display last night told me you already seem to know what you're doing."

"It was fun," I allowed, not wanting to say much more than that. I really didn't want to give him the impression that I wanted to repeat the experiment anytime in the near future.

"Well, I think we'll still take it easy today." His phone buzzed in his pocket, and he frowned. "Who the heck would be calling this early in the morning?"

About all I could do was lift my shoulders. I knew in my own family, we'd always tried to avoid making calls before ten in the morning, since witches and warlocks often had erratic schedules and tended to be late risers, but I doubted that the whole world operated that way.

When he pulled the phone out of his pocket,

his frown deepened. "It's the property management company. Guess I'd better take it."

Property management company? I hoped there wasn't anything wrong, like the Texas oil guy had decided to sell after all and we needed to get out ASAP. That would really stink.

"Hi, Cristina," Simon said. "What's up?" He waited for a moment, obviously listening to her reply. "Oh, sure. In the office? Okay. I'll bring it in later. Sure. No problem." After taking the phone away from his ear and replacing it in his pocket, he told me, "I guess the owner left something in the desk drawer in his office. Cristina wants to see if I can find it and bring it to her."

"Ah," I replied, relief running through me. Just a simple errand. We weren't about to be booted out on our ear. Yes, I knew we couldn't stay here forever, that we'd have to be on our way in less than a week, but at least that gave me some time to mentally prepare for the transition.

"You don't mind?" Simon asked. "I'll have to go into town to take Cristina the envelope she wanted, which means I'll be gone for about an hour."

"It's okay," I assured him. "I'll just watch TV or something." I took a sip of coffee, then asked, "What do you think is in the envelope that's so important?"

"I don't know. I doubt it's anything related to

the house—all those files would be electronic. Since we're talking about a Texas oil tycoon here, I bet he just realized he left an envelope stuffed with hundreds in his desk drawer and doesn't want the caretaker messing with it."

That made some sense, I supposed. "Well, when you take it in, you can prove how trustworthy you are."

"I doubt they'd notice," Simon responded. "They're sort of paying me to be trustworthy."

Fair enough. I glanced out the kitchen window; the clouds of the day before had disappeared, and the sky was gloriously blue again. It might be warm enough to go for a walk in the gardens, which seemed like a good idea to me. I could use the fresh air, and a walk would definitely be more beneficial than sitting on my butt and watching television until Simon got back.

After that, we chatted a bit about some places we might go if we wanted to get out for a while— a winery up the road in Pojoaque, a backroads trail that eventually spat you out somewhere close to the ski area above Santa Fe—while we got breakfast ready. After we were done, we got the kitchen cleaned up, and Simon disappeared for a moment to go look for the envelope Cristina had requested. When he reappeared, he had it in his hand.

"Just what I thought," he said, holding the

unsealed envelope open slightly so I could see the thick wad of bills tucked inside.

"Damn," I said, looking at the cash in some astonishment. My family had money, but they weren't exactly the type to leave large stacks of cash lying around.

Simon's expression was solemn. "We witches and warlocks have our world, and the rich have theirs, I guess." He ran a thumb over the edges of the bills, then tucked the envelope flap back inside. "I can't really relate."

"Neither can I."

"I'd better get going." He pulled a set of keys from his pocket using his free hand, then went on, "When I get back, we can decide if we want to work with more magic, or whether you'd rather get out and about. Either one is fine by me."

"I'll think it over while you're running your errand."

A brief flash of a smile, and then he was gone. I'd be lying if I said I didn't feel somewhat relieved by his absence; although I'd started to feel a bit more normal as the morning wore on, I still couldn't quite shake the memory of that dream, of him touching me, nearly entering me. A dream didn't necessarily have any bearing on reality, and yet it was difficult to keep myself from wondering if the real life experience of intimacy with Simon would be anything like what I'd encountered in my dream.

I wasn't sure I wanted to explore that line of thought right then. Getting some fresh air seemed like a good idea. I needed to get myself centered again, especially if we ended up working with magic once Simon got back.

When I opened the kitchen door, I could tell that the long-sleeved T-shirt I wore definitely wouldn't be enough to keep me warm. The day promised to be mild, but it was barely nine o'clock in the morning, long before the peak heat of the day. I hurried back to my bedroom and got my jacket from where it hung in the closet there, then slipped it on. No need to go all the way back to the kitchen to let myself out, though; I went into the garden via one of the French doors that opened off the long hallway.

The morning air was brisk against my face and smelled faintly of decaying leaves and damp grass. Had it rained overnight? I couldn't really tell, since there weren't any puddles around, but the air definitely felt more moist than usual.

Hugging my jacket against myself, I set off, following the path as it wound through the garden. I didn't have any fixed destination, but I thought I might like to head toward the rear of the property. Simon and I had mostly stuck to the area right off the kitchen and near the garage, but the land here was really extensive, probably at least ten acres, if not more.

When I came around a corner of the house, I saw that off in the distance, close to where the rail fence enclosed the property, there appeared to be another structure of some sort, maybe a shed for storing some kind of farm equipment. This place was definitely big enough that it would require a riding mower to keep up all those acres of grass, something you didn't see all that often in either Arizona or New Mexico, where the water costs to maintain that sort of lawn would be prohibitive.

Since I didn't have any particular goal in mind, I figured I might as well go over to the shed and see what I could find there. If nothing else, it would be a good, brisk walk, and would take up a decent chunk of time.

The morning breeze played with my loose hair as I strode across the frost-yellowed grass. I breathed in deeply, glad I'd come out here. It felt better than I had hoped, to be out in the fresh air and the morning sunlight. The walk seemed to help knock some of the cobwebs out of my brain, to dispel the last echoes of that unsettling dream about Simon. I really needed to let it go. I couldn't control what my subconscious might decide to dredge up while I was asleep, after all.

Up close, the shed seemed bigger than it had appeared from far away. It was definitely large enough to house a riding mower, probably two or more. As far as I could tell, it had been intended for that purpose, since one side was accessed by a roll-up garage door. The opposite side of the structure had a regular door, and the other two walls had three rectangular windows in a neat row.

I figured it couldn't hurt to peek inside. If there was a riding mower, maybe we could take it out for a little spin on the back forty here. It would be something fun to do to kill some time.

Besides, I'd always wanted to go for a ride on one of those things.

I had to stand on my tiptoes to peek inside. At first I saw nothing except some spiderwebs, and felt a slight sense of disappointment at realizing that I wouldn't be able to go for a ride on a mower after all. But then, as I was able to focus better on the dark interior of the building, I realized it wasn't completely empty. Against the opposite wall was a low table draped in black cloth, and on that table was a pair of tarnished silver candelabras, each of them equipped with three black candles. In between the two candelabras was a silver bowl with oddly shaped handles that looked almost like ears, and lying next to the bowl was a long knife with a curved, wicked blade.

Cold ran through me. I might not have known all that much about the sort of magic which required this type of setup, but I sure as hell knew it wasn't the kind of magic my parents practiced. It was dark...dark and forbidden.

My thoughts went immediately to Simon, although I tried to tell myself that he didn't necessarily have to be the person who'd put those ominous objects inside the shed. For all I knew, the Texas oil guy dabbled in black magic—specifically, spells to maintain and enhance his wealth. Such a theory wasn't outside the bounds of possibility, was it? I wanted it to be true...needed it to be true. My heart began to hammer in my chest, even as I tried to rationalize the situation as best I could. It had to be the owner of the property who'd put that stuff in the shed. Simon couldn't have had anything to do with such evil...could he?

Footsteps crunched on the dry grass, and I whirled. Standing a few paces away from me was Simon, an enigmatic smile touching his mouth.

"Hello, Miranda," he said. "I see you've found my temple."

16

FAREWELLS

Rafe

HE STARED AT THE MIRROR, TRYING FOR THE fifth time to get a decent Windsor knot in his damn tie. If it had been for any other occasion, he would have just said screw it and gone with an open shirt under his suit jacket, but Rafe didn't think that was a very good way to honor his cousin Marco. Truth be told, Marco probably would have gotten a good laugh at seeing Rafe all dressed up, stiff and uncomfortable in the only suit he owned, so maybe he should just say the hell with the tie.

Then again, Genoveva would throw a fit if he turned up looking like that at his cousin's funeral.

Grimly, Rafe went back to struggling with the recalcitrant oblong piece of silk. He knew that a good portion of his current foul mood had nothing to do with the tie, and everything to do with the complete strike-out he and Cat had suffered the day before when they'd gotten back from Albuquerque. Both of them had been so certain that, armed with an image of Simon, they'd be able to find someone who'd interacted with him, who'd had some kind of clue that would lead them to where he was currently hiding with Miranda.

But although Mark, the guy at the wine tasting room, had said that yeah, he knew Simon Gutierrez, it was only because of the ad Mark had placed on a local e-bulletin board to get someone to work there for a few days while he was off visiting family in Chicago. "He had experience working at wine tasting rooms in Arizona," Mark said. "A couple letters of recommendation, which was why I thought it was okay to let him cover for me."

"Did he say where he was from, exactly?" Cat asked.

"Um…Tucson? Sorry," Mark added with a rueful smile, while at the same time looking at Cat with interest, "I didn't pay that much atten-tion. He seemed competent, and I needed to get out of town, and there wasn't anyone already working here who could cover those hours for me. Did you have a problem with him or something?"

"No," Rafe had said quickly, "he, uh—he left his wallet in my father's restaurant, and so we were trying to find him. It had some cash and an expired driver's license with an old address, but the only thing that seemed recent was a business card from the tasting room here."

"Oh, bummer," Mark said. "Sorry, but I don't know where he was going after he was done here. I guess back to Tucson?"

Rafe and Cat had thanked him and left. They both knew there wasn't any point in asking Daniel to look up "Simon Gutierrez"—that name had to be just as fake as the "Robert Marquez" alias Simon had used to book the Airbnb.

The ghosts weren't any help, either. Oh, Annalisa had seen him, of course—they already knew that. But the other restless spirits who haunted the streets of downtown Santa Fe couldn't offer anything of value. They'd seen Simon, but only going up to the flat where he was staying, or working at the tasting room, or once or twice coming back from getting himself some takeout at one of the restaurants in the immediate vicinity.

"Might as well have been a ghost himself," Rafe grumbled, taking another pass at that damn tie. Good thing he'd given himself plenty of time to get ready, although Genoveva expected both him and Cat to be at the chapel early, as befitted the children of the *prima*. No doubt Louisa and Malena were already there, properly dressed, children in their church outfits with not a hair out of place. His two older sisters always had been better at playing the game than he or Cat.

The doorbell rang. Rafe cursed, then left the tie hanging around his neck as he went downstairs to answer the door. He and Cat had already decided they would drive together in her car, since parking was so tight at the chapel. Apparently Genoveva had fussed a bit at that idea, because she'd wanted Rafe to come to the house so he could come along with the rest of the family, but he'd put his foot down, even though he knew he was already in his mother's bad graces, thanks to missing most of the vigil held for Marco at the funeral home the evening before. At least this way he and his younger sister could have some autonomy if they needed to leave before the reception following the funeral was over. This event would take place at the *prima's* house, as was only befitting such a solemn occasion.

When he opened the door, Cat stood outside, looking very church-ready and unlike herself in a fitted black sheath dress and a string of pearls he guessed she'd borrowed from their mother. A prim little black bag hung from one arm.

"I hate this," she said, not bothering with even a "hello" as she walked past him into the hallway.

"I hate that Marco's dead and how no one seems to be talking about how *weird* that is, for someone his age to just pass away like that, and I hate that I have to play dress-up just to keep Mom off my back. Does she really think that either God or Marco gives a shit what I'm wearing to the funeral?"

"I know," Rafe said wearily. He wasn't too thrilled about the whole thing, either, but there wasn't much he could do about it. The wrongness of Marco's passing chafed at him, too, although he couldn't quite articulate precisely what was bothering him so much. The doctors hadn't had to do a full autopsy, because a post-mortem of the heart showed that Marco had an undiagnosed valve defect, and that was apparently why he'd thrown a clot and had a stroke, followed by a catastrophic heart attack. On the surface, it was all very plausible, albeit tragic.

Cat let out a sigh. "Let me fix that tie for you," she said, then stepped closer so she could make some order out of the chaos hanging around his neck. In less than a minute she'd achieved a very respectable Windsor knot, and gave it a final tug so it was properly tight.

"Where'd you learn to do that?" Rafe asked, impressed despite himself.

She wiggled her fingers at him. "Magic hands," she replied, then added, "I went through this spell in high school where I was obsessed with knots. Rope, macrame, ties, if you could put a knot in it, I messed with it. Anyway, I guess the motor memory hung on." A glance down at the slim, elegant watch on her wrist—also borrowed from Genoveva, Rafe was sure—and she said, "We'd better get going. It's already ten-fifteen."

"All right." A funeral was the last place he wanted to be, but he knew he had to be there for his cousin…just in case Marco really was looking down from heaven and watching to see what all of them were doing. Besides, Daniel would be there. Rafe hadn't heard from his cousin, but it was still early in the day. If Daniel had heard anything about the database image search, he might have decided to wait to relay that information until he could see Rafe in person—a conversation that probably would have to be delayed until the reception and an opportunity to speak privately presented itself.

Holding back a sigh, he followed Cat out to her SUV, then got in the passenger seat. "Loretto Chapel," she said clearly and distinctly, and the Mercedes' self-driving mechanism kicked in, sending them over to Paseo de Peralta so they could loop around downtown and come in at the right angle to get to the chapel's parking lot.

Neither one of them spoke. Rafe knew his sister had to be almost as frustrated as he was about their failure to turn up any leads the evening before. It had begun to seem that no matter what they did, they couldn't get past the veil of anonymity Simon had drawn around himself. And until they were able to dig up something about him that was true, that was *real,* it didn't seem likely they had any chance of locating Miranda.

When they pulled into the chapel's cramped parking lot, Rafe spied his father standing in the empty space next to the one where Genoveva's big gray Mercedes sedan was already parked. Good thing, too, because every other spot was already filled.

Genoveva stood off to one side, elegantly attired in black, the coral cross that had been a family heirloom for five generations hanging around her neck. Next to her was Sophia, also in black from head to toe, the severe costume making her look even more frail and slender than usual. She wore a black hat and veil, although such head coverings hadn't been required by the church for decades.

Cat took manual control and pulled into the space their father had been saving for them. His face was calm and sad, a contrast to their mother, whose dark eyes were snapping sparks even at this distance. Most likely she wasn't very happy about her two younger children being some of the last to arrive.

However, even she seemed to reconsider the wisdom of chewing out her kids in front of the grieving Sophia, because she only said, once Rafe and Cat had gotten out of the SUV, "Good, you're here." The word *finally* hung in the air between them, although she didn't say it out loud. "Your sisters are already inside with their families. Go ahead."

Apparently the tie had passed muster. Rafe nodded at his mother but didn't reply, then murmured a quiet greeting to Sophia before he and Cat went ahead into the chapel. It was already full, with several rows of Castillos standing in the back. Despite his irritation earlier, he couldn't help but be moved by this show of clan support for their lost cousin. Marco had been taken from them far too soon, and they clearly wanted to show him their grief and their love.

Cat at his side, Rafe walked down the aisle to take his place in the front pew, albeit off to one side so there was enough room for his parents and Sophia to sit. As he'd guessed, Louisa and Malena and their husbands John and Oscar were already sitting down, their small children firmly placed between them in order to keep fidgeting at a minimum. Malena's daughter Elisa was only two, and

Rafe wondered if she even understood anything of what was happening.

Well, if she didn't, that would make two of them. Rafe couldn't make sense of any of it, either. He stared at the shining mahogany casket placed in the center of the altar, surrounded by banks of white lilies and orchids, and scowled. Marco shouldn't be in that damn box. He should be off with his cousins and friends, maybe fishing, which seemed to be his favorite thing to do other than sampling as many of New Mexico's local brews as possible. Instead, he was gone, snuffed out as though he'd never been here at all. Anger flooded through Rafe, even though he wasn't sure exactly what he was angry at. The universe, maybe.

The low murmur of voices in the chapel died down as Genoveva and Eduardo and Sophia entered. They took their seats at the far right end of the pew where the rest of their immediate family sat. As if on cue, the organ began to play, and the bishop himself, attended by several priests, came down the center aisle, censers swinging, filling the air with the faintly cloying scent that always evoked a faint sense of guilt within Rafe. These days, he only came to church when forced into it by family obligations. Although most of the members of the Castillo clan didn't seem to recognize the dissonance, he couldn't help feeling there was something a bit off about being a practicing Catholic and a full-fledged warlock.

The service felt as though it was dragging on forever, but Rafe knew that was only his own impatience. He had to hold back an ironic smile as his father went up and read from Lamentations: *My soul is shut out from peace; I have forgotten happiness.*

Well, wasn't that the damn truth. He knew he hadn't had a moment's peace since Miranda disappeared from his life on Sunday afternoon.

More readings, more hymns, everyone so solemn and sober-faced, the air heavy with incense. It was so not Marco that Rafe could feel himself scowling all over again. His cousin might not have been Irish, but a good old-fashioned rowdy wake would have suited him much better.

At last, though, that part of it was over. Then there came the mass exodus to the cemetery, the coffin lowered into the ground, Sophia weeping as Eduardo and Genoveva flanked her, clearly ready to hold her up if she should collapse. Watching all this, Cat quiet and moody at his side, Rafe couldn't help but experience a traitorous sense of relief once the mourners recited the Lord's Prayer together and the bishop had delivered his final blessing. Only the reception to get through now.

While he hadn't exactly looked forward to the reception at his mother's house, at least there he would have a chance to talk to Daniel...or so he hoped. First, though, came the weary standing at the entrance with his sisters and parents, solemnly greeting everyone who came through the door, which took a good twenty minutes. He hated these rituals but knew his mother clung to them, and so he stood there with as much grace as he could muster, telling himself he was doing this for Marco, even though his cousin probably would have laughed at the whole procedure, remarking that all it really did was prevent people from getting to the food and drink after being put through the wringer for the past few hours.

Finally, the last Castillo cousin had come through the door, and Rafe excused himself and headed into the crowd in search of Daniel. Before he'd taken two steps, however, the phone in his jacket pocket buzzed. Who would be calling now, when he was already surrounded by so many of his family members?

Thinking it might be a client, he ducked down the hallway into his mother's study and pulled the phone from his pocket. At first he didn't recognize the number on the screen. Then he realized it was from an Arizona area code, and a mixture of worry and annoyance churned in his gut.

Angela...or possibly Connor. What the hell were they doing calling now, of all times?

Ignoring them and letting it go to voicemail probably wouldn't be a good idea, since he had the feeling they'd only keep calling him until he answered. Taking in a bracing swallow of air, he touched the phone's screen to accept the call. "This is Rafe Castillo."

"Rafe." Connor Wilcox's voice, tight with repressed anger. "You want to tell me what this garbage is that your mother sent us this morning?"

"Um...I don't know, sir. What did she send you?"

"An obviously doctored image that she claimed was from your wedding. But anyone with two eyes to see could tell it was pasted together—for God's sake, the image of Miranda was one that your sister sent right before the ceremony. What the hell is going on?"

Oh, shit. *Shit.* Rafe had known from the start that this insane idea of his mother's was going to get them all in trouble, but he also knew he had no way of dissuading her. And what the hell had she been thinking, sending that thing the very morning of Marco's funeral?

She probably realized she needed to follow up, Rafe thought, *and went ahead and sent it because she thought it was fine.* He knew he should have asked to see the photo in question, but with everything that had been going on, such a minor detail had completely slipped his mind.

"This really isn't a good time," he said, hedging while he tried to come up with some kind of plausible excuse. "I'm at the reception for my cousin's funeral."

A brief silence. Then Connor said, sounding a little less angry, "I'm sorry to hear that, Rafe. Especially so soon after your *wedding*."

There was no missing the emphasis Connor had put on that last word, and Rafe couldn't help wincing. "Um, about that—"

"What about it?"

The steel underlying those three simple words made Rafe glad that roughly five hundred miles separated him from Connor Wilcox. "The wedding didn't happen. Miranda teleported away, and, well, we don't really know where she is."

As terrible as those words had sounded in his mind when he'd rehearsed what he might have to say to Connor and Angela, they sounded about a thousand times worse when actually spoken out loud. Rafe waited, gut clenched, for Miranda's father to respond.

Another of those long pauses. At last Connor said, "You mean my daughter has been missing for three days now, and you didn't think to get in contact with us?"

In the background, Rafe caught pieces of a furious whispered exchange, as though Angela and

Connor were having a *sotto voce* argument they didn't want him to overhear. "Well, we—"

"Rafe, tell us what happened." Angela's voice, sounding more worried than angry.

"It's complicated."

When she replied to that comment, her tone was noticeably sharper. "Everything's complicated. You need to do better than that."

"There was something of a scene at the ceremony. My family and I believe I was caught in some kind of a mind-control spell or something. Miranda used her teleportation power to get away. I can't really blame her for that."

"Wait…she teleported?" Shock was clear in Connor's voice; of course he couldn't have known about the strange, erratic powers Miranda had developed during her time here in Santa Fe.

"Yes, sir. It, uh, it happened once or twice before that."

A long silence as Connor appeared to digest that piece of information. Then, "Who cast the spell?"

"We don't know. That is, I think it might be a warlock named Simon, but we don't have much more information about him than that. We're trying to track him down now."

"Unsuccessfully, I assume."

"So far. Look—" Rafe gathered a breath and went on, "I suspect this guy might be a de la

Paz warlock who had a crush on Miranda. Did you ever hear anything about something like that?"

"No," Angela said at once. "Miranda didn't go down into de la Paz territory very often, so I can't even think of how she might have attracted the attention of one of their warlocks. I also don't know of anyone named Simon, but I'll check with Zoe Sandoval to be sure." A long pause, during which Rafe could hear another round of heated whispering between the McAllister *prima* and the Wilcox *primus*. "But since it seems you've managed to lose our daughter, Connor and I think we'd better come to Santa Fe and help with the search."

Oh, God. Genoveva would blow an absolute gasket if that happened, even though she'd basically brought this current crisis on herself. If she'd just held off on sending that goddamn doctored photo….

Trying to keep his tone calm, Rafe said, "Unless you have a magical ability that lets you know where your daughter is at all times, I'm not sure how your being here is going to help. My cousin is a private detective and is running a search on Simon's image as we speak. Once we find him, I'm pretty sure we'll find Miranda as well."

"Why would she even go off with this person?

If things went as badly at the wedding as you hinted, why didn't she come straight home?"

The accusation in those words was clear enough. "I don't know for sure," Rafe replied. "She had an acquaintance with Simon, but I don't think she realized he was a warlock. He was friendly to her. Otherwise, I can't really comment on her motivations."

Silence, followed by a slight rustle coming from the phone's tiny speaker, as if Angela had handed off the phone to her husband. Sure enough, it was Connor's voice Rafe heard next. "This all sounds extremely strange, Rafe. And now you say one of your cousins has passed away?"

"That doesn't have anything to do with Miranda's disappearance," Rafe said hastily. "Marco had a congenital heart defect."

"Oh." A hesitation, and Connor went on, sounding slightly awkward, "Well, I'm sorry to hear that. And although our first instinct is to hop on the next plane and go to Santa Fe to look for our daughter, Angela and I know you're right about one thing—we don't know what we could do to aid in the search. Our combined powers are strong, but the one talent we've never been able to master is the Sight, and that's about the only thing that's going to do Miranda any good right now."

"Thank you for understanding, sir."

"Not so fast. You have two more days. If you

don't find our daughter by then, we're coming to Santa Fe, even if it doesn't seem as though it would do much good. But it would be better than sitting here and waiting and wondering."

Two days. Miranda had already been gone longer than that, but Rafe had to hope he'd find her before the deadline arrived. Something had to give.

"I think we'll find her before then. My cousin Daniel is very good at this kind of thing." At least, Rafe had to hope he was. He didn't know all that much about the sorts of cases his cousin handled, but a plush office like his seemed to indicate he did more than follow cheating husbands and wives around Albuquerque.

"Let's all hope he is. And when you find something, you call us. Immediately."

"I will."

"Until then."

The call ended there, and Rafe expelled a breath. He supposed it could have gone worse—at least he'd been granted a two-day grace period—but now more than ever they needed to step up the search.

As he slipped his phone into his pocket, he headed back into the hall. He'd barely made it into the living room before he bumped into his oldest sister Louisa, the *prima*-in-waiting, who looked supremely irritated with him. In that moment, with her hair pulled up into a French twist and her mouth pressed into a thin line, she very much resembled their mother.

"Just where the hell have you been?" she asked in an undertone.

"I had to take a call."

"*Now?*"

"It was Miranda's parents."

"Oh." The expression of annoyance vanished, to be replaced by one of concern. "What did they want?"

"They weren't too thrilled by that little Photoshop job our mother tried to fob off on them. I managed to talk them down, but if we don't find Miranda soon, they're going to be on our doorstep, breathing fire."

"Oh, hell." Louisa tucked a stray strand of hair behind one ear, then glanced over her shoulder at the crowd in the living room. Genoveva and Eduardo stood near the fireplace, talking quietly with Sophia and an elderly cousin from Pecos. Seemingly satisfied that their parents were occupied for the moment, Louisa went on, "We can't let that happen. You know how Mom thinks she can handle everything on her own. She's going to go nuts if two of Arizona's clan leaders suddenly show up here."

"Yeah, I know." Privately, Rafe thought it might do Genoveva some good to get knocked down a peg or two by the northern Arizona *prima* and *primus*, but he knew better than to say such a thing to his sister. "I was actually going to talk to Daniel, see if he's found anything yet."

"Okay. I think he was in the dining room the last time I saw him."

After delivering that helpful piece of information, Louisa moved back out into the living room, pausing to exchange a few words with a relative, then stopping to check in with her husband, who was clearly in charge of keeping an eye on their two children so she could be free to circulate. Watching her, Rafe thought again how she was the perfect choice to be *prima*-in-waiting. Her talents were strong, but more than that, she seemed to instinctively know how to handle people, to be in command. Or maybe it wasn't instinct at all, but only a lifetime of watching her mother operate.

Either way, he knew Louisa wouldn't say anything to Genoveva about the phone call from Miranda's parents—not yet, anyway. She'd wait to see how it all shook out before issuing any warnings.

In the meantime, he needed to find Daniel.

On his way to the dining room, however, he found himself waylaid by Tony, who grabbed him by the sleeve. "Hey, Rafe," he said. "After this, a bunch of the cousins were going to go to Antonia's brew pub, have kind of a wake for Marco. Say you'll come."

It did sound like the kind of gathering Marco would have appreciated, a lot more than this quiet gathering with its finger sandwiches and pitchers of iced tea and crystal bowl of punch. But with everything that was going on, Rafe realized he couldn't make promises he didn't know if he could keep. "Maybe," he allowed. "I've got some stuff I need to handle, but—"

"You should. It would look weird if you weren't there."

That was only the truth. His cousins would expect Rafe to come to such a gathering—he'd been close in age to Marco, and they'd usually hung out when he came down to Santa Fe from Taos. They didn't exactly share confidences, but they'd always gotten along. A sudden thought struck Rafe. "Hey, Tony—did Marco ever talk about a girl named Tess? An old girlfriend or something?"

Tony appeared puzzled, then shook his head. "No. I mean, his last girlfriend was a civilian named Barrie. She lived in Arroyo Seco, just outside Taos. But they broke up about three or four months ago, I think. Why?"

"Just wanted to make sure we didn't leave anyone out when we were inviting people to the funeral," Rafe said, which only made his cousin appear that much more confused. But before Tony could ask any more questions, Rafe had turned and begun to pick his way through the crowd, intent on locating Daniel.

As he went, he thought about how he wished he could just get out of here, go someplace to clear his head. Being around too many people started to get on his nerves after a while, and the best cure was generally some time spent outdoors. Most of the fall color would be faded by now, but he'd always liked the old forest road that cut down from the ski area above Santa Fe to Tesuque.

The second that thought passed through his head, Rafe came to a dead stop. *Tesuque.* Of course. That's what Marco had been trying to tell him. He hadn't been whispering the name of a former lover. He'd been trying his damnedest, using every bit of the meager strength that remained to him, to tell Rafe and Cat that Miranda was somewhere in Tesuque.

Daniel forgotten for the moment, Rafe scanned the crowd of Castillos that filled the bottom floor of the house, looking for his sister. He needed to find her so he could get her car keys from her. Then he could go find Miranda.

This prospect seemed a little daunting at first view, simply because, although Tesuque was a small village compared to Santa Fe, it still contained enough individual properties and small private lanes that tracking Miranda there wouldn't exactly be a cut-and-dried proposition. However, at least he knew what to look for now. Rafe was sure that, having once detected the trail of evil Simon seemed to leave behind him, he could do it again. And once Rafe found it in Tesuque, he knew that trail would lead him right to Miranda.

Ah, there was Cat over by the window, talking to two of the cousins who were supposed to be Miranda's bridesmaids. Rafe hurried to her, then bent and murmured in her ear, "I need to borrow your car key."

"My what?" she responded, giving him a startled glance, even while Maria and Ylena looked on with some curiosity.

"I think I know where Miranda is."

Cat's eyes widened, and she said to Maria and Ylena, "Excuse me for a sec." Taking Rafe by the arm, she led him away from the window, over to the foyer that separated the living room from the dining room. "What are you talking about?" she asked once they were safely out of earshot.

"It just sort of came to me in a flash. Marco wasn't trying to say a girl's name that day in the hospital—he was trying to say 'Tesuque.'"

His sister didn't look quite as impressed by this insight as Rafe had hoped she would be. "Are you sure?"

"Of course I'm not *sure*," he snapped. "But it

makes more sense than anything else we've been able to come up with."

"If Miranda is really with this Simon person, why would they be staying someplace so close to Santa Fe? You'd think the smart thing to do would be to get as far away from us as possible."

"I have no idea. That's not the issue here. The issue is that my car is a mile away at my place, so I need to borrow yours and go take a look."

"And bail out in the middle of the reception? Mom will have your head on a platter."

"Right now, I really don't care," Rafe said. "We've already wasted enough time. I need to see if this hunch is correct or not. Now, are you going to lend me your car key, or am I going to have to call a Ryde to take me to my house so I can get the Jeep?"

"Oh, all right," Cat replied, both her tone and expression resigned. "It's not as if I need it right now anyway." She opened the small purse that still dangled from her arm, then pulled out the fob for her Mercedes SUV. "What am I supposed to tell Mom?"

"With any luck, she won't even notice I'm gone."

Cat pulled a face at that comment. "Give me a break, Rafe. She's going to notice the second you step out the door."

"Make up something. I don't care. Tell her

there was something I left at my house that I'd meant to give to Tony. Whatever it takes."

"Okay." She gave his arm a nudge. "Go ahead. I can tell you're foaming at the mouth to get out of here."

Rafe shot her a grateful smile, then headed back toward the kitchen, figuring it would be less obvious if he slipped out by way of the back door. To his surprise, he nearly bumped into Daniel as he exited the kitchen, cell phone in hand and a grave expression on his face.

"I was just about to come looking for you," Daniel said. "I got a call, so I thought I'd better take it in here, where I wouldn't be disturbing anyone. It was my secretary Gina. She wanted me to know she was sending a packet on Simon."

"You found something?"

"The automated searches found something. As soon as it came in, she called, since I'd told her to let me know the minute we had any kind of update." Face grim, Daniel extended his phone to Rafe. "You're not going to like this."

Tense with foreboding, Rafe took the phone from Daniel and looked down at the screen. There was a picture of Simon, probably from a few years earlier. Underneath was a lot of text, apparently from an arrest for breaking and entering into an empty house. However, the crime itself wasn't what made Rafe's blood run cold. No, it was

Simon's full name, spelled out directly below the photo.

Simon Luis Escobar.

No. No way. Rafe glanced up from the phone and saw Daniel watching him, concern in his eyes. "I know. 'Escobar' is a name everyone hoped they would never hear again."

It couldn't be a coincidence. But how?

No, *how* didn't matter right now.

"I have to go," Rafe said, his voice hoarse as he shoved the phone into his cousin's hand.

Then he was running across the kitchen, opening the back door and letting it bang shut behind. A voice in his head was shouting, *Hurry, hurry, hurry....*

As he opened the door to Cat's SUV and flung himself inside, he prayed that he wouldn't be too late.

17

ECHOES

Miranda

Mouth dry, all I could do was stare at Simon. "T-temple?" I stammered.

"I know you saw it, Miranda." He was still smiling, his entire attitude relaxed. Apparently, he wasn't at all put off by my presence so close to his sanctum. "Would you like to go inside? I was going to show you at some point anyway…once I thought you were ready."

I wanted to retort that I would never be ready for that kind of terrible magic, but my tongue seemed to be sticking to the roof of my mouth. At last I was able to swallow. Then I said, "What are you doing messing around with that kind of stuff, Simon?"

His head tilted slightly. "I hope you're not

going to get all sanctimonious and start lecturing me about the left-hand path, or whatever it is you McAllister witches call it. After all, your own uncle dabbled in some pretty dark enchantments."

"And paid the price for it," I said, surprising myself with my daring.

Simon came close, wrapped the fingers of his left hand around mine. More than anything, I wanted to pull away, but the cold fear coiling in my belly kept me from being quite that bold. A bird sang in a tree somewhere across the field, but even that innocuous sound only served to remind me of how alone we were out here. "I will pay no price," he said. "All I'm doing is claiming my birthright."

"Your 'birthright'?" I repeated, trying to ignore the harsh sensation of his fingers clamping down on my hand. "I'm pretty sure the de la Pazes don't mess around with this kind of magic, either."

A chuckle escaped his lips. "Ah, Miranda, that was just another story I told you. I'm no de la Paz. My real name is Simon Luis Escobar."

No. The cold in my center spread outward through my body, freezing all my limbs in a kind of numb terror. That wasn't possible. How could it be possible? The dark warlock Joaquin Escobar had died before I was born, and his only son, Matías, had died even before his father's passing.

"You look confused," Simon said. He reached up with his free hand and touched my cheek, and I couldn't help flinching. The half-smile he'd been wearing that whole time abruptly disappeared. "What, you don't want me now that you know who I am? That shouldn't change anything, Miranda. I'm still the friend who's protected you, taught you…loves you."

He bent and touched his lips to mine. At once I was nearly overcome by a sensation of wrongness, of being consumed by something cold and evil. My whole body wanted to rebel, and yet I somehow knew that if I tried to openly defy him, I would only provoke the sort of confrontation I wasn't certain I could win. Yes, my powers had grown exponentially over the past week—thanks to Simon, much as I hated to admit it—but I still didn't know whether they would be enough.

If he noted my revulsion, he gave no sign of it. A satisfied expression on his face, he pulled away and straightened up, then reached over to touch my hair. "Good," he said. "You don't know how hard it's been, making myself wait for you. Now there's no reason to wait any longer."

Oh, Goddess, he didn't mean what I thought he meant, did he? Once again revulsion rose up in me, but I pulled in a breath of cool morning air and told myself I needed to stay calm. "I guess not," I said, my tone deliberately casual. "Only…I don't understand. How can you be Joaquin Escobar's son?"

He shook his head. "I have a lot to tell you, Miranda. Let's go into the house, though. It's too cold to keep standing out here. The last thing I want is for you to get sick."

His fingers twined with mine again, and he began to lead me toward the house. I wished I had the courage to tear myself from his grasp and take off running. Where exactly I would run, I had no idea, since I wasn't even sure how close the nearest neighbor was. Not that it mattered; anyone living nearby would be a civilian, and therefore of as much help as a bucket of water in a raging forest fire.

We went in the house, and he guided me into the living room and sat me down on one of the couches. "Your hands are cold," he said. "How about some more coffee, or tea? I don't think there's any hot chocolate."

"Tea," I said faintly. Although coffee was my morning drink of choice, I had a feeling if I tried to drink any, I'd be sick to my stomach. Tea seemed a bit more manageable. And maybe while Simon was occupied with making the tea, I could make a run for it.

Even as the thought crossed my mind, I knew I wouldn't try to flee. For one thing, I very much feared that Simon would be able to easily catch up with me. Also, as much as I hated to admit it, I wanted to hear what he had to say. I still couldn't quite get my brain to process the revelation that he was Joaquin Escobar's son, Joaquin Escobar, the dark warlock who'd nearly had all the Arizona clans under his thumb in addition to the Santiagos, the California clan he'd infiltrated first and made his own.

So I sat on the couch like the coward I was, listening as Simon moved around in the kitchen and heated some water for my tea. A century later —or maybe more like five minutes—he came back in with a mug of the same heavy biscuit-colored stoneware as the plates we'd eaten our breakfast on. The tea bag was still in it... Darjeeling from Republic of Tea. Had he left the tea bag there to reassure me that he hadn't messed with it in some way, given me a potion to make me more cooperative?

"Here you go," he said, pressing the mug into my chilled fingers.

And you know, it did feel good. I held on to the mug, willing some of its warmth to penetrate the icy fear that seemed to have invaded my entire body. Maybe I could just hold on to the mug but not actually drink from it. "Thanks."

He smiled and sat down next to me. Too close to me, but I knew I wouldn't protest. Not yet. I needed more information, and didn't want to upset him. After seeing that terrible temple, I knew he must be capable of all sorts of horrible things…if provoked.

"My mother is Marisol Valdez, the *prima* of the Santiagos," he said. He'd brought a glass of water for himself, and he took a sip of it before he set the glass down on the coffee table and continued, "Of course, for a long time, I didn't know that. I thought my mother was Olivia Gutierrez, a *nunca.*"

So that was why he'd told me his name was Simon Gutierrez. It probably had been for most of his life, no matter what his birth certificate might have said. Was his legal last name really Gutierrez, or Valdez? I somehow doubted the *prima* of the Santiagos would have allowed him to be called Simon Escobar. He'd probably adopted the name once he was squarely on the same dark path as his father.

"A *nunca* like me," I murmured.

"No, *not* like you," Simon replied, a flash of anger coming and going in his too-black eyes. "Your magic was only hidden, not nonexistent like my sister Olivia's."

"I thought you said Olivia was your mother."

"I said I *thought* she was my mother." He went quiet for a moment, expression grim, as though he revisited unpleasant memories he had done his best to shove away somewhere in the dark. "My real mother was pregnant with me when my father died, but she hid the pregnancy from everyone in the clan. When I was born, she smuggled me out, had my half-sister Olivia tell everyone I was her second child with her civilian husband."

"I'm sorry," I murmured, and I realized I was. Simon might have been the son of the devil, but no innocent child deserved that kind of treatment.

Simon appeared grateful for my response, because he reached over and took my free hand for a moment. I had to force myself to stay still, but my forbearance seemed to have worked, because he seemed slightly less tense as he went on, "It happened. Problem was, my powers started to show up early, when I was only around nine years old. It soon became clear enough that Olivia and her husband couldn't handle me. When I was ten, I got sent to live some other relatives in Orange County, a Santiago witch and warlock who were supposed to be pretty powerful in their own right. That went on for about four years. Then they said I was too much to handle, too, and that was when Marisol was forced to step in and take me to live with her." His mouth twisted. "My *mother*. Of course, she didn't come out and tell me the truth right away. I always thought she was detached because I was the problem child no one wanted to deal with, and I did my best to behave myself around her—tried to keep my powers in check, tried to be a good student in the civilian schools she sent me to. But then one day after I'd been living with her for about three years, I overheard her arguing with her cousin Lucinda about the situation, and that was when I realized what they'd done to me."

Oh, Goddess. Part of me wanted to give Simon a hug and tell him I was sorry for the way his family had deceived him. But how could I allow myself to feel pity for him when I knew he'd been dabbling in black magic? For that matter, exactly what the hell kind of spells *had* he been casting out in that shed?

Since I wasn't sure what to say, I settled for giving him a sympathetic nod, during which I hoped I wore an appropriately understanding expression on my face. It seemed to be enough, because after a brief pause he continued with his story.

"I confronted her, of course. And she broke down in tears and told me she'd only done what she thought was best for me, that although she couldn't allow herself to get rid of me before I was born, she also knew she couldn't bear to look at me and see anything of my father in my face. I told her she was weak and wasn't fit to be *prima,* and I took my stuff and got out. I've been on my own ever since."

I couldn't imagine having to live on my own when I was just seventeen. At the same time, I was afraid to ask how he'd gotten by. I supposed he could have stayed in Santiago territory, since his ability to hide his warlock powers would have allowed him to blend in with the civilian population. And I also guessed that he wouldn't scruple at breaking a few laws to get the things he wanted for himself, whatever he needed to survive. Still, it must have been a terrible and lonely existence.

To cover my confusion, I lifted my mug of tea to my lips and took a large swallow. By that point it was only lukewarm, but it was still soothing enough going down my throat, and it tasted fine. I didn't think Simon had done anything to it. Since he didn't seem inclined to say anything else, I knew I needed to speak. So I uttered the first words that came to my mind. "But why me?"

"Because I knew there was something special about you. I'd heard Lucinda and Marisol talk about you, about how it was a shame that you didn't have any magical gifts when your parents were so powerful. It made me think, and wonder." His dark eyes fastened on me, and I didn't know how to look away. "After all, we're not so very different, are we? You and I—we're both the children of a *prima* and a *primus* pairing. Even at seventeen, I knew I was stronger than anyone in the Santiago clan, stronger even than my birth mother. Why was I that strong, when you didn't appear to have any powers of your own? It didn't make sense. So I traveled to de la Paz territory, where no one knew me. It was easy enough to gain access to their libraries—with my own talents hidden, they thought I was just another civilian house cleaner or gardener or pool guy. I was basically invisible to them. I read, and I learned. That part of what I told you was true enough. I did read accounts of people like you, people whose magic came to them much later than it should have. It just needed…waking up."

"And were you the one who did the waking?" I asked, not sure whether I really wanted to know the answer to that question. Still, I also knew I couldn't avoid the truth forever.

"Yes," he replied at once. Gently, he took the mug from my hands so he could clasp them between his own. Those long fingers of his were very strong, and I knew I probably wouldn't be able to pull away—even if I'd been crazy enough to provoke him so openly. "I made an amulet filled with certain powerful herbs, and I wore it under my shirt when I met you on the Railrunner. If you truly had been a *nunca,* those herbs wouldn't have had any effect on you. But because your powers were only dormant, it brought them to life. That was why you began to feel the effects almost immediately, why you were able to talk to ghosts, why you could suddenly teleport. That was all because of me."

His grip on my hands tightened as he said that last sentence, and the intensity of his gaze only increased. Again unsure as to how I should I respond, I said, "Then I owe you a lot of thanks. I would have gone my whole life without realizing there was magic in me if it hadn't been for you."

I'd only been trying to keep him from suspecting how much I wanted to get away, but clearly he took my words as something else altogether. At once he pulled me toward him, kissing me again, his hands sliding up my arms. And once again I experienced that sense of wrongness, of horror. It was far more than just being kissed by someone I really wasn't attracted to. It was more that the magic in me recognized the power in him as something dark and twisted, something that could never walk in the light.

He held the kiss for a long time, so long that I wondered in some despair what he would do if I began to gag, since I could feel my entire body beginning to recoil, desperately trying to get some kind of space between us. At last, though, he lifted his mouth from mine. "You feel it, Miranda?" he asked. "This is why I came here to be with you. I knew you had powers that were the match of mine. And that's exactly what we should be—a perfect match, a *prima* and *primus,* just like your parents, just like mine. Together, we can do anything, *be* anything."

"I'm not a *prima*," I protested, my voice shaky. I had to pray he thought its unsteadiness was only due to the effect of his kiss, and not because I was using every amount of will I possessed to prevent myself from either throwing up or fleeing the room. "I'm only a witch."

He reached over to push a lock of hair away from my cheek. How could his touch be so tender when I knew the soul within had to be black as night? "No, Miranda, you are not *only* a witch. You're a witch that the world has never seen before. Don't you understand? My father proved that it's easy enough to take a clan for your own, and he was only one man. You and I working together—we would be unstoppable."

"Oh, no." I couldn't bear to be sitting next to him for one second longer. Ignoring the possible consequences, I got to my feet and went to stand over by the fireplace. "You can't think I would ever do something like that, Simon."

"Why not?" He rose as well and came toward me, thus rendering my minor retreat basically not a retreat at all. "Look at those asshole Castillos. They treated you like crap, especially Genoveva. Wouldn't you like to see her begging for your forgiveness, cowering in front of you? That could happen. It would be easy for the two of us."

"I-I'm not that person," I said, wishing my protest didn't sound so pathetic and weak. "I mean, I would be the first person to admit that I'm not a fan of Genoveva Castillo. But that doesn't mean I want to grind her under my boot heel. And there are people in the clan who are really nice—Rafe's sister Cat, and his cousin Tony, and the girls who were supposed to be my bridesmaids. I couldn't possibly hurt any of them."

For a moment, Simon didn't reply. He just stood there and watched me, his expression almost unreadable. Then, to my surprise, he smiled. "And this is why I love you, Miranda. You're a good person. I gave up being a good person a long time ago, mostly because everyone expected the worst of me. Maybe I wouldn't do that to the Castillos…if you asked nicely."

"Then please don't," I said. My voice was almost a whisper. "I don't want anything bad to happen to them."

"Well…."

From the way he stopped after that one syllable, I knew he'd already done something terrible. My gut clenched, but I made myself ask the question. "What did you do, Simon?"

His gaze slid away from me. One hand tapped against the heavy plaster of the mantelpiece. "I've done a lot of things, Miranda. Most of them were to make sure I survived. Lately, it's been to make sure that you and I would be together. Like the cat."

"'The cat'?" I echoed, then stared at him, eyes narrowing with suspicion. "You sent that cat when I was staying in Genoveva's casita?"

"I *was* the cat," Simon said, pride clear in his voice. "Unlike your former fiancé, I don't have any size limitations when it comes to shapeshifting. It was an easy way to keep an eye on you—or to make sure you didn't have any contacts I didn't want you to have. Why do you think I scared you into dropping your phone? You were about to call your parents and possibly blow the whole thing."

There hadn't been many times in my life when I was rendered speechless, but as I looked at Simon, I couldn't think of any coherent way to respond. I'd let that damn cat wander all over the casita. Had it ever seen me when I was getting out of the shower? I didn't think so—I was fairly sure I'd always kept the bathroom door closed—but just the mere suspicion that Simon might have already seen me naked was enough to make me feel nauseated all over again. Then I realized his last sentence didn't even make sense. "If you didn't want me contacting my parents, then why that whole production of taking me to Walmart so I could buy a new phone? My mother and I have been talking and texting just fine for the past few days!"

His mouth curved into a smirk. "Have you?"

"What do you mean?"

"You thought you were calling your mother's number. In reality, all your calls and texts were going straight to my phone. I was the one responding, not your mother."

This revelation was so astonishing that again I could only stare at him, flabbergasted and outraged at the same time. "But—"

"But nothing. It was a simple little spell, really, even the times when I had to disguise my voice to fool you into thinking you were talking to your mother. I needed to make sure your parents wouldn't come here to Santa Fe and stir up any trouble. If you'd really been in contact with your mother and told her what you told me, you know she and your father would have been here in a heartbeat—literally, since of course they don't have to wait to take a plane like most people would."

This was all insane. Or rather, Simon had to be insane. I wouldn't argue that the Santiagos had done a piss-poor job of managing the cuckoo that had been dumped in their nest, but on the other hand, no sane person would have gone to all these machinations just to get close to one particular woman, no matter how powerful her magic might be. All this plotting and planning, all to make sure I would be his. Unfortunately, in all that scheming, he'd left out the most important part of the equation.

Me.

Only a crazy person could have believed I would go along with all of this. Simon might have done everything he could to learn about me, about my background, but he sure as hell had never figured out that I wasn't the sort of person who would ever think it was okay to lie and cheat and scheme, all to achieve some terrible end of world domination, or at least domination of whatever corner of the witch world he thought he could seize for himself.

"Yes, you've been very clever," I said, my tone hinting that I wasn't nearly as impressed with his cleverness as he wanted me to be. "Any other revelations you'd care to share?"

His mouth tightened, irritation clear in every line of his face. Then he said, "Just one, I think. A minute ago, you were saying you didn't want anything to happen to the Castillos. I don't really understand your loyalty to a clan that only looked at you as a bargaining piece, not a person, but—"

"*Tell me.*"

That awful smirk returned. "The Castillos had a man whose gift was locating missing items or people. Marco. The first time Rafe and his sister asked him to help find you when you disappeared, I was able to keep you blocked so he couldn't track you down. After this last time, though, when you teleported away from the wedding ceremony, I could tell he was trying harder than ever, was going to break through my defenses if I wasn't careful. So I gave him a little stroke to keep him off my back."

"You *what?*" Now I really did feel like I was going to be sick. Shaking my head in horror, I began to back away from Simon—only to bump into the coffee table and stumble and nearly fall. He caught my arm before I took a tumble, though, and continued to hold on to me, his grip like a band of iron around my bicep.

Tone as casual as though he was discussing the weather, that terrible smile still playing around the corners of his mouth, he said, "I gave him a stroke. It was easy enough. I figured he'd just be in a coma long enough for the two of us to finish our work here, and then we would disappear and we'd be too far away for him to find us. Problem was, I hadn't really counted on how goddamn *stubborn* he was. Even in a coma, he was fighting me, trying to tell someone where they could find you. The strain was too much, and his heart gave out."

"You killed him!" I twisted in Simon's grip, then realized I didn't need to fight him at all. I could teleport the hell out of here, go to the Castillos, tell them where to find the dark warlock who'd taken shelter so near them. All I had to do was imagine myself standing in the chilly living room of Genoveva's house, and then—

And then...nothing. I was still trying to pull myself from Simon's grasp, still standing a few feet away from the coldly elegant fireplace of the house he'd taken for his use.

"Oh, no, Miranda," Simon said. "Did you really think it would be that easy? Your powers are strong, but I can still block them if I have to. The last thing I want is you disappearing on me. As for Marco, well, I didn't *really* kill him. Yes, I made him have a stroke, but if he hadn't struggled so hard, hadn't tried to get the word out about where you were, then he wouldn't have had the heart attack that killed him. It was just a terrible accident."

He truly believed that. I could see it in what looked like the genuine regret in Simon's eyes. Of course, it could all be an act, but I didn't think so. In his mind, he was innocent. It was Marco's fault that he was dead, since he hadn't just lain there peacefully in a coma the way he was supposed to.

"You're crazy," I whispered.

Simon shook his head. "Hmm...no, I don't think so. It's easy to call someone crazy just because you don't like how they do things or because their worldview is different from yours. But I didn't kill him. I haven't killed anyone... although I really did want to kill that useless fiancé of yours. He didn't appreciate you. But I—*I* appreciate you, Miranda."

His eyes glittered, and he pulled me toward him. I knew I could put up a fight, but I wasn't strong enough to match him physically, and since he was able to block my powers somehow, I couldn't use them to get away or to hurt him enough that I might have a chance to flee.

Hands gripping my shoulders, he shoved me over to the couch, the cushions hitting the backs of my legs. I wriggled in his grasp, sure now of what he planned to do. After lying and stealing and committing murder, what was a little rape, after all?

I had to do something, even if I couldn't win.

My knee came up into his groin, but I might as well have ground it into a metal plate for all the good that effort did. Pain lanced up and down my leg, and I let out a gasp.

"That won't work, either," he said. "Give it up, Miranda." Tone softening, he added, "I don't want to force you. I want you to want this. You *should* want this. No one will ever love you the way I love you. No one will ever do for you what I've done. I just need you to be mine, Miranda. That's all. Mine completely."

"Never," I ground out from between clenched teeth. "I'll never be yours, you sick bastard!"

"Oh, yes, you will be," he said, "even if you don't think so now."

And he shoved me down on the sofa, his weight pinning me down, preventing me from getting away.

No escape. Nothing I could do to stop him.

Oh, Goddess....

18

TRANSFORMATIONS

Rafe

HE BARRELED DOWN BISHOP'S LODGE ROAD heading out of Santa Fe, the warning light on the dashboard flashing at him, scolding him for using manual control in a restricted area. Rafe knew he was probably picking up a new speeding ticket every time he passed an automated checkpoint, but right then he couldn't give a rat's ass. He'd gladly pay the fines, and as for the black marks on his record, well, those could get quietly erased. Just another perk of being a Castillo.

The name kept dancing in front of his eyes, taunting him, tormenting him.

Simon Luis Escobar.

How the hell could Joaquin Escobar have had a son that age? Rafe supposed Simon could have been born outside the United States, just like Escobar's evil witch daughter, the one who'd been responsible for a trail of bodies in the Tucson and Phoenix area more than twenty years ago. For some reason, though, that explanation didn't seem to fit, and it definitely didn't explain why Simon had come after Miranda, unless it was out of some strange need for revenge. If that were the case, though, you'd think he would have tried to strike against her parents, since they were the ones directly responsible for Escobar's death.

And, to a lesser extent, Rafe's own grandmother. If simple revenge was Simon's only motivation, he could have easily killed Rafe when he had him under that mind-control spell. That didn't seem to have been what Simon was up to, however. Actually, it appeared that almost everything he'd done had been part of some grand scheme to lure Miranda into his web.

The thought of her being with Simon Escobar this whole time with no idea of who he truly was didn't make Rafe's blood run cold. No, instead he was burning with rage, every muscle tense with the need to strike out, to do whatever he must in order to get Miranda safely away from the dark warlock.

Easier said than done, unfortunately. Once he was past Santa Fe's city limits, Rafe slowed infinitesimally, just because the road began to narrow here and also grew gradually more winding. The last thing he needed was to T-bone some poor slob whose only crime was pulling out of their hidden country driveway at the last minute.

All right, think. Rafe didn't know Tesuque like the back of his hand, the way he did Santa Fe, but he guessed that Simon had to be holed up in one of the properties away from Bishop's Lodge Road, or Tesuque Village Road, the two main arteries that ran through the small settlement. There were a lot of high-end mini-ranches and downright estates out here, mostly because they provided a way to be out of the bustle of downtown Santa Fe but still close enough that you could be in town for a five-star dinner within about ten minutes.

He adjusted the nav so he could get a top-down view of the entirety of Tesuque, or at least the portion on the east side of Highway 84. For some reason, he thought Simon would have chosen a place here, probably because it was easier to find a property tucked away in the foothills. The other part of the village was a little too exposed.

Distracted by studying the nav, he almost missed the stop sign at the intersection with Tesuque Village Road and had to slam on the brakes. A cloud of dust and tire smoke rose up around him, and he growled a curse. Luckily, no one else had been at the crossroads, so even if he had blown through the stop, he wouldn't have suffered any ill effects...except probably another moving violation.

Then he felt it, or smelled it, even above the scent of burning rubber—that hint of evil, the same dark, oily residue of black magic. It led away from the center of the tiny village, off a secondary route called Griego Hill.

Thank God. Rafe turned right and followed the road as it wound up into the hills. Here, a good many of the trees still retained their fall foliage, although he spied just as many leaves on the ground as there were on the trees. He couldn't allow himself to enjoy the beauty of the autumn splendor that surrounded him, however. All his focus had to remain fixed on the faint, terrible trail he was following.

And then it was gone. He stomped on the brakes and paused there for a moment, idling, his senses reaching out and finding nothing. Damn it. There must have been a driveway or side road he'd missed, a nearly hidden intersection where Simon would have turned off from the main road.

Cursing under his breath, Rafe wheeled the SUV around and began slowly driving back in the direction from which he'd come. At least this wasn't a well-traveled road; it wasn't as though he was preventing anyone from coming through here at a more reasonable rate of speed.

There. He stopped at a narrow lane, the only entrance into what appeared to be a large property with expensive split-rail fences enclosing the entire substantial piece of land. And there was the gate just a few feet beyond the turn-off, no flimsy wooden thing but a heavy barrier of laser-carved iron. A sign just above the gate proclaimed the place to be Daybreak Ranch.

Well, shit. Big and sturdy as Cat's Mercedes SUV might be, there was no way he could drive it through that gate, even if he backed up and tried to break through it at speed. Just as well that he hadn't bothered to try, because he knew his sister would kill him if he did anything so reckless with her precious vehicle.

Rafe sat there for a moment, studying the gate and the sign above it. As far as he could tell, there didn't seem to be any security cameras posted here. And the fence wasn't *that* high.

The urgency driving him didn't allow any room for hesitation. Maybe if he sat here and thought about it for a while, he could come up with a better plan. Then again, maybe not.

There was a lot to be said for the element of surprise.

He turned off the engine and shoved the key in his pocket, then got out of the vehicle. A quick glance up and down the road told him there was no one around to witness his trespassing, so he went to the fence and climbed over, then kept moving.

The lane continued through the property, curving here and there, but more or less heading straight to a cluster of buildings about a quarter-mile away. As he'd thought, this place was *big*. Although Rafe didn't track property values the way some of his Castillo cousins did, buying low and selling high, he knew this place had to be insanely expensive, judging by the size of the tract it was situated on. In the grand scheme of things, that didn't matter so much, but he still had a hard time figuring out how Simon Escobar had managed to get his hands on it. More mind control? Maybe.

With a grinding anger in his gut, Rafe thought it was just the sort of place Simon would use to try to impress Miranda. They could have been getting pretty cozy here over the past few days.

No, he didn't want to think that. She had to have been hurt by the terrible things he'd said, but Rafe had to believe she wouldn't immediately go into Simon's arms. But if this wasn't some kind of a love nest, then what had they been doing here, hidden away from everyone?

He paused for a moment, taking shelter in a stand of pine trees that bordered a large pasture. From here, he could see that the cluster of buildings included the main house, done in the New Mexico territorial style with a peaked roof and covered patios all around, another smaller house similar in design to the main structure, and then a detached garage and a small building that probably was a shed or a workshop.

Rafe focused his attention on the main house, guessing that must be where Simon and Miranda were located. His vantage point didn't allow him to see anything of what might be going on inside. Everything seemed calm and still, but that didn't mean much. For all he knew, Miranda wasn't even here. Escobar could have taken her someplace for the morning, maybe out to breakfast or hiking or God knows what.

This was the right place, though. The stink of evil was so strong, Rafe didn't even have to shift into coyote or wolf form to be able to smell it, rank and heavy, like the spray from some foul, terrible creature. For some reason, it seemed to be concentrated on a small structure he could barely spy, way out on the back pasture. A place of ritual magic, he guessed, but he decided to ignore it for now. He doubted that Simon would have allowed Miranda anywhere near the place, since the only way he could hope to persuade her to be his would be if he managed to conceal what he truly was from her.

A low growl escaped his lips, and he wondered

for a moment whether he should shift into animal form. No, that wouldn't work; he'd have to slip out of his clothes and leave them here, and that thought was completely unappealing. Besides, he always thought better as a human, although it wasn't as if his mind became wholly animal once he had shifted. He always retained something of himself, enough to get back to his natural form.

In this case, though, he thought it was probably better to keep his wits about him, and stay human.

There were enough trees on the property that it wasn't too difficult to slip from one to another, using them as cover while he came closer and closer to the house. Now he could see there was a garden to one side, a few late hollyhocks and marigolds still hanging bravely on, although the rest of their compatriots seemed to have succumbed to autumn's frost. He also was able to see that a long hallway extended down one side of the house, with French doors opening onto the garden. Those same doors allowed him a glimpse inside, although he couldn't see much except a couple of long tables set up against one wall, with large paintings hung over them.

The tree that sheltered Rafe now was the last one between him and the house. He would have no further cover once he slipped away from it. Then again, he had no idea what kind of powers

Simon possessed. For all Rafe knew, the other warlock had been aware of his presence from the time he'd left the SUV parked out on the side of the road.

Anyway, they were going to confront one another sooner or later. Rafe couldn't stand here dithering about having adequate cover for the final leg of his approach. He just had to go for it.

A deep breath of the cool late morning air, and then he was running through the garden, pounding over the gravel walks that separated the neat beds of flowers and vegetables. Up the stairs now, hand already on the handle of the French door. It opened easily enough—yes, it had been locked, but Simon hadn't put any other safeguards in place. Was he really that cocky, or had he simply thought Rafe would never be able to track him down here?

All those questions fled his mind, though, as he heard the sounds of an angry confrontation coming from somewhere down the hallway. Miranda's voice for sure, and Simon's as well. Just hearing those insinuating tones was enough to make the hair on Rafe's neck stand up. He recognized that voice all too well—the voice that had told him to betray his fiancée, to throw away the delicate beginnings of a love he had only begun to acknowledge.

Without thinking, he flung himself down the

hallway, feet pounding on the brick floors. He emerged into what had to be the living room, a coolly formal space in what were probably intended to be soothing shades of cream and beige and gray. However, what he saw there only made his blood boil that much more.

Miranda was writhing on one of the sofas, pinned beneath the dark warlock, who had grasped both her wrists in one hand while pushing up the long-sleeved T-shirt she wore with the other. Rafe caught a glimpse of a black lacy bra, then didn't wait to see anything more. He launched himself at Simon, grasping him by the collar of his shirt and flinging him backward with a strength he didn't even know he possessed.

The other warlock hit the edge of the heavy plaster mantel and gave a satisfying little grunt of pain. At once Miranda leaped up from the couch and rushed toward Rafe, grabbing his arm so she could pull him away, as if she knew he planned to continue his attack.

"You can't fight him," she gasped. Her eyes were wide with fear, her full mouth somehow tender and bruised, as though Simon had forced a few kisses on her before Rafe got there to tear them apart. "He's too strong."

"Yes," Simon panted, one hand going back to touch the spot where his spine had connected with the mantel. "She's right. Nice of you to come charging in here like a hero out of an action movie, but it's not going to do any good."

With his other hand, he made a strange circling gesture. At once Rafe felt something like an invisible hand catch him by the arm and spin him backward with enough force that he went flying over the arm of the couch and dropped to the floor below. As pain shuddered through his shoulder, he heard Miranda cry out—and then she, too, made a strange gesture with both hands, almost as though she was pushing the very air in front of her.

Whatever she'd done, it seemed to have some effect, because Simon was pushed back into the fireplace once again, this time with so much force that the plaster of the mantel actually cracked, and a large piece from the edge fell onto the rug. He stumbled and dropped to his knees, the breath going out of him with a shocked "woof" of a sound.

At once Miranda was beside Rafe, her hand going around his bicep so she could help haul him to his feet. "Come on," she said in a fierce whisper, and began to tug him toward the door.

"Not so fast," came Simon's voice from behind them.

It was as if they'd walked into a wall of glass. Now it was Rafe's turn to make a grunt of surprised pain—as if he wasn't already hurting enough from that tumble he'd taken over the arm of the couch.

"You think I'm going to let you take her from me?" Simon asked, his voice taut with anger. "After everything I've done to get her here, to get her to see what I could offer her? You don't deserve her, Castillo. You never thought about her, thought about what she felt, what she needed. You only thought about what *you* wanted."

Rafe wanted to shout out his denial, but as much as he despised the Escobar warlock, he knew there was some truth in the other man's words. He turned slowly, meeting Simon's black glare. "Maybe so. But what about what *Miranda* wants? From what I saw when I walked in here a minute ago, she didn't look too happy about being with you."

"No, I wasn't," she said. Her eyes might as well have been pools of green fire, they were so filled with fury. "I don't want you, Simon. You lied to me over and over again. You've *hurt* people —good people who didn't deserve what you did to them."

He stepped closer, hands knotted into fists at his side. "You don't know what you're saying, Miranda. You just need to let me have some time with you so I can show you—"

"Show me what? How to use black magic to

get what I want? I'm not that kind of witch, Simon. I've told you that already."

Looking at Miranda then, at the way she stood there like a queen, head high despite her disheveled hair and smeared makeup, Rafe knew he loved her, knew that he probably didn't deserve her but would do whatever he could to make her happy.

First, though, they had to get the hell out of here.

And he knew what he had to do.

"I don't *need* black magic," Simon snapped. "My powers are strong enough that I can get what I want all on my own."

"Then what's with the shed? The candles? The bowl? If you're so powerful, why all the gimmicks?"

Miranda was playing a very dangerous game by confronting Simon like that, but the worry that coursed through Rafe wasn't enough to prevent him from focusing on his own plan. As far as he could tell, Simon wasn't even paying attention to him, had his gaze fixed entirely on the woman who stood before him, as if he thought that he could bend her to his will merely by staring at her.

Maybe he could. Rafe still didn't know how Simon had managed to make him say those terrible words at the cathedral. So far, it seemed as if Miranda was immune to that kind of mind control, but who knew how long she could hang on?

Transforming inside his clothes was uncomfortable, but he could do it if he had to. Luckily, his power allowed him to shift instantaneously. It wasn't like the movies, where werewolves always seemed to have these long, painful transitions. One second he was a man; the next, a large Mexican gray wolf burst forth from within his discarded clothing and leapt for Simon's throat.

The warlock put up both hands to defend himself. All that gesture accomplished, however, was to allow him to get knocked off balance and topple to the floor, his head missing the coffee table by mere inches.

Too bad. If he'd managed to brain himself, it would have been much better for everyone involved.

Rafe's teeth sank into one of Simon's forearms. The taste of the dark warlock's blood made Rafe want to gag, for it was just as tainted as the rest of him, black and foul, more like the ichor of an insect than the blood of a true human. Still, that wasn't enough to make him back off. Instead, his teeth sank in even more deeply as Simon let out a groan of pain.

But then—then the warlock was lifting his free hand, making the same odd circular gesture he'd performed a few minutes earlier. In the next instant, Rafe was torn away from Simon's arm and thrown through the air, landing a few yards away with a painful thud on the brick floor. Whimpering, he forced himself to his feet and began to limp back toward his adversary.

He didn't get very far before Miranda came to him and sank her fingers into the thick fur at his neck. "Don't do it," she whispered. "He'll kill you."

"I'm glad to see you're coming to your senses," Simon remarked. He was standing again, ignoring the blood that coursed from the gash in his forearm and dripped onto the expensive rug beneath his feet. "Step away from that creature, Miranda. Step away, and come to me."

"No," she said.

A flash of irritation crossed Simon's lean features. "Stop acting like an idiot, Miranda. You're strong, but you're not strong enough to defeat me. You couldn't even get away from me a few minutes ago when you tried."

"You're right," she replied. "I couldn't then. But I thought about it, and I figured out what you were doing. So I can teleport now."

In the next instant, she had dropped to her knees and wrapped her arms around Rafe's neck. Before he could even blink, the coolly elegant room and the infuriated warlock standing in it had disappeared, and then Rafe whirled through darkness for an infinitely long split second before they reappeared, crouched on the floor in his own living room. He blinked at her in surprise.

"Can you turn back into yourself now?" Miranda asked, and got wearily to her feet. "I think we need to talk."

19

DARKER PATHS

Miranda

As I watched, the wolf turned back into Rafe—a very naked Rafe. True, he was sort of crouched down, so I couldn't see *everything,* but....

It was hard to say who was more embarrassed, Rafe or me. Even as hot blood flooded my cheeks, he muttered, "Um, give me a minute," and fled for the stairs. However, his haste didn't prevent me from getting a very good look at his muscular bare ass as he ran down the hall.

Well, then.

I ran a hand through my hair and sort of stumbled over to the couch so I could sit down. Everything had happened so fast, it was hard for me to register the fact that I was now sitting in Rafe's living room. I'd managed to flee from Simon before he could stop me.

I was safe. More than that, Rafe was safe, too...because I'd used my powers to get us both way from Simon. As frightened as I'd been—as I still was—I couldn't quite prevent a flush of happiness from filling me at that realization.

Well, we were safe for now, anyway. I wasn't about to fool myself into thinking that he couldn't track me down; with all the research Simon had done on me and the Castillos, I figured it was a pretty sure bet that he knew exactly where Rafe lived. True, he might not have guessed that we'd come here first, might have thought we'd go straight to Genoveva's place, but I couldn't count on him looking elsewhere before he turned his attention to Rafe's home.

I needed to do something.

Like so many spells or powers or whatever you wanted to call the magic I'd begun to practice, I'd never tried this one before. However, I knew it existed, because it was the talent that my cousin Caitlin's husband Alex had been born with.

Closing my eyes, I imagined an invisible bubble of protection encasing the house, securing everything within against magical attack. Or rather, this bubble was supposed to protect against any kind of assault, magical or not, but I sort of doubted that we had to worry about being assailed by the local SWAT team or whatever. Once it was in place, I felt as though I could breathe a little more easily. I didn't know for sure whether Simon could get through the shield I'd created or not— he was so *very* strong—but it was better than sitting here and doing nothing.

Rafe come down the stairs then, barefoot, dressed in a pair of faded jeans and an army-green henley shirt. He was so amazingly handsome— and so reassuringly *not* Simon—that I wanted to go and throw myself into his arms. But I hesitated, not sure what I should do. He'd been horrible to me at the chapel, so why had he suddenly come running to my rescue? Guilt? I couldn't think of any other reason why he would go to so much effort to save me.

Before I could do or say anything, he'd come over to the couch and sank down next to me, his hands reaching for mine. They were warm and strong, and I never wanted him to let go.

"I am so sorry, Miranda," he said, sincerity ringing through every syllable. "At the chapel— that wasn't me. That was Simon's words coming out of my mouth, the words he wanted me to say so you would go running to him. I would never say anything like that to you because it would all be lies. I did want to get married—I *do* want to get married."

Of course. I should have known that Rafe's rejection had only been another one of Simon's maneuverings. The relief that rushed over me was so intense, tears sprang to my eyes and began to flow down my cheeks.

"Don't cry," he whispered. "Don't cry, Miranda—it's all going to be okay."

Then he was kissing me, mouth pressed against mine with all the passion and tenderness I'd remembered but had thought must only be a cruel dream. This was the real Rafe, the man I'd allowed myself to fall in love with.

I wanted nothing more than to be there with him forever, his arms around me, every touch, every kiss helping to erase the darkness in which Simon had tried to drown me. Deep down, though, I knew this was only a pleasant interlude. I knew the man who had tried to steal my heart would not let it go this easily.

"Rafe," I said at last, once I was able to regain my breath. "We really do need to talk."

He pulled away from me, but with clear reluctance. "I know. It's just—I thought I had lost you. We couldn't find any trace of you, and nothing we tried worked. Even Marco—" He stopped then, face going very still, as though he was struggling with emotions he didn't quite want to face.

"I know," I said quietly. "Simon told me."

"He told—" The words broke off as Rafe stared at me, terrible comprehension flaring in his warm brown eyes, so different from Simon's cold black ones. "Simon killed Marco to keep him from telling us where you were."

"Yes. That is," I went on, "he says he didn't mean to kill him. He sent the stroke that put him in the coma, but the heart attack came from Marco struggling to get you the information you needed. Not that it makes any real difference, as far as I'm concerned. I'm so sorry, Rafe. I feel like this is all my fault."

"Your fault?" he repeated, with some incredulity. "How can any of this possibly be your fault, except that you had the bad luck to attract the attention of a psychopath like Simon Escobar?"

"Wasn't that enough?" I replied, guilt twisting within me. "If it hadn't been for me—"

"You can stop that right now." His tone was firm, and he reached out to touch my cheek briefly, the tenderness of even that soft brush of his fingers against my skin enough to send a ripple of warmth all through my body. "Because I could say, well, if it hadn't been for my mother insisting on having you come here, then Simon Escobar would have had no reason to hurt Marco, would he? How far back do you want to cast blame?

There's no point, because the only person responsible for all this is Simon. Full stop. Understand?"

"Yes," I said meekly, and Rafe actually chuckled.

"Meekness doesn't really suit you, sweetheart." He leaned over and kissed me, a soft and gentle kiss that was still somehow a promise of much more. "You were pretty impressive back there, you know. What was that thing you did with your hands to push Simon away?"

"Oh, that."

"Yeah, *that.*"

"I don't know, exactly," I said. "That is, my magic seems to work differently from most people's. I just sort of have to think of something, and I can make it happen. When I saw Simon attack you, I knew I could probably do something similar. It was sort of like this toy my parents gave me when I was a kid—it looked like a plastic cone, and it had a plastic bladder inside and some elastic you pulled. When you let go of the elastic, it created a sort of air bomb. I mean, it pushed the air so that you could actually feel it hit you. I just imagined the same sort of thing, only a lot harder. And it seemed to have worked."

Rafe was shaking his head. "You're amazing."

"Not as much as you might think." I took a breath, then went on, "I wouldn't be able to use any of these powers if Simon hadn't showed me how to access them. That doesn't mean I forgive him, but…." I let the words trail off, not sure what I was trying to say. Rafe watched me with understanding in his eyes, and he waited patiently for me to continue. Rubbing my damp palms on the knees of my jeans, I said, "Even with all that, even with finally being able to tap into my powers, I still couldn't get away from Simon on the first try. Before you even got there, I tried to teleport away from him, and it was as if he'd blocked my powers. It was terrible. I'd never felt so helpless."

Spots of anger burned on Rafe's high cheekbones. "When I see him again, I'm going to kill him."

As angry as I was, I didn't know whether that was the solution. Also, even through my love for Rafe, I knew he wasn't strong enough to take Simon down. He'd gotten lucky back there at the house and had caught him off guard, but I couldn't count on that happening a second time.

"We'll worry about that later," I said.

He let out an angry breath, but at least he didn't try to argue. "If he was blocking you from teleporting, how were you able to do it that last time when you got us out of there?"

"Like I said, he'd let his guard down. He was

in a lot of pain from your attack, I think." I stopped, remembering that horrible moment, remembering also how the magic had flowed through me, strong and sure. "And I sort of felt how he was managing to block me, and I maneuvered around the block. That's all."

"As I said, you're amazing." He scrubbed a hand over his face. "Oh, shit."

"What's the matter?" I asked, concern flooding through me. "Are you hurt after all?"

"No, I'm fine." A rueful glance down at the clothes he was wearing, and he added, "It's just that I left my clothes on the floor of Simon's living room. And I left Cat's SUV sitting on the side of the road by the front gate to the property. She's going to fucking kill me."

"I doubt it," I said. "It's just a car. I'm sure she'd be much more worried about your well-being."

"Maybe. Still, I hate to think that Simon can get at it. I mean, the key fob was in my goddamn jeans pocket."

Which meant Simon could happily drive the SUV right off a cliff if he felt like it. However, I wasn't sure he would do something like that—not because he had a problem with destruction, but because the Mercedes would have been sitting out there long enough that someone might have noticed. I thought it far more likely that he would call the sheriff's department and complain about someone abandoning their vehicle on his property. That way he could maintain the law-abiding façade he'd worked so hard to establish.

However, since Rafe had left his clothes behind, that meant he'd also left his wallet, the keys to his house, his phone…everything. "What does your wallet look like?" I asked.

"What?"

"Your wallet. Describe it."

"There isn't much to describe—" he began, then broke off, comprehension spreading over his features. "You're going to try to get it back?"

"If I can," I replied. This flexing of my powers was still very new to me, and I still didn't have a clear grasp of what I could and couldn't do. Still, I could teleport myself and another person at the same time. Moving a small object like a wallet didn't seem like that big a deal. "The car is one thing. But your identity is in that wallet, and I have a feeling we're going to have enough to deal with in the very near future without having to get you a new driver's license and credit cards and all that."

"You have a point. Well, it's brown leather, a simple double fold about yay big." He described the wallet's rough dimensions by making a square with this thumbs and forefingers. "The edges were starting to get worn, the dye rubbing off. I don't carry cash, so it just had my I.D. and a couple of credit cards in it, which means it was pretty thin."

"Thanks, Rafe." I sent him what I hoped was a confident smile, although I didn't feel all that confident. But I had to try. I visualized his jeans lying on the floor of the living room at the house in Tesuque, and realized the easiest thing to do would be to bring them here, rather than just the wallet. That way, I could recover his wallet, house keys, phone—and the key fob for Cat's Mercedes.

Assuming, of course, that Simon hadn't pounced and begun rifling through the discarded pants as soon as we'd disappeared. I hoped his anger and his frustration would vent themselves in other ways, though.

Another breath. Okay, Rafe's jeans, faded Levi's that had started to go a bit ragged at the hem. For all the Castillo wealth, he obviously tended to wear his clothes until they began to fall apart, probably because he couldn't be bothered to go shopping.

And instead of them lying on the floor of the house Simon had borrowed or stolen or cajoled out of the property management company—I still wasn't sure which—suddenly those jeans were draped over Rafe's lap. He gave a start of surprise, then flashed me a grin that had both relief and admiration in it.

"Wow," he said, running a hand over the faded material before he reached into the back pocket and pulled out a wallet that exactly matched the description he had provided just a minute earlier. "I'm going to have to find a different adjective than 'amazing' to describe you, Miranda. The powers you've developed over the past few days—I've never seen anything like it. And here"—he set the wallet down on the coffee table and fished around for something in one of the jeans' front pockets—"here's the fob for Cat's Mercedes. I'll text her and tell her to send the auto club to tow it back to the house. I doubt Simon will interfere with them if he's as concerned about his public image as you seem to think he is."

"Fingers crossed," I said. "He might have already called someone to have it towed, because he knows that will inconvenience us. I wonder if he knows it's Cat's car and not yours?"

"I have no idea." Rafe picked up his wallet and placed it in the pocket of the jeans he now wore. "He does seem to know more about all of us than I would like. But I can't do much about that." His gaze met mine, intent, worried. "What's our next step?"

"Well, you'll need to let Genoveva know that I'm back, and safe," I replied. "But first I'd really like to call my parents and tell them I'm okay. Simon tricked me into thinking I was communicating with my mother, but it was really him the whole time."

A scowl creased Rafe's brows. "That's pretty low, but about what I'd expect from him." He got his phone out of the jeans I'd recovered from Simon's house, unlocked it, and handed it over to me. "They'll be relieved to hear from you. They knew you were missing, knew the Castillo clan was doing their best to locate you, but...."

"But you probably had a lot of fun convincing them to let you handle it, rather than have them come here and try to help," I finished for him, and he gave me a rueful smile.

"Yeah, something like that. They gave me two days."

"Well, now you don't have to worry about it, because I'm here." I reached over with my free hand and touched his arm briefly, then punched in the number for my mother's cell. It picked up on the first ring.

"Rafe? Have you heard something?"

She'd answered so quickly, I wondered if she'd been sitting there, staring at the screen, willing Rafe to call her. "No, Mom. It's Miranda. I'm fine."

"Oh, thank the Goddess." My mother let out a little huff of a breath. "Where are you?"

"I'm at Rafe's house. We were able to get away from Simon."

"This Simon person. Who is he? I checked with Zoe because Rafe thought he might be a de la Paz, but she'd never heard of him."

"He's—" I paused and looked over at Rafe, and he gave me an encouraging nod. "Mom, he's Joaquin Escobar's son."

"Goddess…."

That was about my reaction when I'd learned the truth about him. "How was that possible, though? I mean—"

"Marisol was pregnant when your father and Isabel Castillo and I rescued her from Escobar. We never heard anything further about the child, though, so everyone just assumed she—well, we all thought she must have ended the pregnancy. Who could have blamed her?"

Who, indeed? The thought must have crossed her mind many times, but I supposed that Marisol, being a good Catholic in addition to being the *prima* of her clan, had decided she couldn't go through with it. Instead, she'd done everything she could to hide the truth of who Simon really was.

Since I hadn't responded right away, my mother went on, her tone musing, "Even his name was a clue—Simón Santiago was the consort of the former *prima*. I suppose Marisol gave her son that name in some kind of twisted tribute. I don't understand how they could have kept his existence a secret this whole time, though."

"Because she gave him to Simon's half-sister Olivia to raise. Then it sounds like he got bounced around the clan when he turned out to be too much for her to handle. No one knew he was Marisol's."

"He told you that?"

"Yes. He—" I honestly didn't know how much I should tell my mother. There were things that, frankly, I didn't want either her or my father to know. "He confided in me because he thought he was in love with me, thought we were going to be some kind of perfect match—you know, the son of a *prima* and a *primus* and the daughter of a *prima* and a *primus*. But I didn't feel the same way. Rafe came and rescued me."

"Rafe?" my mother said, disbelief clear in her voice. It was obvious enough that she hadn't expected too much from my Castillo fiancé.

"Yes," I said firmly. "We got out of there. And we're definitely going to get married, although we don't know when that's going to happen. We need to deal with this Simon situation first."

"Your father and I—" my mother began, but I didn't let her get any further than that.

"Let us handle it," I said. "I'm pretty sure the

resources of the entire Castillo clan are enough to handle one bastard of a dark warlock, no matter how powerful he might be."

"'Us,'" she responded, her tone musing. "You already think of yourself as a Castillo?"

I looked over at Rafe, who was sitting quietly, letting me have my conversation with my mother. He must have been burning to get in contact with his own family, and yet he had let me reach out first, as if he knew my family was the one that needed the most reassurance. "Something like that," I said. "Anyway, we're on top of this. Of course, I'll be in touch if we need help." I paused, then asked, "Is Dad there?"

"No, he went up to Flagstaff for the day—he needed to finish winterizing the house there. He'll be upset that he missed your call."

I was also unhappy that I wouldn't get a chance to talk to him now, but I reassured myself that I could call him the next day. Sooner or later, I'd have to get a new phone—a *real* phone, not one that Simon had hexed.

Which reminded me that, while I'd retrieved Rafe's jeans and all the valuables contained in them, I hadn't done anything to get my own stuff back. Everything I owned was hanging in the closet at the house back in Tesuque, and my purse was still sitting on the dresser. Great.

"I'm bummed about it, too," I said, bringing

myself back to the conversation with my mother. "But I'll call again tomorrow. I need to go, though."

"All right, Miranda." A little pause, and she added, "Tell Rafe thank you from all of us. We're so grateful for what he did."

"I will, Mom. Love you." I pressed the button to end the call, then handed the phone back to Rafe. "Well, that's settled. Of course, I just realized that all my belongings are still at Simon's house. I need to try to get them back."

"Well, considering the way you basically snapped your fingers and made my jeans reappear, that doesn't sound like it should be too much work."

I hoped not, although in this case I'd be retrieving a bunch of items, not a single pair of pants. Still, the principle should be the same. I shut my eyes for a moment, thinking of my clothes hanging up in the closet, the weekender bags on the shelf above them, the toiletries in the bathroom. Since I'd never been upstairs in Rafe's house, I didn't know what the bedrooms looked like. I'd have to have everything appear here and then move it later.

When I reached out with my magic, though, it was as if I had hit a blank wall. Again and again I attempted to push through and lay magical hands on the items I needed, and again and again

I was thwarted. At last I let out a frustrated breath and said, "I think the little stunt with your jeans pissed Simon off. He's not letting me through to get my stuff."

He frowned. "You're sure?"

"Pretty sure. I can try again later, but I think for now we'll just have to write it all off. I can call the bank and cancel my cards, and I needed to get a New Mexico I.D. anyway, but literally all I've got right now are the clothes on my back."

"We can take care of that," Rafe said, his tone reassuring. One hand reached out and took mine, strong and warm and comforting. "I'll take you shopping just as soon as I talk to Cat. I'll get you anything you need."

A part of me worried that it wouldn't be safe to venture out into Santa Fe, but I tried to tell myself that Simon wouldn't attempt anything in front of a bunch of civilians…would he? Anyway, I could take that invisible bubble of protection with me. I needed to go out, if only to get some new underwear and a toothbrush.

"Thanks." I squeezed his hand. It felt so good to be here with him, to know that he loved me and wanted to be with me, that all of these other minor annoyances were just that—annoyances that could be handled easily enough.

His phone buzzed, and he looked down at the screen. Letting go of my hand, he swiped the screen to accept the call and mouthed *it's Cat* at me. I nodded, thinking that was just about perfect timing. He could let her know that he'd gotten me away from Simon, and then the two of us could go shopping. Yes, we'd need to sit down with Genoveva and Louisa and the rest of the clan's strongest witches and warlocks, and begin to prepare for what was about to come, but surely the world could spare me an hour to get some replacement underwear and toiletries.

"Hey, Cat," Rafe said. "Great news. I—" He stopped there abruptly, face going stony and cold, so without expression that he was almost unrecognizable. "When?" A long silence as he listened to his sister's reply. "We'll be right over. Just—just hang in there." He ended the call and set the phone down on the coffee table, then stared at it as if he'd never seen it before.

Fear lanced through me, although I still had no idea of what was going on. "Rafe? What is it? What's the matter?"

He stared at me for a moment, still with that horrible stony expression on his features, the one that turned his face into that of a stranger. The room was so quiet, I thought I could hear my heart beating in my chest. What was wrong? Why was he looking at me like that?

At last he said, "My mother is dead."

And as I looked at him in horror, I realized this was far from over.

One way or another, Simon would have his revenge.

The Witches of Canyon Road series continues with *Mysterious Ways.*

ALSO BY CHRISTINE POPE

THE WITCHES OF CANYON ROAD

(Paranormal Romance)

Hidden Gifts

Darker Paths

Mysterious Ways (July 2018)

DJINN DOMINION

(Paranormal Romance)

Stolen

Forgotten (June 2018)

Driven (August 2018)

THE WITCHES OF CLEOPATRA HILL*

(Paranormal Romance)

Darkangel

Darknight

Darkmoon

Sympathetic Magic

Protector

Spellbound

A Cleopatra Hill Christmas

Impractical Magic

Strange Magic

The Arrangement

Defender

Bad Blood

Deep Magic

Darktide

Books 1-3 and Books 4-6 of this series are also available in two separate omnibus editions at special boxed set prices. Chronicles of Cleopatra Hill includes the series' two "back in time" novellas, *Bad Blood* and *The Arrangement*.

THE DJINN WARS*

(Paranormal Romance)

Chosen

Taken

Fallen

Broken

Forsaken

Forbidden

Awoken

Illuminated

The first three books of this series are also available in
an omnibus edition at a special low price!

THE WATCHERS TRILOGY*

(Paranormal Romance)

Falling Dark

Dead of Night

Rising Dawn

THE SEDONA FILES*

(Paranormal Romance)

Bad Vibrations

Desert Hearts

Angel Fire

Star Crossed

Falling Angels

Enemy Mine

The first three books of this series are also available in an omnibus edition at a special low price!

TALES OF THE LATTER KINGDOMS*

(Fantasy Romance)

All Fall Down

Dragon Rose

Binding Spell

Ashes of Roses

One Thousand Nights

Threads of Gold

The Wolf of Harrow Hall

Moon Dance

The Song of the Thrush

Books 1-3 and Books 4-6 of this series are also available in two separate omnibus editions at special boxed set prices.

THE GAIAN CONSORTIUM SERIES*

(Science Fiction Romance)

Blood Will Tell

Breath of Life

ABOUT THE AUTHOR

Christine Pope has been writing stories ever since she commandeered her family's Smith-Corona typewriter back in the sixth grade. Her work includes paranormal romance, fantasy romance, and science fiction/space opera romance. She fell under the Land of Enchantment's spell while researching her Djinn Wars series and now makes her home in Santa Fe, New Mexico.

Christine Pope on the Web:
www.christinepope.com

 facebook.com/ChristinePopeAuthor

 twitter.com/ChristineJPope

pinterest.com/ChristineJPope

www.ingramcontent.com/pod-product-compliance
Lightning Source LLC
Chambersburg PA
CBHW021126260626
47169CB00005B/1468